Captive

CAPTIVE

DAVID ELLIS

TENTH STREET PRESS

THIS EDITION

© Copyright 2013 David Ellis

Published by Tenth Street Press   2013

Original cover art & design by Tenth Street Press

ISBN: 0-9923034-0-0

ISBN13: 978-0-9923034-0-2

TENTH STREET PRESS Ltd.
MELBOURNE LONDON
www.tenthstreetpress.com
Email:contact@tenthstreetpress.com

For Henry, and long may our travels continue.

Thursday, February 3, 2011

Popham Street N1 is a typical street of Victorian houses in Islington, north London, situated about two miles north of Kings Cross station and four miles south of Karl Marx's final resting place in Highgate Cemetery. The houses were built at the turn of the 1900s to house the more prosperous families of Islington and usually consisted of three stories with a couple of rooms on each floor. Property developers seized upon these houses with gusto to convert into apartments and it's in number 58, on the second floor, that Hugo Brown and Ben Cavendish share a rented apartment. They met about two years ago at a party organized by someone they'd never met who had two friends independently acquainted with Hugo and Ben who invited them along. It was love at first sight across the living room floor and their relationship took off within hours of that first meeting.

And while it's yet another cliché, Hugo and Ben really do look like the dream couple. Both are 26, tall and good-looking, but Hugo has the edge with his lean, naturally muscular physique, wavy blond hair that flops over his forehead and blue, come to bed eyes. Ben, on the other hand, has short dark brown hair, gray-brown eyes, a well-defined body and a six-pack that comes and goes dependent on his attendance at the local gym. Sex is important in their relationship but Ben invariably takes the lead, often to Hugo's annoyance. He's also not as monogamous as Hugo would like him to be although Hugo isn't exactly a stranger to erotic fantasies that involve straying from Ben and the bed they share. Hugo also has the trump card in the form of the more than generous proportions of his penis, which Ben remains in awe of to this day and positively worships.

Hugo's background is that of the aspirational middle class: the bright, golden-haired youth from a loving, caring family attending a minor but decent public school, then Oxford University, and finally ending up in the refined world of the Courtauld Institute, London, where he's an assistant curator in fine art. In many ways, he's a product of institutions, albeit the best institutions that England has to offer. He isn't really remotely career driven; preferring to go with the flow than rocking the boat, although a friend and colleague at the institute named Alexander is always goading him to make more of himself. Alexander is also hopelessly infatuated with Hugo and never stops trying to get him into bed.

Ben couldn't be more different. Born with a silver spoon in his mouth and a family lineage that goes back centuries, Ben was destined for great things simply because that's what was expected in his family. Unfortunately for his parents, he rebelled in a big way when attending Eton College and afterwards, and his family spent a lot of time and effort extracting him from relationships that went sour and business ventures that went bust. In the end, they more or less gave up and his mother retreated to her usual solace of charitable activities, religion and the Women's Institute. Sadly, her charitable disposition doesn't extend to his sexuality, life style or relationship with Hugo, despite the fact that meeting Hugo helped to ground his excesses and get him a good job as an advertising executive which suits his more extravert personality.

But tomorrow is probably the most important day of their life, as they're having their civil partnership ceremony. It was Ben that actually proposed to Hugo just a few months ago and the last few weeks have been a flurry of organizing and rather more bickering than usual. Hugo actually paid for an advert in The Times to announce their wedding, although Ben was quick to point out that none of their families would read it as they either read the right-wing Telegraph (Ben's family) or the liberal Guardian (Hugo's family). That didn't go down well, as paying for the advert used up the last of Hugo's meager pay for the month.

"Oh God, I can't believe it!" exclaimed Hugo. "We're actually getting married tomorrow!"

"Weird, isn't it," replied Ben. "All these years of going on about gay lib and celebrating queerness and now we're about to become hitched according to an ancient heterosexual tradition."

"Well, you could at least sound a bit more romantic about it!"

"Sorry, sweetie, it's just my pre-nuptial jitters and thinking about relatives being there."

"Come here and show me your love again." Hugo slid out of his pajama bottoms and lay back on the bed with a coquettish grin and a growing erection.

"Isn't this against the wedding rules?" asked Ben with a smirk.

"Doesn't the condemned man deserve a last fuck before he meets his end?"

"Which end were you thinking of?"

"That depends on which one of us is going to be the lady of the house."

"I think we know the answer to that," replied Ben, quickly removing his bathrobe and leaping on top of his husband to be. They kissed and tongued and enjoyed the sensation of their dicks growing between them. Ben raised himself up and looked at Hugo's dick which had sneaked up his abdomen to at least an inch past his belly button.

"Someone ought to write a book about your dick," said Ben. "Perhaps it could be called 'The Adventures of Hugo and his Humongous Penis'. With photos, of course, and perhaps scratch n' sniff as well. And it would definitely have to be pop-up too."

Hugo laughed. "So what adventures do you have in mind?"

"Well, this, for instance," said Ben, sinking his mouth onto Hugo's thick 10 inches until it disappeared down his throat. He came up for air. "That's its disappearing trick." He looked at Hugo's dick from the side. "And that's your dick pretending to be a stalagmite or perhaps a rocket about to blast off into outer space."

"What if it wanted to blast off into this inner space?" asked Hugo, gently teasing Ben's anus with a finger.

"I think I can do better," said Ben. He licked a finger and pressed it against Hugo's opening. Hugo started stroking the head of his dick which had oozed a drop of pre-come. Hugo put his feet on his lover's broad shoulders and Ben eased his dick into Hugo's smooth white ass. They looked into each other's eyes and shared the feeling of intense desire. Hugo arched his back and moaned with pleasure. They fucked with a much-practiced combination of Ben's thrusts and Hugo's sinuous pelvic movements. Without breaking the rhythm, Ben bent down and wrapped his lips around the corona of Hugo's dick, tonguing and sucking the pre-come that was still oozing. He felt Hugo's fingers exploring his perineum and working their way downwards to touch the head of his dick as he momentarily pulled out. Ben pushed back in and he felt Hugo's sphincter contracting around his dick and knew he was just seconds away from coming. Hugo's fingers grasped Ben's buttocks and pulled him in as deep as he could go. Their simultaneous ejaculations shuddered through their bodies and Ben swallowed every drop of Hugo's spunk as his dick blasted its thick, milky juice into his mouth.

"Wow, that was amazing," said Ben, licking his lips. "Who needs a milk delivery when they've got your juice on tap?"

"You're not so bad yourself, lover," said Hugo, lying back thoroughly sated. "So what other adventures do you have in mind for my dick?"

"Well, who knows what'll happen on our honeymoon. I hear that Cape Town guys are very sexy."

"You don't mean a threesome?"

"Perhaps even an orgy."

"God, you're incorrigible."

"But you love me for it, sweetie."

The two of them fell asleep with limbs wrapped around each other and lips touching, their dicks resting happily until the next bout of lovemaking. Hugo was dreaming about the ceremony, reception and their honeymoon in the warm sun of Cape Town. Ben's dream was much the same but there was something niggling in the back of his mind which made him uneasy.

Friday, February 4, 2011

Hugo and Ben are sitting down for breakfast, still in their bathrobes, and are trying to synchronize looking through various lists and other paperwork with eating mouthfuls of muesli.

"Be careful, that's some milk you've just dropped on my mother!" exclaimed Ben, brushing away a splatter of milk that had landed on the seating plan.

"You think she'll turn up, then?" asked Hugo.

"I know she's said some vile things about us but I bet she won't pass the chance of a meal that she doesn't have to pay for."

"God, she can be a cow."

"And with a bounteous supply of milk if you can get on the right side of her."

"So what do I have to do to get on her right side?"

"Appeal to her vanity, sweetie, and smile your lovely smile."

"You mean, like last night?"

"Smile, yes; humongous erection, no. Now, to matters in hand."

"I thought we'd moved on from my erection."

They both laughed.

"So we're agreed the seating plan is okay unless there are any no-shows?" asked Ben.

"Yes, it should be fine," said Hugo. "And anyway, your best man should be able to take care of any last minute changes unless he imbibes too much champagne."

"I wouldn't bank on that, sweetie, and he might just pipe up and say he's the lawful impediment."

"What? Because you fucked him last week?"

"Well, he is the ex who insists on being resurrected from the grave."

"Don't we know," said Hugo with a withering look. "Just because it was your stag do it doesn't mean you have to shag the first thing you see on two legs."

"Do I smell burning martyr, dearest?"

"And you better have used a condom if you want our sex life to continue unimpeded."

"Of course, silly. I may be a rutting stag but I'm not that stupid."

They returned to their bowls of muesli.

"So what about the flight?" asked Hugo.

"We're all checked-in. It's BA0059 and take-off is at 7:30 p.m. I managed to get us seats on the upper deck, so there shouldn't be any screaming kids," replied Ben. "Thank God your dad paid for business class seats."

"Yeah, at least he's not a stingebag like your mum."

"That's a bit below the belt."

"Yeah, your ex would know all about *that* region of your body."

They glared at each other momentarily before taking a sip of coffee.

"And which terminal?" asked Hugo.

"Terminal 5," replied Ben, "and we can drop off the car in short-stay parking."

"So nothing should go wrong."

"Unless one of us gets our knickers in a twist. Speaking of which, we ought to get our glad rags on as the car will be here to collect us in an hour."

They left the kitchen, Ben holding Hugo from behind and pressing his dick against his sexy butt. They waddled their way into the bedroom where their suits were laid out on the bed. They stripped off their bathrobes and took in each other's bodies.

"So this is the last time I'll see you naked and single," said Ben.

"That's some thought," said Hugo, grinning at Ben.

"Do we have time?" asked Ben, looking hungrily at Hugo's huge dick that seemed to be reaching out like some alien life form eager to make first contact.

Hugo looked down at Ben's dick which clearly wanted to complete the greeting. "It's tempting, lover, but let's wait until later. And anyway, it's said to be bad luck to have sex on your wedding morning."

Ben shrugged and went into the bathroom for his shower. Hugo double-checked the clothes laid on the bed.

"Okay, your turn now," said Ben, toweling his hair dry as he came back into the bedroom.

Hugo stepped into the shower stall and turned on the faucet, watching the threads of water emerge from the shower head, streaming down his body over the lingering length of his dick and then splashing to the floor below. He enjoyed the attention that Ben gave to his dick but he'd never really seen it as that special. He was amused by the idea of the book, though.

When Hugo emerged from the bathroom he saw that Ben had finished dressing and was admiring himself in the full-length mirror. Yes, he'll definitely do, thought Hugo. He went up behind Ben, nuzzling his ass with his dick and kissing him on the neck.

"God, you're gorgeous," said Hugo.

"You're not so bad yourself," said Ben, running his hands through Hugo's damp hair. "Okay, time to put some clothes on, Hugo Brown."

Hugo finished drying himself and slowly dressed, aware that Ben was watching every move. Both had decided to wear the same outfit of a gray Armani suit, white shirt and pink tie, but Hugo would be the one who'd stand out in the wedding photos, with his blond hair and languorous look giving him the look of someone who'd just stepped off a catwalk. Ben wanted there and then to take a photo of him as the Mapplethorpe model, with zipper open and dick hanging down, but that would have to wait until later.

They stood side by side looking at themselves in the mirror: well-matched as a couple both in and out of bed, but with their own individualities and idiosyncrasies. They turned to each other and kissed.

"Will you marry me, Hugo Brown?" asked Ben.

"You try stopping me, Benjamin Cavendish," replied Hugo.

The sound of the doorbell ringing stirred them back into reality. They grabbed their wallets and door keys and made their way downstairs to the waiting limo.

The limo they'd booked for the short journey was from a company called 'Camp Cars' who guaranteed to be gay friendly and were well used to antics on the leather seats in the back. The driver on this occasion was someone that Hugo knew from taxi journeys to and from the Courtauld and he rushed to open the car door when he saw them come down the steps hand in hand. Ben could see net curtains twitching up and down the opposite side of the street and he gave a queenly wave.

"Such a beautiful couple you make," said Pieter the driver, tears brimming up and reaching dramatically for a handkerchief.

Hugo thought Pieter looked rather splendid too, as he'd dressed for the occasion in a double-breasted limo driver's outfit complete with black tie and hat.

With his passengers safely strapped in the back seat and tears mopped, Pieter set off for the short drive to Camden Passage. Hugo and Ben had debated long and hard about the venue for their ceremony. Islington Town Hall in Upper Street had been the first option but they'd been put off by the warning on the council's website that "ceremonies running over half-an-hour incur extra cost" which gave them the impression of being cogs in an assembly line. They eventually plumped to have it in Frederick's restaurant in Camden Passage which was just a stone's throw from Upper Street, but with the advantages of their ceremony being the only one happening that day and everything occurring under the one roof. They'd already met with the registrar who'd be conducting the ceremony and were pleased by the positive vibes they'd picked up from her which seemed at odds with what had been reported in the press about a homophobic colleague.

They arrived at Frederick's exactly on time at 10:30 a.m. for a preliminary meeting with the registrar and to complete paperwork. This was after being greeted warmly at the door by the manager and a glass of champagne put in their hands. Despite the warmth emanating from everyone, their nerves were starting to kick in and Ben was feeling distinctly queasy. Hugo seemed to sense this and held Ben's hand while they were waiting for the registrar to arrive. The door opened and she bustled in with her assistant, beaming a smile that immediately put them at ease.

"Hugo and Ben, it's good to see you again. This is my

assistant Carly and she'll be making sure I don't make any mistakes. Can we just confirm the words you've decided to use?"

Hugo extracted some sheets from his inside pocket.

"This is the format we'd like to use. It's basically what we went through with you at the Town Hall with some minor changes, but all the legal bits are still where they should be." He handed the registrar her copy. She glanced through it and then slipped the pages into plastic covers.

"That looks fine. As you know, I'll be making an address to your guests and witnesses, which includes the question about any lawful impediment. I presume that nothing has happened since we last met that changes that?" She looked inquisitively at Hugo and Ben.

"No," they said together after looking at each other briefly.

"Excellent. Then I'll take you through your vows. Don't worry about remembering the lines, as I'll say them and then ask you to repeat them. If you make any mistakes just repeat the word again. Following that, I'll ask your guests to stand for the exchange of the rings. Do you each have rings or is your best man responsible for them?"

"Ben has his best man and my sister is my best woman," said Hugo.

"I like that," said the registrar. "Next there's the declaration of your commitment which is essential for the civil partnership to be valid. Finally, there's the signing of the register and then your civil partnership becomes recognized in law. So do you have any last minute questions?"

Hugo and Ben looked at each other and replied: "No, we're ready."

As if on cue, Ben's best man, Jonathan, stuck his head around the door.

"Sweeties, everyone's here."

"Does that include my mother?" asked Ben.

"Even her," said Jonathan.

"Is she smiling?" asked Hugo.

"Almost," replied Jonathan, "but more of a knowing smile, as if she doesn't really believe what's about to happen and is expecting divine intervention to put things right."

"That's my mother," said Ben. "I just hope she doesn't insist on praying for our salvation half way through the ceremony."

Jonathan handed the two of them a spray of miniature white lilies which they put in their buttonholes. The three of them followed the registrar and her assistant up the stairs to the ceremony room from where they could hear expectant chatter. The registrar went in first and Jonathan was instructed to open the doors when it was time for Hugo and Ben to enter. They smiled at each other and held hands like lovers on their first date.

As the doors were opened and they walked in, Hugo and Ben exchanged fleeting looks with their guests on either side. Hugo's family had beaming smiles and his mother was already dabbing away at a tear. Ben's family appeared rather more reserved and his mother was looking straight ahead. Hugo noticed that Ben had been looking at her and they exchanged a rueful smile. The registrar smiled at them and commenced the ceremony:

"Good morning, ladies and gentlemen, my name is Florence Josephs. Welcome to Frederick's for the civil partnership ceremony of Hugo Brown and Benjamin

Cavendish.

"The place in which we are now met has been duly sanctioned according to law for the registration of civil partnerships. You are here to witness the formation of a civil partnership between Hugo Brown and Benjamin Cavendish. If any person present knows of any lawful impediment to this partnership they should declare it now."

There was a brief, pregnant pause and a bead of sweat appeared on Ben's upper lip. The registrar continued:

"Hugo Brown and Benjamin Cavendish have chosen to pledge themselves to each other by committing to a legally binding contract. Hugo and Ben will now make their vows."

Hugo and Ben turned to look at each other. The registrar addressed Hugo first:

"Hugo, will you repeat after me: I choose you above all others to share my life. I promise to honor this pledge as long as I live. I call upon these persons here present to witness that I, Hugo Brown, take you, Benjamin Cavendish, to be my life long partner."

Hugo repeated the words, looking intently into Ben's eyes, and somehow managed to get the words out faultlessly despite his nerves.

The registrar turned to Ben:

"Now, Ben, will you repeat after me: I choose you above all others to share my life. I promise to honor this pledge as long as I live. I call upon these persons here present to witness that I, Benjamin Cavendish, take you, Hugo Brown, to be my life long partner."

Ben repeated the words but Hugo couldn't help but notice that he seemed even more anxious than him. He smiled at him to give encouragement.

The registrar smiled and said: "You may now exchange rings."

Hugo's sister handed him the ring and he put it on Ben's finger: "I give you this ring as a token of my love. Wear it with pride and happiness now and always."

Ben then took the ring from Jonathan and placed it on Hugo's finger: "I give you this ring as a token of our love. Wear it with pride and happiness now and always."

"Please all stand for the declaration," said the registrar. "Hugo, please repeat after me: I declare that I know not of any legal reason why we may not register as partners in law. I understand that on signing this document we will be forming a civil partnership with each other."

Hugo repeated the words.

"Now, Ben, please repeat after me: I declare that I know not of any legal reason why we may not register as partners in law. I understand that on signing this document we will be forming a civil partnership with each other."

Ben did the same.

The registrar completed the ceremony: "Hugo and Benjamin, it is now my pleasure to tell you that you are now partners in law. You may kiss each other if you so choose."

Hugo and Brown paused for a moment, then smiled broadly and kissed each other firmly on the lips. Both would have admitted afterwards that kissing each other in front of their family and friends was really the best part of the ceremony. However, there was one member of the happy gathering who was neither family nor friend and uninvited. He'd dressed to avoid recognition and slipped out as Hugo and Ben exchanged their kiss and the tearful guests applauded. He wasn't moved to tears but he was excited. He had arrangements to make. There was no doubt that they made a very attractive couple. He was becoming aroused at the thought of them in bed together.

Once downstairs for the champagne reception, Hugo and Ben shook hands in turn with their line-up of guests, exchanged long forgotten anecdotes and stories, and posed in multiple permutations for the photographer. Despite the chilly February weather, a feeling of warm affection permeated throughout until anyone came into the vicinity of Ben's steely gazed mother. Hugo thought it was particularly inappropriate for her to have a cross ostentatiously on display around her neck.

The reception segued into the lunch and all the guests sat down for the three-course meal which Hugo had carefully planned to take into account all known dietary restrictions. Hugo had decided his nerves would get in the way of saying anything meaningful, particularly without the benefit of PowerPoint, so only Jonathan and Ben were giving speeches. Ben, on the other hand, felt entirely at home speaking in public and saw it rather like pitching for an advertising campaign. It was the Jonathan's turn first and he tinged a teaspoon on his glass.

"As many of you will know, Ben and I go back a long way and if I wanted to I could probably make him very, very embarrassed. I won't, of course, although there was that occasion when he and a bellboy got stuck in an elevator in a New York hotel after the elevator got confused about whether it was meant to be going up or down with all the hot action going on." Everyone laughed and Ben did indeed blush. Ben's mother looked horrified and wondered what was coming next. "As you can see, they do make the most handsome couple and you can see why Hugo was offered a modeling contract when he was a freshman at Oxford. But the catwalk wasn't his thing and he chose to strut his stuff academically, which a certain Mr Sewell has been particularly delighted to behold." This time it was Hugo who blushed. "But now that I've done what I promised I wouldn't do by embarrassing them both and thereby satisfying the esteemed tradition of the best man's duty, I'd like to ask you to raise a toast to the happy couple: to Hugo and Ben and to a long and happy life together. But please, don't have any babies."

Glasses were raised: "To Hugo and Ben."

Ben stood up, looking less confident than Hugo had expected. He squeezed his hand to give him reassurance.

"That's a hard act to follow and I hope that Jonathan appreciates his gift of a replica of the object that gave Elton John so much pleasure." Half the guests laughed and half didn't have the faintest idea what he was referring to. "Of course, I'm referring to a golden... framed picture of Madonna... on stage in New York and wearing Jean-Paul Gaultier." Ben's mother looked affronted but everyone else laughed. "As Jonathan has said, Hugo is a prince among men and I suppose I should be thankful that Mr Sewell didn't come across him in the Courtauld Institute, as I'm sure he'd have had a certain part of him pickled in Victorian aspic for display on his mantelpiece." Very few of the guests had first-hand experience of what Ben was referring to but most of them guessed and laughed loudly. "And I promise that we won't be making babies but I'll check before we head for Cape Town that Hugo has been taking the pill."

Hugo laughed along with everyone else but felt ill at ease about the stereotyping of his role in their relationship.

So more champagne was consumed, promises were exchanged to keep in touch with distant relatives, and the time came for Hugo and Ben to return to 58 Popham Street and then to drive to Heathrow for their evening flight to South Africa. Pieter returned in the limo as arranged, loaded the trunk with their wedding presents, and opened yet another bottle of champagne as soon as the last photos had been taken of the happy couple and Hugo's mother had wished them 'bon voyage'. They arrived back at home just in time for a quick change and general turnaround but certainly not enough time to have sex. They kissed each other deeply and put the rest of their nuptials on hold until they were in the hotel in Cape Town.

London Heathrow Terminal 5 gleamed impressively in the late afternoon sun as Ben drove up to departures. Bags dropped off, they went through the fast track lane for their boarding passes and passports to be checked and then joined a blissfully short queue to go through security. Ben passed through unhindered but Hugo set lights flashing and he was instructed to go through a walk-in full body scanner and then had a very thorough frisk from a security guard. "It's that WMD in your jeans that did it," Ben whispered just out of earshot of the guard. The two of them giggled and headed in the direction of the South Gallery lounge. This was their first taste of the business class experience and they were momentarily in awe of the luxury on offer which seemed a million miles away from cattle class at 3:00 a.m. This impression was briefly dented by an obese Russian traveler vomiting down her front just feet away from where they were sitting, but once they'd moved away from the sight and smell and had glasses of champagne in their hands, the club class equilibrium was restored. The plane was boarding just as they arrived at the gate and they joined the fast track queue. Climbing up the stairs to the upper deck on the 747 added to the excitement of their journey. Ben had pre-booked seats 63J and K, which was a pair of seats facing each other with a reasonable degree of privacy, although not to the extent that there was any chance of them joining the mile high club.

Halfway through the dinner service an announcement went out on the intercom: "We're sorry to interrupt you, but British Airways and the crew would like to congratulate a young couple, Hugo and Ben, on the upper deck, who are flying with us this evening after having their civil partnership ceremony today. We're sure you'd all like to join us in a toast to them if you have a glass to hand." Rather sweetly, and totally unexpectedly, Hugo and Ben heard a ripple of applause which seemed to spread from the bowels of the plane upwards. They stood up in their seats and gave little bows. A steward appeared and handed them a bottle of champagne 'with the complements of the captain'. A short time later, the captain actually emerged from the flight deck and shook their hands. Hugo really couldn't think of a better way of starting their legally sanctioned life together.

Saturday, February 5, 2011

The plane touched down just after 9:00 a.m. As Hugo and Ben walked down the steps towards the entrance leading to immigration, they could see Table Mountain with its fluffy covering of cloud sinking off the edge into the brilliant azure sky. Processing through immigration seemed endless, with the queue of half-asleep visitors performing what seemed like a slow version of the conga without the customary hands on waists. Ben tried to hold hands with Hugo but it was the wrong time and place for a display of their affection. After waiting for their bags to be deplaned and delivered to baggage reclaim, they finally got to the airport exit 60 minutes after landing and they then looked for a taxi. The journey to the Nelson Lodge Hotel was brief and they were dropped outside the grand entrance just before 11:00 a.m.

Too early to check-in, they left their bags and went in search of a coffee on the nearby Kloof Street. Having found a convenient deli, they sat opposite each other, sipping their espressos, touching fingers across the table and rubbing legs together underneath. Both became aware that their button flies were in danger of popping open. As they stood up, Ben gave Hugo a look of dramatic surprise and handed him a napkin to hold over his heavily bulging crotch. Hugo blushed and giggled and briefly considered ripping his jeans open.

In fact, Ben would have done precisely that given half a chance. The nearest the two of them had come to airing their sexuality publicly was last year while spending a weekend in Amsterdam, in an unusual place which translated from Dutch as the 'Come Again Garden', but commonly referred to as the 'Come Garden', on account of its policy of inviting single men and couples to have al fresco sex and then leave biodegradable tissues on the ground to nurture the grass and plants. But years of middle class indoctrination and a thick mantle of respectability had made that impossible for Hugo even when looking at Ben's near perfect body.

Walking back to the hotel, they were both aware of feeling extraordinarily horny and the bulging of their jeans must have been obvious to anyone passing by. Indeed, Hugo did get a few lustful looks when passing the Studio 91 entrance where a gaggle of men where queuing to get in for their auditions. Arriving back at the hotel, they were able to complete their check-in. An immaculately dressed porter took their bags and escorted them to room #202 on the second floor overlooking the pool and gardens.

Their immediate response on the door being opened was to wonder whether they'd been given the wrong room, as the show of opulence took their breath away.

"Wow!" exclaimed Hugo.

"Are you sure this is the right room?" asked Ben.

"Absolutely, sir," replied the porter. "You've been upgraded to one of our senior suites."

The porter left, leaving them to take in their surroundings. Apart from a king size bed, there was an adjacent lounge area with a three-seater couch and a large flat screen TV. When Ben went over to look at it, he noticed that it was displaying a message: "Many congratulations to the two of you. I hope you enjoy your room upgrade. I'll see you later. M." Ben's immediate thought was that this must be a message from Hugo's mother.

"Come and see this, sweetie," he called to Hugo. "Your mother paid for the upgrade."

Hugo went over and looked at the screen. "I don't think it's her. I mean, why would she say something about seeing us later?"

"Yes, you're right. Perhaps it's a secret admirer of yours from Kloof Street."

They both giggled but Ben was still wondering who 'M' might be.

"Lunch?" asked Hugo.

"Later," said Ben, bending down and putting his face to Hugo's crotch.

"Okay, but let's shower first," said Hugo.

The two of them undressed and went into the vast, gleaming bathroom complete with a double power shower. Ben was initially reluctant to use the bidet but relented and then joined Hugo in the shower. They let the powerful jets of water strip away the sweat and grime of the long flight and commenced their first lovemaking as a legal couple, gently touching and kissing. Partially toweled dry, they flopped onto the king size bed, Ben astride Hugo and then Hugo on top of Ben. Ben looked momentarily confused by this change of tactic.

"I meant what I said in the vows, lover," Hugo said. "I want us to share everything." He licked his index finger and teased Ben's anal opening. He sniffed the finger and put it to Ben's nose. "That's your smell."

Ben did the same to Hugo and they shared the musky odor. "I prefer yours," he said.

Hugo's dick tensed. Ben savored the sight and sensation of its length and girth, taking it in both hands and stroking it slowly up and down. He bent forwards to lick the opening and then around the thick rim, tasting some lingering saltiness. Hugo's dick bobbed higher and a bead of pre-come emerged from the tip. Ben sucked greedily and he felt a shudder go through Hugo's body. A moan of pleasure escaped from his lips.

"My turn," said Hugo softly. They exchanged places and Hugo allowed the head of his dick to pulse against Ben's opening. Ben's dick bobbed expectantly and Hugo traced the length with his tongue, feeling the veins distending under the built-up pressure, and he then took in the entire length to the back of his mouth and beyond. Ben sighed, and to his surprise, he felt Hugo's dick entering him with only the slightest, momentary discomfort. He leant back and allowed it to slowly fill him. Hugo bent forward to kiss Ben, his dick still inside and throbbing against his prostate. Ben lifted his body up until the head of Hugo's dick almost emerged and then he lowered himself again. Hugo bent forward and the two of them rolled over. Hugo slowly pulled out of Ben and then immediately pushed back in with short, staccato movements. He took hold of Ben's dick and matched his strokes with those of his dick. Sensing that Ben was near to coming, he withdrew out and switched to a 69 position. Hugo and Ben stroked and sucked greedily and they were rewarded with fountains of creamy come.

"Wow," said Ben, "I didn't know being fucked could be as good as that."

"Thanks, lover," said Hugo, "that was amazing."

The two them lay back on the bed, utterly spent, with the sheet entwined around their legs. There was a knock on the door. Ben called out "Come in!" and a waiter entered carrying a bottle of champagne and two glasses. "With the compliments of the management," he said, hardly giving the naked couple a second look before putting down the tray and closing the door.

"Cute," said Ben.

"Very," agreed Hugo.

After showering and changing, Hugo and Ben sat on their terrace enjoying the champagne and the view of the hotel's tree-lined gardens.

"It's so peaceful here," said Hugo.

"But you know what happens behind bushes," teased Ben.

"No!"

"I promise. It's mentioned in the Spartacus guide: a quick cruise followed by a lengthy afternoon tea with cream cakes."

"You daren't!"

"Okay, I promise I won't."

Hugo and Ben walked downstairs hand-in-hand to the restaurant for lunch. This display of their affection had been Ben's idea and he'd persuaded Hugo to agree to this by saying that he'd go on a trip to Robben Island if Hugo agreed to cast his reserve aside for once. They'd dressed similarly in loose-fitting white shirts and chinos and the impression created was of a handsome, fashionable gay couple who'd every right to demonstrate their love on the first day of their honeymoon. Indeed, as they made their way to their allotted table, they turned the heads of at least 75 percent of the guests and 100 percent of the male waiting staff.

The next five days passed in a well-choreographed pattern of lovemaking, indulgent meals in Cape Town's trendiest restaurants and an assortment of touristic activities, including going up Table Mountain and making the boat trip to Robben Island. Although both agreed that the vast, flat expanse at the top of Table Mountain was the most impressive thing, a close second on Ben's list was the five minutes he spent ogling the blond-haired operator of the rotating cable car there and back. The fact that he seemed oblivious to being an object of lust only made him more desirable in Ben's eyes. The trip to Robben Island the following day did an effective job of denting Ben's ardor: while Hugo saw something of a monastic simplicity in the eight feet square cell with its steel bed, slit-like window and slopping-out bucket, Ben was horrified by the idea of constraint and felt sure he'd go crazy in such an environment.

Later that afternoon, and probably as a way of proving the point of not being locked-up and therefore free to do whatever he wanted, Ben persuaded Hugo to join him in some canoodling on a swing seat on a veranda set back from the pool area. Even Hugo agreed that this was relatively low risk given that most of the guests were partaking of afternoon tea at the time. What started off as fairly innocuous kissing and cuddling quickly became sucking and tonguing, and then full-on pummeling of Hugo's ass as Ben almost dislodged the seat from its moorings with his thrusting.

Their ejaculations weren't captured on camera, but the rest of the young couple's al fresco lovemaking was watched with intrigue on a monitor screen in the hotel's security office. Ben's ability to fuck a swinging sex object so effectively was particularly interesting to the man watching. He looked forward to reacquainting himself first-hand with Mr Cavendish's sexual athleticism.

Thursday, February 10, 2011

The penultimate day of Hugo and Ben's honeymoon was heralded as usual by the intense South African sun shining on their faces through the windows of their suite. Hugo sat up, stretched his arms and looked out of the window. For the first time in the week, Table Mountain was free of its blanket of cloud, which seemed to augur well for the rest of the day. Ben stirred and stroked Hugo's back.

"Penny for your thoughts, darling," he said.

"I was just thinking that the sight of Table Mountain without its cloud cover must mean something good," said Hugo. "I wish we could stay another week in this gorgeous place."

"So do I, sweetie, but there's the small matter of work and paying back AmEx for our reception and honeymoon."

Hugo groaned.

"So, are you ready for some breakfast?" asked Ben.

As if on cue, there was a knock on the door and their breakfast was wheeled in, including scrambled eggs with smoked salmon trout and a couple of glasses of champagne. The cute waiter smiled at them.

"In bed or out of bed?" he asked.

"That depends on whether you're joining us," said Ben with a seductive smile.

"God, you're a slut," said Hugo, glaring at Ben. He turned to the embarrassed waiter: "Don't take any notice of him. We'll have breakfast in bed, please."

The waiter carefully put the trays on their laps, doing

his best to avoid touching the bedding and particularly the mound of bedclothes where Ben's erection was pushing upwards.

"Down, boy!" whispered Hugo, who by now was getting thoroughly irritated by Ben's flirtatious behavior.

The waiter finished arranging the breakfast items and left the room, turning briefly to smile at Hugo. Hugo smiled back without really thinking about what he was doing.

After breakfast and showering, Hugo and Ben sat down to plan the rest of their last full day together in Cape Town.

"Ben, I really need to spend some time on the talk I have to give at the Courtauld the day after we get back, so you go out by the pool and top up your tan. We'll have lunch on Kloof Street."

"That sounds good with me, but I'll need to see your dick struggling to be contained in your speedos sometime today."

"I'll see what I can come up with. Happy tanning. And don't go into the bushes."

Ben grinned and kissed Hugo on the cheek as he left the suite and went down to the pool in his bathrobe, wearing just his speedos underneath.

Hugo turned to his laptop and the talk he had to prepare. His job as assistant curator at the Courtauld Institute wasn't exactly onerous, but from time to time he had to prepare lectures to give to various visiting parties and his anxiety levels invariably went through the roof. On this occasion, it was a rehash of something he'd done before on a particular period in the life of the French artist Nicolas Poussin. He could have done this almost in his sleep but his dedication to his work required him to go over the material again and add to his previous meticulous research.

Ben, on the other hand, was now busily sunning himself on the lounger after lengthy anointing with SFP16 cream. He enjoyed watching the reaction of others as he smoothed the cream over his body, particularly when he pulled down the waistband of his speedos and touched the tip of his semi-erect dick with his fingers.

In fact, Ben's audience extended wider than he imagined. Two men watched him from behind bushes in the hotel's verdant gardens and were enjoying his blatant exhibitionism. They licked their lips in anticipation and rearranged their jeans.

In the meantime, Hugo had pretty much completed his update of the PowerPoint presentation and was pleased to have found a jpg file of a rare Poussin work that had been bought and hidden away by a Russian oligarch. There was a knock on the door and Hugo went to answer it.

"Sorry to disturb you, sir, but can I collect the breakfast things?" asked the waiter who'd previously arrived with their breakfast.

"No problem, come in," said Hugo.

"I hope I'm not being out of turn, sir, but I couldn't help but notice certain tensions between the two of you."

"It's that obvious, is it?"

"Well, it was pretty clear when I was setting breakfast."

"Sorry, he's a bit like that."

"But you love him, don't you?"

"Christ yes, but his dick has a mind of its own sometimes."

"And what about you, sir, what would you really like?"

"That's a good question. I'd certainly like to have more control of what he does with his dick."

"And what would you like from me, sir?"

"Come closer," said Hugo, feeling both amazed and excited at the direction this encounter was taking.

Hugo examined the waiter's face, seeing a delicate mouth with full lips, a slightly snub nose, sparkling blue eyes beneath blond lashes and the curls of his sun-bleached hair. He reached down and put his hand against the waiter's crotch. The waiter sighed and put his mouth against Hugo's, his tongue insistent and searching.

They slowly undressed each other, the waiter surprised by the beauty of Hugo's olive-tinged whiteness and Hugo relishing the naturally tanned and toned body of someone with exactly the right genetics. But Hugo's genes were clearly superior when it came to a certain part of their bodies. The waiter gazed in wonderment at Hugo's dick.

"That's really something, sir," he said, closing his hand around the head and just managing to touch his fingers against his thumb. "I'm negative, by the way."

"So am I," said Hugo, smiling.

"Let's bareback." He held Hugo's dick with both hands.

"Are you sure?"

"Oh yes. I don't think a condom would fit your dick, anyway."

"Naughty but nice."

"Very nice," the waiter replied, smiling and rapidly stripping off the rest of his clothes.

The waiter turned around and parted his pert, tanned buttocks with both hands. Hugo let his dick glide up and down the cleft and then he bent down and tongued the inviting opening. He licked his fingers and added saliva to the pre-come on his dick. He pushed the tip of his dick against the entrance, willing the sphincter to open sesame, and then gently pushed in three-quarters of his length. They groaned in unison. Pulling out, he teased the waiter's anus with short stabs before plunging in again, feeling his rectum responding to being stretched by the large foreign object. He pulled out and the waiter turned around to envelop his dick with his mouth, eagerly trying to swallow the full length.

"Let's move to the bed," said Hugo.

The waiter lay on his back with his legs in the air and ass curled up, ready and waiting. Hugo teased the opening again and then started fucking the waiter with a ferocity and intensity that surprised him. The waiter also looked momentarily surprised by the change in Hugo's fucking but that turned rapidly into sighs of unadulterated pleasure. He pulled out and moved up the waiter's body. He sank down slowly onto the waiter's dick and then ejaculated all over his face at precisely the same time the waiter came inside him.

Hugo lay on the bed watching the waiter change back into his clothes. "Do you provide that sort of special room service often?"

"Actually, sir, you're the first."

"I'm honored. But why me?"

"Oh we could see you were special the first day you were by the pool. We had a bet on who would have you first."

"How will you prove it?"

"Easy," he said, pulling out a cell phone. He pressed a key and Hugo heard the sound of them having sex. He took a photo of Hugo lying on the bed. "That's the icing on the cake," he added.

"You bugger," said Hugo with a smile, standing up and going to the sideboard. He handed the waiter a 500 rand note.

"I can't possibly take that," said the waiter with a look of surprise on his face.

"I insist. Will your absence have been noticed?"

"By everyone I would think. They've been watching the pool and had instructions to phone me if your friend moved from the pool."

"Very cunning," said Hugo, impressed by the upstairs downstairs skullduggery. "May I know your name?"

"It's William, sir," replied the waiter.

"Well, thank you, William. Your room service was quite outstanding."

"Thank you, sir, but the pleasure was all mine. Have a safe trip back."

The waiter left, finally completing his appointed task of removing the breakfast trays, and Hugo went across to the window to check on Ben's progress with his quest for bronzed perfection. He saw that Ben was still on the same sun lounger but had turned over onto his front and had pulled down his speedos below his buttocks which were uplifted into the shape of a golden, but furry, peach. He really has no shame, Hugo thought, although no less desirable and gorgeous for it.

Desirable is also what the two men hiding in the bushes observing Ben thought, particularly when he turned over and exposed his buttocks to the sun. The pool area had emptied as guests made their way inside for lunch. The time had come for them to make their move.

Hugo felt guilt for what had just occurred in the bedroom but also felt excited. He wasn't sure when and how he would tell Ben but he could always rationalize it by saying that it was because Ben had fucked Jonathan on his stag night. However, there was no doubt that he was an utter hypocrite for accusing Ben of having unprotected sex when he'd been guilty of doing precisely that just minutes ago.

Hugo showered again and dressed. He returned to his laptop to put the finishing touches to his talk. He checked his watch and saw that it had just gone 1:00 p.m. He closed the lid, picked up the room keys and left to find Ben and go for lunch.

When Hugo got to the pool area, he was surprised to see that Ben was no longer on the sun lounger. He looked down the length of the pool and couldn't see him there either. Wherever he'd gone, Ben had left behind the book he was reading, the sun cream, his aviator sunglasses and the hotel's bathrobe. He bent down and touched the beach towel that Ben had been lying on and felt lingering dampness from his sweat. Perhaps he'd simply gone for a pee. Hugo waited for twenty minutes but Ben didn't return. He picked up the paperback. 'Looks Could Kill' was the title and the page he'd been reading related to the disappearance of the main character. A chill sensation went up and down his spine. Hugo looked around for some sort of clue as to where Ben had gone but couldn't see anything. He bent down and sniffed the towel: the combination of Ben's natural odor and aftershave was unmistakable. A touch on his shoulder made him start and he turned around fully expecting to see Ben with a mischievous look on his face.

"Apologies for disturbing you, sir," said the good-looking, besuited hotel manager, "but might I have a word with you in private?"

"Is it about Ben? Has someone seen him?" asked Hugo earnestly.

"No, sir, it isn't about your companion. Perhaps you would accompany me to the office."

Hugo stood up, glanced around again, and reluctantly followed the manager back into the main building and his office, which was surprisingly utilitarian with none of the chintzy splendor of the rest of the hotel. The solid wooden desk was free of adornments apart from a PC, a phone and a photo of a handsome, smiling man with a beard. "Please sit down, Mr Brown. May I offer you some coffee?"

"No thanks. Look, I'm really concerned about what's happened to my partner. He's been gone for 30 minutes now and all he had on were trunks and flip-flops."

"Pardon me for saying so, Mr Brown, but might that have something to do with your, er, indiscretion with a member of our waiting staff?" asked the manager with a half-amused smile.

"Oh God, I'm sorry. I hope I haven't got him into any trouble."

"Not exactly, sir. These things happen from time to time. And to be frank with you, our low wages do tend to lead some of our more attractive male staff into supplementing their pay packets with generous tips for services rendered. But I do think that guests should be more prepared to ensure that such encounters are safe. I suppose in future it might be wise if our staff had access to a supply of condoms in case of emergencies."

"He's all right, isn't he?" asked Hugo with concern in

his voice.

"Nothing that a day's rest won't cure, Mr Brown. He was complaining of a rather sore bottom, I believe. And he might be busy putting together something rather interesting for YouTube."

Hugo blushed and fidgeted, trying to avoid looking at the manager.

"Now to the matter of your missing friend. Could it be that he'd entertained similar ideas of extramarital activities? Boys will be boys, after all."

Hugo was becoming slightly perturbed by the direction this conversation was taking and the lustful look on the manager's face.

"No, I'm sure he wouldn't have got up to anything. We were just about to go for lunch anyway. Look, I'm sorry again for what happened with the waiter, but I really need to get back to the pool to wait for Ben."

"Very well, sir, and please let me know if there is anything we can do to help." The manager stood up and offered his hand. "My name is John Bredenkamp, by the way."

He shook the offered hand and noted that it felt as damp as his. They exchanged brief but meaningful eye contact.

Hugo left the office and returned to the pool side. The time was approaching 2:00 p.m. Ben's sun lounger remained exactly as it was when he'd left it. He thought back to what the manager had said and decided to explore the surrounding gardens. He walked away from the pool side in an obvious direction towards some evergreen bushes that were about 20 feet away. These certainly provided privacy for those using the pool but also provided cover for anything that might be happening behind them. Hugo was aware that the hotel's gardens were a popular cruising ground despite the presence of security guards at the main entrance and patrolling the grounds. As he walked around the bushes, he half-expected to see Ben engaged in some impulsive tryst but no one was there. However, when he looked down at the ground, he could see that the grass had been flattened. He looked around to check for any used condoms but surmised that they were probably removed as quickly as they were deposited by the ever-vigilant gardeners. But he did find a couple of cigarette butts, and when he bent down to pick one up, he thought he detected some residual warmth. Hugo walked further into the garden and found one of the gardeners raking up fronds from the giant palm trees.

"I'm sorry to bother you but I'm looking for my friend. You couldn't have missed him as he only wearing trunks and flip-flops. He's about my height with dark hair. He was last by the pool over an hour ago."

"Sorry, boss, no see your friend," replied the gardener, who looked surprised to have been spoken to by a guest.

"Thanks anyway," said Hugo.

Hugo retraced his steps back to the pool. The loungers were starting to fill up as guests returned from lunch. Hugo took the lounger next to Ben's and pulled the umbrella stand over to give some shade from the sun. He sat and waited, ever-vigilant, like a pet dog awaiting its owner's return. The sun dipped in the horizon and cast mysterious shadows in the surrounding greenery. At one point, Hugo thought he saw movement and his pulse rate momentarily accelerated in anticipation, but he was mistaken and the shadow moved on to a new patch of greenery. 6:00 p.m. came and went and the pool area cleared for the day. A few guests looked in his direction as they departed, wondering what the young man was doing sitting on his own with such a worried look on his face. Hugo knew that he couldn't stay outside indefinitely, but he wasn't sure what to do with Ben's things on the lounger and was worried that staff would remove them and take them in as lost property. He found a pen and paper in his pocket and scribbled a note saying

"PLEASE LEAVE - ROOM #202" and hoped that would suffice, both for staff and for Ben, should he return before dark.

Hugo went inside and knocked on the door of the manager's office. He heard a female voice call out "Come in!" and he entered. The woman occupying the manager's chair was wearing a black trouser suit and she had her hair pulled up into a bun.

"How may I help you, Mr Brown?" she asked with a sincere looking smile.

"You know my name," said Hugo.

"Of course. My colleague made me aware of the events of the day. Has your friend still not returned?"

"No. I'm really getting worried now. It's not like him to go off for hours. I just don't see where he could have gone hardly wearing any clothes."

"Yes, it is rather strange. Perhaps security could help, as there are cameras covering most areas of the hotel."

"That sounds a good idea." Hugo looked relieved that someone was at last taking him seriously.

The manager picked up the phone and dialed. "Is that security? Good. It's the manager here. I need a check on activity in the pool area between 12 and 1 today..." She looked at Hugo for confirmation and he nodded. "... I'm interested in the movements of a guest wearing swimming trunks who disappeared during that period of time and hasn't returned. Can you call me back when you've checked? Good. Thanks." She looked sympathetically at Hugo. "I'm sure if there's anything to find it'll be on the tapes."

"Thanks," said Hugo before bursting into tears and finally letting the emotional turmoil of the day come to the surface.

The manager came round to his side of the desk and grasped his hands. "I'm really sorry for you. It's not exactly the best way to end your holiday."

"What if he doesn't turn up tomorrow?" asked Hugo, his tears subsiding.

"Look, try not to think about that. We're not going to chuck you out and we're happy to contact the airline if it comes to that."

"What's your name?"

"I'm Martha, Martha Jones."

"Thank you so much, Martha."

The desk phone rang. "Yes?" asked Martha. "Okay, okay, that's helpful. We'll come and look at the video." She looked at Hugo, her warm smile replaced by a steely look. "There's something on the video. You'd better come with me."

Hugo followed Martha out of her office across the lobby to a door marked 'Security'. Inside, Hugo could see rows of screens monitoring the public spaces inside and outside the hotel. The two security guards on duty seemed to be particularly interested in whatever was playing on a screen labeled 'Pool 4' in the middle of the bottom row. Martha motioned Hugo to watch what was playing.

"This is the freeze-frame video from the pool area where your friend was last seen. It's jerky because the shots are taken only every few seconds," she explained.

Hugo could see numbers at the bottom of the screen which included the date and time down to the second. The loop set up by security started at 12:30:00 and showed a few guests on loungers. Towards the top left, Hugo could see Ben lying on his back with the jerky freeze-frame giving the impression of him trying to find a comfortable position. At around 12:40:00, Ben turned over on his front and pulled down his trunks. Hugo noticed the security guards sharing a look. Then at 12:51:00, when other guests had left the pool side, Hugo saw a figure appearing right at the top of the screen, although the image was indistinct. At this point, Ben seemed to take notice and he sat up and put his flip-flops on. As he walked over to the figure, he could be seen pulling up his trunks. Ben and the figure then disappeared off screen and the video looped back to the beginning.

"What do you think?" asked Martha.

"Well, that's definitely Ben," replied Hugo, "and what's on the video fits with what I noticed when I went to see where he might have gone. There was certainly no sign of any struggle, and when I went around the bushes to where that figure appeared from I could see that the grass had been flattened and there were cigarette butts on the ground."

"So you think someone could have been watching from behind the bushes and then came out for him when the coast was clear?"

"Something like that."

"Could he have known that man?"

Hugo shook his head. "I really don't see how; we haven't met up with anyone else while we've been here."

"Well," said Martha with a sigh, "It seems we have a missing person. I'll call the police." She turned to Hugo: "And I suggest you get something to eat. We might be in for a long night."

***

Ben regained consciousness and was aware of a pounding headache and discomfort in multiple parts of his body. He didn't understand why he couldn't see anything and couldn't move his limbs. He seemed to be bound to something metal and was reclined almost to the horizontal. He momentarily thought that Hugo must be playing some sort of game but his senses quickly told him that he was in a foreign environment that was cold and damp and far removed from the hotel. He shivered. He remembered seeing a man near the bushes by the pool wearing a tight t-shirt and enticingly bulging jeans who made a gesture with his fingers to come to him. He recalled seeing a second man behind the bushes and the excited anticipation of a threesome but everything went blank after that.

He could feel rough material on his face and something pressed into his mouth. He tried speaking but grunts emerged. He was also aware that he was entirely naked and could feel a cold draft rustling hairs on his arms, chest and legs. A more acute ache in his pelvic region became increasingly insistent and he recognized that his bladder was about to burst. He gave in to the need and voided his bladder, hearing and feeling the liquid trickling down his legs onto the floor below. He heard noises of someone moving a few feet away and a voice muttered "Dirty queer." A feeling of dread descended into his bowels and he almost lost control. He tried to ask "What do you want? Who are you?" but grunts were the only sounds he could make. The covering over his head was removed and he felt a loud, stinging slap to his right cheek. He saw that he was in a small square room with a low ceiling and a single light-bulb overhead that cast ominous shadows into the gloom around him. Five feet away, he noticed the man who'd enticed him away from the safety of the hotel. His dark hair was cut short and his intensely green eyes bore into him. He wore a white t-shirt which was stretched tightly over a muscular chest. He held a camcorder in his right hand and his left hand stroked a sizeable erection that poked out through the open flies of his jeans. Ben suddenly felt a hand grabbing his hair and forcing his head backwards. A second erect penis entered his field of vision. The gag in his mouth was abruptly replaced by the penis which forced its way to the back of his mouth and down his throat. He gagged painfully and tried to resist but his head was yanked back further. Suddenly the penis was withdrawn and the owner ejaculated over Ben's face, covering his eyes, nose and mouth with semen. The penis was thrust back into Ben's mouth. "My turn now," he heard from the other side of the room.

***

Hugo found an empty table in the restaurant and ordered a salad. He was relieved to see that William the waiter wasn't on duty. He had little appetite and toyed with the food, his mind overwhelmed with doom-laden scenarios which were compounded by being on his own and so far from home. Martha the manager came over to his table and let him know that the police had arrived. He left the table and followed her back to her office. She introduced the Detective Inspector from the Cape Town Central Police Station. He was thickset with short blond hair and eyes set a little too close together, but his manner seemed relaxed rather than confrontational.

"Mr Brown, my name is Jim van der Merwe and, as you've heard, I'm a Detective Inspector from Cape Town Central. I gather from Ms Jones here that your companion - a Mr Benjamin Cavendish - has been reported missing. Perhaps you could summarize for me the events of today."

"Okay, I'll do my best," said Hugo, "but I'm almost at my wits' end worrying about him." He paused to gather his thoughts. "Well, today was the last day of our honeymoon - we had our civil partnership ceremony back in London last week - and I stayed in our room after breakfast to do some work on my laptop while Ben went down to the pool to sunbathe. I looked out of the window just before quarter to one and could see him lying on his front on the lounger. I had a shower, changed and went down to the pool to find him so that we could go out for lunch. He wasn't there and had left his sunglasses and other belongings behind. I waited for some time and then looked around the gardens to see whether I could find him. When I looked behind the bushes nearest to the pool, it seemed that someone had been standing there and there were a couple of cigarette butts on the ground. I then returned to the poolside and spent the rest of the afternoon waiting for him. It was only at about 6:00 p.m. when it was getting dark that I went in to get help and that's when I spoke with Ms Jones here."

"Interesting," said the DI, who'd been making notes as Hugo was speaking. "And during the time you were on your own, did anyone else come to the room?"

Hugo blushed. "Well, a waiter came to collect the breakfast things," he replied.

"So he left immediately and then you were on your own again?"

"Well, not exactly," said Hugo, now looking extremely embarrassed.

"Actually, Detective Inspector," interjected Martha, "the minor issue that Mr Brown is referring to has already been dealt with by my colleague John Bredenkamp earlier in the day."

"It may well have, Ms Jones, but I would still like to hear from Mr Brown about what transpired." He turned again to look at Hugo. "Mr Brown?"

"Er, I had sex with the waiter. That's all. I gave him a tip and then he left."

"And you mentioned all that to the manager?"

"Yes, he came looking for me at the poolside, as he must have heard about my, er, indiscretion."

"Mr Brown, wouldn't it be reasonable to assume that two people who've just got married - including two people of the same sex - would only have sex with each other?"

Hugo blushed again. "Well, ordinarily we *are* monogamous but, er, occasionally our relationship becomes a bit looser than that."

"Like this morning?" asked the DI.

"Like this morning," agreed Hugo.

"So isn't it possible that Mr Cavendish was doing exactly the same thing as you? Perhaps he even returned to the room briefly and saw you engaged in your extramarital activity and decided to get his own back?"

That thought hadn't crossed Hugo's mind until then. "But I'm sure he didn't. And I don't think he'd just have walked back to the pool without saying something."

"But you can't be sure, can you?" pressed the DI.

"No, but I think I can be sure that Ben wouldn't walk off - even if it was to have sex with a stranger - in just his trunks and flip-flops, leaving everything else behind and then not return for..." He looked at his watch.".....over seven hours. And on top of that we're due to fly back to the UK tomorrow. It really doesn't make sense to me."

"Thank you for your candor, Mr Brown," said the DI with a less inquisitorial tone to his voice. "To be equally candid with you, I'm inclined to agree, but you must appreciate why I might have reservations." He turned to Martha. "I gather that your video surveillance shows Mr Cavendish apparently going off with another man without any obvious coercion at about the time that Mr Brown mentioned."

"It appears so, although the surveillance doesn't cover the gardens, so we don't know what happened next," she replied.

"Do you still have the belongings he left behind on the lounger?" asked the DI.

Martha nodded and pointed to a small pile of things on a table.

"And that includes the towel he was lying on?" he asked.

"Yes, plus a hotel bathrobe."

"Right," he said, standing up, "we need to get the sniffer dog here while the scent is still reasonably fresh. I'll go call the station." He left the office, nodding at Hugo and Martha on his way out.

"Phew," sighed Hugo, running his hands through his hair, "that was difficult."

"All in all, I think you got off quite likely," said Martha. "Some of our police are pretty homophobic and wouldn't have second thoughts about locking you up for further questioning. But for now, I need to make my own notes, so I suggest you try to get some sleep and we'll meet in the morning. What time is your flight?"

"Not until the evening."

"Okay, that gives us plenty of time to make arrangements if it comes to that. Good night, Mr Brown, and please try not to worry too much." She extended her hand and Hugo grasped it in both of his.

"I'm really grateful, Martha. Thank you."

Hugo went upstairs to their room and looked out of the window. The moonlight was shining on the pool and the lights dotted around the gardens created an inviting atmosphere. He could see couples walking around, glasses in hand, blissfully unaware of the unfolding drama. He wondered how the hotel would explain to guests the presence of the police and the imminent arrival of a sniffer dog.

He thought of Ben and wondered what he'd got himself involved in, wittingly or unwittingly. Before meeting Ben, there'd been occasions when his liaisons had taken an unforeseen turn but he'd never felt that unsafe or unable to extricate himself. He knew that Ben's past had a darker side that he sometimes felt compelled to reengage with and he wondered whether that's what had happened at the pool side. He remembered a news report some years ago of a woman being kidnapped in Johannesburg just hours after arriving from the UK and then being subjected to a 14 hour ordeal of gang rape. It was terrifying to think that Ben might have become caught up in something like that himself but almost more frightening that some part of him might actually be enjoying it.

***

"Yes, I can assure you that all precautions have been taken... Yes, he's negative and I have a copy of the test result should you require it. And as requested, a very thorough clean has been performed, so absolute satisfaction is guaranteed. But you must understand that such perfection comes at a price: 10,000 rand per participant is what I have in mind... I'm pleased that you agree... Yes, he is quite exceptional: prime British meat, as one might say...Very good, I'll see you and your colleagues later."

***

Ben thought he must have dozed off. He was still naked but now seemed to be enclosed in a harness suspended from something. His legs were separated as far apart as they could go. He tested the restraints around his wrists and ankles and found himself rocking to and fro from the exertion. His head was enclosed in a tight-fitting hood that smelt of leather. There were holes for him to look out of and to breathe. His mouth was partially held open by something attached to the hood. He heard shuffling and whispers from the other end of the room and then the sounds of clothes being taken off. The harness was abruptly adjusted and he felt he was being tipped upside down. He could see the floor below and the wall in front but everything else was outside his limited field of vision. He saw the bottom half of a man's torso silhouetted against the wall. An erect penis was shoved into his mouth without any warning and his head was pulled back hard. Simultaneously, he was aware of forced entry into his anus and pain as his sphincter was stretched into submission. He rocked back and forth in the harness as he was assaulted from both ends. Abruptly the two men withdrew but were swiftly replaced by two more penises. The grunting and thrusts increased in volume and frequency and he felt a liquid sensation in his rectum. The man in front of him forced his penis in deeper and ejaculated into his mouth. Ben wanted to spit it out but a hand was put over his mouth.

And so it continued until all the men were spent. Ben lost track of the time and how many penises his body had unwittingly serviced. Zippers were pulled up, clothes put back on and the room emptied. The harness was adjusted so that he was now facing upwards. For a moment, Ben was left alone, aware of the ache in and around his ass and the lingering taste and smell of semen. He felt what must have been semen seeping out of his anus onto the floor. Despite the ordeal, he was aroused and his dick stiffened. The door opened and he heard a pair of feet walking towards his right. He heard a faucet turning and the sound of water splashing on the floor. The spray of water was suddenly directed onto his body and over the hood. He gratefully swallowed the drops of water entering through the hole in the hood.

"Aren't you the thirsty one," said a voice on the right. "I'll remove the hood."

The man removed the hood and Ben immediately recognized him as the one wearing the tight t-shirt from yesterday, although he was now entirely naked. Ben looked into his eyes and felt the unnerving combination of fear, desire and excitement. His dick responded accordingly.

"Very impressive," said the voice. "You're a fast learner. If you behave, you'll be rewarded. If you resist, you'll be punished. It's time for your first lesson."

The man removed the shackles restraining Ben's wrists. Ben held them up to his face to examine the red marks from the constant chafing. He ran his hands over his face and scalp as if to confirm that nothing had been altered when he was unconscious. Ben could see the man's right hand stroking his penis and he brought it up to Ben's mouth. Ben took hold of it with his hands and guided it into his mouth, teasing the circumcised head with his tongue and then moving his head backwards and forwards as the man introduced it further and further into his mouth. Ben took hold of the penis in his right hand and stroked it with increasing frequency while licking the tip with his tongue. After some minutes, the man ejaculated into his mouth and Ben sucked hungrily on the source of liquid. The man pulled out and looked down at Ben who was licking his lips.

"Now it's time for your reward." The man moved in between Ben's legs and bent down to examine his penis. He put a finger to the pre-come on the tip and licked it. He teased Ben's anus with the finger and felt the wetness from the semen leaking out. He tongued the entrance, relishing the musky, aromatic smell. Ben groaned with pleasure. The man switched his attention to Ben's penis which by now was begging for attention with pulses of contraction. Almost immediately, Ben exploded into the man's mouth as it moved up and down the shaft. Without saying anything, the man stood up and bent over Ben's face, letting the semen drop into Ben's open mouth. Ben swallowed the sustenance gratefully. The man stood up and looked down at Ben.

"What do you want from me?" Ben asked.

"Well, apart from your body, I'm not at liberty to say at the moment."

"But why me?"

"That should become clearer with time, Mr Armstrong."

The man refastened the shackles around Ben's wrists and he adjusted the harness so that Ben was back in his original position. Ben noticed a camcorder on a tripod to the left. The man removed a videocassette, then dressed and left. Ben felt guilty for what had happened but knew he was powerless to do anything about it. He felt warm liquid seeping out of his anus onto the floor. He thought of Hugo and wondered what he was doing following his disappearance from the hotel. He'd do anything at this moment to hold Hugo in his arms and be away from all of this. He sobbed quietly, frightened of annoying the man with the strange green eyes who'd just rewarded him for good behavior. Ben closed his eyes and was grateful to no longer have the hood covering his face.

Friday, February 11, 2011

Hugo's sleep alone in the king size bed was uneasy. About an hour after turning in, he was woken up by the sound of a dog barking, which he thought must be the sniffer dog doing its job and responding to Ben's scent. Disconcertingly, he'd found himself dreaming of exotic couplings with the waiter and the handsome hotel manager. Waking up from such an erotically charged dream, Hugo's response was to stretch out his hand to touch Ben's furry chest. Finding his absence in their bed jolted him back to reality. He thought back to their first day in the hotel when the two of them enjoyed their first lovemaking as newly-weds. He felt his dick straining against the bed coverings. He sighed and reached for the phone to order breakfast. He dozed for a few minutes and then got up and walked naked to the window. The pool area looked no different to the day before and it was almost as if the hotel had decided to erase the events of the previous day.

There was a knock on the door and he called out "Come in!" He turned around and was surprised to see William the waiter walking in with the breakfast tray. William looked embarrassed and seemed to want to beat a hasty retreat.

"Gosh, I'm sorry. I'd forgotten I had no clothes on." Hugo grabbed a sheet to wrap around his waist.

William stared at him, looking forlorn and vulnerable. "I know I shouldn't have come to your room again, sir, but I feel so bad about your friend disappearing. Perhaps if I hadn't been here, you'd have been by the pool and he'd never have gone missing." He started sobbing.

"Come here, William," said Hugo softly, extending his hands out towards him.

William slowly came forwards to him, unsure how to respond. He stood about a foot away and they looked into each other's eyes. Hugo brushed away William's tears with his fingertips.

"How old are you, William?"

"22."

"I'm 26, the same age as Ben." He turned his face towards the pool and felt tears welling up.

William touched Hugo's face. "Can we start again? Just as friends, I mean. I really would like to help you if I can."

"I'd like that, William. I think I'm going to need friends to get through this." He leant forwards and kissed William gently on the lips.

"Time for breakfast, I think," said Hugo, removing the sheet and getting back into bed.

"And would sir like his breakfast in or out of bed?"

"In bed, I think, William. My name is Hugo, by the way."

"I'm pleased to meet you, sir. Would you care for milk in your coffee?"

***

Ben thought he must have dozed off, because he suddenly became aware of a young male voice saying "Mister, mister." He turned his head to the right and saw a teenage boy, fully clothed, holding out a tumbler of water. The boy seemed unperturbed by Ben's predicament and held the tumbler to Ben's parched lips. Ben eagerly drank until the tumbler was empty.

"Where am I?" he asked the boy.

"Sorry, mister, I can't say, I was just told to give you the water."

The boy turned and left without looking back. Ben closed his eyes again, grateful to have had his thirst relieved. He heard the door opening and recognized the footsteps. The man with green eyes was back in the same t-shirt and jeans and he was carrying a number of camcorders and tripods. He set up one on the floor in between Ben's feet and the other two on either side of Ben's face. He pressed buttons on all of them to start them recording. He adjusted the harness so that Ben's head was tilting towards the floor. Ben opened his mouth in expectation of the hood being put back on.

"I don't think the hood will be necessary, Mr Cavendish," said the t-shirt man. "And anyway your face is far too handsome to keep it hidden away."

"Thank you, sir," said Ben.

"It's time for your next test. I'd like to introduce you to someone we call the 'Milkman'."

The door opened again and Ben heard bare feet walking towards him. The man was tall and muscular with a shaven head. The light from the overhead bulb glistened on skin that was like polished ebony. The man was sporting an erection that was beyond anything Ben had ever imagined even in his wildest fantasies. At well over 10 inches in length and with a girth the size of Ben's wrist, it hung down virtually to the man's knees, swaying as he walked like a cobra entranced by a snake charmer. The man came round to Ben's right side and he slapped his appendage against Ben's face.

"Open wide," commanded the t-shirt man.

Ben responded without hesitation. He looked up and saw that another camcorder was pointing at his face. The ebony-skinned man was now standing astride Ben's chest and priming his penis for the strike. He plunged his massive erection into Ben's mouth. Ben felt hands behind his head forcing the penis against the back of his mouth and down his throat. Just as he felt he was about to pass out from lack of air, the man withdrew. He moved to the other end of Ben's body, separated Ben's buttocks and spat onto the cleft. Holding onto one buttock with his right hand and his erection with his other hand, he moved the head up and down the cleft, teasing the sphincter to open. He eased his penis into Ben's anus and rectum surprisingly gently but then commenced a jackhammer action of deep, fast thrusts that took Ben's breath away. After barely a minute of this he withdrew and returned to standing astride Ben's chest. Without even being told, Ben opened his mouth as wide as it would go. The man stroked his erection briefly and then ejaculated a thick geyser of semen into Ben's mouth that seemed endless, threatening to fill his mouth and overflow onto his cheeks. Ben swallowed the spasms of juice hitting the back of his mouth, fleetingly wondering how his system would respond to the vast amount of semen he'd ingested while in this room. The man stood up, stroked the head of his penis for a final time and walked out without saying a word.

The t-shirt man returned into view and smiled at Ben. "Yes, you're a very fast learner. Most don't pass that test. I think it's time for some food for you."

"What would have happened if I hadn't passed the test?"

"I'm afraid you'd have gone right back to square one,

which could of course still happen, but that's entirely dependent on your continuing good behavior. Your food will arrive shortly."

The t-shirt man stopped the camcorders, extracted the videocassettes and then left. The boy he'd seen in the previous intermission between tests walked in with a bowl of something that was steaming and smelt good.

"Mister, you want something to eat?"

Ben nodded hungrily. The boy dipped a spoon in the contents of the bowl and brought it to Ben's mouth. He swallowed the hot contents greedily not worrying whether it was burning his mouth. Ben couldn't easily identify the contents but it was spicy and had meat in it. The boy replenished the spoon and continued feeding Ben until the bowl was empty.

"You want to pee?" the boy asked.

Ben nodded again and briefly entertained the idea that he might be released from the harness, but he felt the boy lifting his penis and putting it in the bowl. "You pee in here," he said. Ben let his bladder empty into the bowl and gave an involuntary moan of relief as the discomfort in his pelvic region subsided. The boy walked over to some sort of sink and emptied the bowl. He returned to Ben's side and said: "You need to sleep." He walked to the door, switched off the light and left Ben on his own in the dark still strung up in the harness.

Ben listened to the sounds around him but couldn't identify anything that gave him any clue as to where he was. With no external light coming into the room, he'd no idea of the time of day. The cold dampness suggested that he might be in a basement, but there was no way of knowing whether he was 100 yards or 100 miles from the hotel. Although he'd endured abuse and degradation that had far exceeded any previous experience, he took some small consolation that he'd not actually been physically harmed. And from the comments made by the t-shirt man and the presence of camcorders during all his ordeals, he figured that his physical attributes were of value to the man. He'd heard of extreme porn being made on demand for the benefit of wealthy clients who got their rocks off from watching the sort of abuse he'd been subjected to. He also assumed that he had been picked out as a suitable candidate during their stay in the hotel. What he couldn't work out was the endpoint of the elaborate game, but he had to hold on to the belief that he was worth more to his captors alive than dead. And he realized that he was grateful to the man for rewarding him for his good behavior and enjoyed being praised for passing the tests. With that thought in mind, he closed his eyes and tried to get some sleep so that he would be best prepared for whatever was to happen next.

***

After breakfast, Hugo showered and shaved and tried to prepare a list of things that had to be done if Ben didn't return in time for the flight. He walked down to the lobby in search of the manager for an update on the police's investigation. He knocked on the office door and was relieved to hear Martha's voice say "Come in!"

When he entered the office, his immediate impression was of a charged atmosphere. The man sitting opposite Martha was middle-aged with a massively spreading abdomen that was poorly constrained by his shiny black suit. He stood up slowly and extended his fleshy hand to

Hugo.

"So this is the young man I've been hearing so much about," he said without a glimmer of sincerity.

Hugo took his hand reluctantly. "And you are?"

Martha responded: "Mr Brown, this is our owner, Mr Carmichael, and I'm afraid he's unhappy with the press coverage the hotel has been receiving." She handed Hugo a copy of the Cape Argus that had Ben's disappearance splashed all over the front page. Hugo glanced at the sensationalist headline:

'GAY HONEYMOONER DISAPPEARS IN NELSON LODGE HOTEL'S BUSHES'.

Fuck, he thought

"Would you know anything about that? Another young friend in the press room, perhaps?" asked Mr Carmichael with a sneer.

"Absolutely not," replied Hugo. "I don't trust the press and I'd certainly never do anything that might jeopardize something as important as my partner's life. In fact, I'm shocked that you'd even consider the idea." He glared at Mr Carmichael.

"I'm reassured to hear that, young man," responded Mr Carmichael, "but nonetheless, you must appreciate that this episode is highly embarrassing for the hotel, particularly as unorthodox sexual practices may be involved. In short, I'm prepared for you to remain here for another 24 hours but after that you will have to leave."

The hotel owner heaved his bulk out of the chair and walked out of the office, leaving Hugo and Martha watching his slug-like exit.

"I can't say I'm surprised," said Hugo, "but what a bastard."

Martha smiled sympathetically. "Hugo, that's business. But as I said before, we won't simply chuck you out. Let me give you an update and then you can decide what you want to do."

"I'd appreciate that." Martha poured him some coffee.

"Well, first things first. The sniffer dog picked up a trail but it ended at a spot where the gardeners park a buggy used to transport garden waste. That buggy has been missing since Ben disappeared. I checked with security at the main gate and they have a record of a buggy leaving at just after 1:00 p.m. with two men in front who dressed like our garden staff. But they can't say where it went after that."

"So Ben could have been in the back of the buggy?"

"That's what it's looking like."

"What do the police think?

"Well, they think his abduction was planned rather than impulsive and their guess is a sexual motive, although they can't rule out a ransom demand."

"So what do the police suggest?"

"Well, they're following leads and obviously looking for the buggy. It's being treated as a kidnap, so there's no question of them not taking it seriously. Their advice is for you to contact the British Consulate who might be able to help you both practically and financially. And you'll need to speak to your airline about your flight this evening."

"Would you be able to help with that? We're meant to be on BA0058."

"Okay, I'll ring them." Martha consulted a list of telephone numbers and dialed the local number for British Airways.

Hugo half-listened to her conversation but his thoughts

were was still reeling from the encounter with the obnoxious hotel owner.

Martha turned to Hugo. "Well, that was easy. Fortunately, your return flights are flexible, so all you have to do is to contact British Airways when you're in a position to fly and that's valid for up to a year."

Hugo groaned. "Christ! I hope he's back from wherever he is before then."

Martha nodded sympathetically.

"And what about my stay here?" he asked.

"Officially, you'll need to leave the day after tomorrow; unofficially, I'm sure we'll come up with something."

"Thanks again, Martha."

"I'm happy to help, Hugo, and I'm really sorry about what's happened."

They shook hands and Hugo returned to the room he'd been sharing with Ben. He looked at Ben's clothes and wondered when he'd see him wearing them again. He decided to get some much-needed sun by the pool and put on speedos beneath a bathrobe. Although feeling slightly guilty at the thought of this indulgence, he rationalized it by considering that he'd be looking out for anything untoward. He'd make more phone calls after lunch although dreaded having to speak with Ben's mother.

Hugo chose the same sun lounger that Ben had been using but noticed that any scent of his partner had long since gone. Taking off his bathrobe, he lay flat and enjoyed the warmth of the sun against his skin. His speedos tightly contained his dick that was expanding with the heat. Having briefly dozed off, a tap on his shoulder alerted him to someone else's presence. Half sitting up and trying to avoid looking into the sun, he noticed that John

Bredenkamp was sitting on the lounger next to him, although this time his hair was tousled as if just washed and he had on a fitted, short-sleeved, white shirt and jeans. He was smiling warmly.

"Mr Brown? Hugo? I'm sorry to disturb you but I feel such a fool for making such a song and dance about the waiter when I should have been listening to your concerns about your friend. I was so sorry to hear from Martha what seems to have happened and I feel guilty about not taking it more seriously. So I'd like to help by offering for you to stay at my place when you have to leave the hotel."

Hugo looked at John uncertainly, trying to gauge his motives. "Was that Martha's suggestion?" he asked eventually.

"Sort of but I was going to suggest it anyway. You seem like a nice guy and I just wanted to help."

"How do I know that I can trust you? For all I know you could be planning to take me to some dark room and have your wicked way with me."

John tried to look shocked but the smile gave him away. He glanced at Hugo's bulging speedos.

"It's definitely tempting but I promise it's not on my agenda. Have a word with my boyfriend if you're not convinced. He's a doctor at the Groote Schuur Hospital. You can call him if you like."

"I saw his photo on your desk. He looked nice."

"He is. He may also have some ideas about what your friend has got involved in. I can take you to our place this evening, if you like.'

"Okay, thanks a lot, but I hope you've got room for all our bags."

"Good. I'll see you in the lobby at 6:00 p.m."

Hugo returned to his room and thought through everything that had happened since they'd arrived in Cape Town just a week ago. Although his world had been turned upside down by Ben's disappearance, this was ironically giving him time to discover more about himself. When he first met Ben, his own sexual experiences had been limited to furtive wanks at school and the occasional, alcohol-fuelled encounter at university. He'd never seen himself as being particularly attractive, so any approach from another man seemed unusual and a source of apprehension rather than excitement. Ben, on the other hand, had experiences up to the hilt and Hugo was bowled over by their lovemaking and particularly the enjoyment he found in being fucked. That had continued unabated throughout the two years of living together, but his rather refined job in the Courtauld Institute provided few opportunities to be more openly sexual despite the effeteness associated with fine art. Ben had also made him aware that the size of his dick was something to be proud of, although he still found it difficult to accept pride in something that he'd just been born with. But from the first time he'd walked down Kloof Street, he'd become attuned to the effect he had on other gay men and found himself glorying in the attention he was getting. And with that new confidence in his sexuality came the need to explore what he did in bed, as Ben discovered to his surprise on their first day in Cape Town and the waiter experienced yesterday morning.

Turning to his laptop, Hugo found the phone number for Ben's mother and the details of the British Consulate. He decided to start with Ben's mother. Checking his watch, he worked out that it would be 10:00 a.m. in the

UK.

"Oh, hello, is that Barbara? It's Hugo, Hugo Brown... Yes, we're still in Cape Town... Look, Barbara, I've got something difficult to tell you and you might want to sit down...Yes, it's about Ben... No, he hasn't been injured or anything quite like that... The thing is he disappeared around this time yesterday from the poolside and we don't know where he's gone... Yes, the police have got involved and he's now officially a missing person. I'm praying that he'll just simply turn up. It's just not like him and I'm really worried sick..." Hugo started sobbing. "... Yes, sorry, I'm still here. Do you want to fly here if he doesn't turn up in the next day or so? ... No? ... Okay, I understand that you've got too much going on... Anyway, I'll keep in touch. Oh, I'm also going to phone the British Consulate...Yes, I'm sure they should be able to help... Okay, goodbye... Bye, Barbara."

That conversation hadn't been easy and Hugo was glad that he'd kept information to the minimum. He was quite sure that any suggestion that Ben had gone off in pursuit of another man would have unleashed a tirade about unnatural sexual practices. He also wasn't surprised in the least that she hadn't taken up his suggestion of flying to Cape Town. It's a pity you can't choose mother-in-laws at the same time as husbands, he thought.

Next stop on his list was the consulate, but he hadn't a clue as to the response he'd receive. He was hoping his accent might help. He phoned the number he'd found on the South African website.

"Is that the British Consulate? Good. My name is Hugo Brown and I'm a UK national staying at the Nelson Lodge Hotel. I need to report my partner Benjamin Cavendish going missing about 24 hours ago... Yes, the police are involved. Could you put me through to someone? Thanks."

Hugo listened to the connection being made and hoped for the best. The woman on reception sounded bored and was probably more used to dealing with missing passports than missing people. The connection was made with a reassuring and very British click.

"Yes, that's correct... Oh, you were already aware of his disappearance. That's good to hear...Yes, I'd be pleased to come to the consulate tomorrow...11:00 a.m. sounds fine. May I know your name? Excellent. Thanks, Mr Anderson. I'm very grateful. I'll see you tomorrow. Goodbye."

That sounded more hopeful. It turned out that the consulate had already been in touch with the police after reading the news report in the Cape Argus.

Finally, Hugo rang his mother.

"Mum? Hi, it's Hugo. Oh, God, Mum, I don't know where to start." Hugo started sobbing again. 'No, no, we haven't split up as such. It's just that the silly bugger went off after someone behind the bushes at the hotel yesterday lunchtime and I haven't seen him since. I suppose he might simply have wanted to screw someone senseless but it's still not really like him as he just went off in his speedos and flip-flops...Yes, everyone seems to be going on about 'boys being boys' but we're on our honeymoon for Christ's sake... Sorry, I didn't mean to raise my voice but it's all getting a bit too much... Yes, I've talked to the police and to the British Consulate... No, the hotel is being fine about things really apart from the stroppy owner. I'm going to stay with one of the managers and his boyfriend who want to help. And the hotel has also contacted BA who'll rebook us when Ben turns up... God, it'd be great if you could come here, but give it a day or two so that you don't have an unnecessary flight. Thanks Mum. Love you lots. Bye."

As expected, his mother's response was poles apart from when talking with his mother-in-law. His mother was the sort of person who didn't bat an eyelid about anything to do with his sexuality and he loved her even more for that.

There was a timid knock on the door and Hugo called out "Come in!"

William the waiter entered, looking shy and forlorn. "I hear you're leaving today to stay with the manager, John Bredenkamp," he said.

"News travels fast," said Hugo. "Can I trust him?"

"He's okay," said William. "His hands wander but we all like him. His boyfriend is nice too."

"Is it really true that I left you with a sore ass?"

William blushed. "Well, not exactly, but I wanted the afternoon off."

Hugo laughed. "I thought it might be something like that."

William looked down at the carpet. "You know, sir, I still feel so responsible for what happened. I wish there's something I could do to put things right for you."

"Well, you could try asking around your colleagues to see whether anyone has heard anything."

"Actually, I did that before I came up to see you but no one seems to know anything. There was a meeting with management early this morning and we were all told to keep quiet. I'd probably get the sack if they knew I was here now."

"What about the other guests? They must have realized something was up last night when the police brought out the sniffer dog."

"Well, I overheard quests talking about the disappearance when I was serving breakfast and lunch, and one couple did ask me directly what had happened after they read the local paper."

"So I'm hardly the most popular guest and I can see why they want to get rid of me."

"Who told you that?"

"The owner, someone called Mr Carmichael."

"Oh him."

"You know him, then?"

"Oh yes, he's also got wandering hands."

"That's not a pleasant thought." Hugo stood up and went to the window to look out at the gardens. "William, is it true that guests come here for a quick cruise followed by a lengthy afternoon tea?"

"Where did you hear that?"

"Ben said the gardens were mentioned as a cruising place in the Spartacus guide."

"Perhaps he was pulling your leg, sir."

"You know, I wonder whether he'd actually planned in advance to go off into the bushes."

"It sounds as if he's someone who enjoys the wild side now and again, sir."

"That's certainly one way of putting it, William."

"And what about you, sir?"

"You probably won't believe it, but Ben was the only one until we had sex yesterday."

William looked surprised. "Gosh, I'm honored, sir."

Hugo checked his watch. "William, I really need to

collect things together before I leave." He reached into his wallet for a business card which he offered to the waiter. "If you're ever in London, give us a ring. I'm sure Ben would like to invite you into our bed again."

William looked at the card and smiled. "I'd like that, sir. I'd definitely like that."

***

Ben woke with a start as the harness was adjusted again. He noticed with relief that his hands were now free. The light was back on and he could see that he was now suspended at a 45 degree angle with his face towards the back wall away from the door. Immediately underneath him and pressing against his crotch there was a pair of male buttocks separated by straps attached to whatever their owner was lying on. It was obvious that the t-shirt man planned for Ben to fuck him. He felt his dick stirring. The rest of the individual's torso and head was hidden from Ben's view. He heard soft moans coming from in front of him. He whispered "What's your name? Where are we?" but didn't get a response. The t-shirt man slapped him hard on the face. The door opened and a pair of feet walked towards his rear. He felt hands separate his own buttocks and something push against his anal opening. He looked down and saw that he was now fully erect. He turned to look at the t-shirt man as if to ask "What do you want me to do?" but the man was continuing to set up various camcorders to record the scene from different points of view. Having done this, he stood at an oblique angle in front of Ben.

"Mr Cavendish, this is your penultimate test. If you fail the test, you'll go back to square one. Do you understand?"

Ben nodded.

"The scenario is simple. You're in an imaginary driving seat and you've a passenger immediately behind you. You've met him before. I want you to fuck the man in front of you and at the same time you'll be fucked by your passenger. But the timing is all important: your passenger must ejaculate on your back first and then you must withdraw and ejaculate over the man in front of you. The twist is that at precisely the time that your passenger ejaculates, the man's neck will be twisted and broken. He won't feel anything as he's already unconscious. You'll feel his sphincter contract around your penis and that's your signal to withdraw and ejaculate."

Ben nodded, realizing yet again he was powerless but utterly horrified by what he was being required to do. He dreaded what would happen if he couldn't perform but the insistent pressure from behind and the sight of the inviting opening in front seemed to be sufficient to maintain his erection.

"Action!" called the t-shirt man.

The man behind entered Ben with minimal hesitation and the momentum drove Ben's penis forward into the parted buttocks in front on him. The pummeling his ass received went way beyond anything he'd experienced before and his dick continued the motion into the unconscious receptacle lying on the bench. After minutes of relentless pounding, Ben sensed that the Milkman was reaching the point of no return and he tried to hold himself back. The Milkman suddenly pulled out and ejaculated streams of warm semen onto his back and then plunged deep inside him again. Ben knew that he wouldn't be able to hold back much longer. He heard a loud snap from in front and the body went limp. He felt the man's sphincter contract around his penis and withdrew and ejaculated over the torso, splattering the material shielding the rest of the body.

"Cut! That's a wrap as they say," said the t-shirt man. "That's impressive, Mr Cavendish. You haven't let me down after all. I'm pleased to see that you're well on the way to attaining the potential that I always thought you were capable of."

"My God!" exclaimed Ben. "I've met you before!"

"Indeed. I seem to remember an interesting series of encounters in an Earls Court basement a scant five years ago. You were younger of course, but just as desirable and I could see then that you had so much potential."

"But how did you manage to keep track of me? And how did you know I was coming to Cape Town?"

"It was remarkably easy on both counts. Your friend Hugo obligingly placed an entry in The Times which included all the details I needed about your ceremony and vacation in Cape Town. And I must say you did make such a handsome couple in your suits. It's such a shame I had to leave before the meal and speeches, but I fear you would have recognized me. And anyway I had so many preparations to make. I trust you appreciated the room upgrade. I couldn't leave my name, of course."

"You were at the ceremony? Oh Christ! I don't believe it!"

"Perhaps I should jog your memory a little more: I am your master, you are my slave."

Ben responded without thinking: "You are my master, I am your slave." He had a glazed look on his face.

***

Hugo struggled with the bags down to the lobby just before 6:00 p.m. He went up to reception to check-out and paid for the extras with his AmEx card. John arrived to take Hugo and his luggage to his apartment. Hugo leaned back in the seat of the Mercedes convertible and thought he could get used to life in Cape Town. John cast admiring glances at his passenger.

John's loft apartment was only a short drive away in Bree Street. He explained as he was driving that Greg had managed to buy it at a knockdown price from a British couple who'd become disenchanted with Cape Town and wanted to get back to life in safe, genteel Surrey. He parked in the garage on the ground floor and helped Hugo carry his bags into the ancient elevator that wheezed its way up to the fourth level apartment. The first sight that greeted Hugo on exiting the elevator was a farmyard scene of papier-mâché sheep grazing on astroturf next to the seven foot high entrance door.

"Welcome to our humble home," said John, as he dramatically slid the huge door open to reveal a double height space that seemed to Hugo to stretch as far and as wide as he could see.

"Wow!" he exclaimed.

"Yes, it's rather something, isn't it," said John.

They dropped the bags and John led Hugo through the open plan living area to the front terrace where his boyfriend was waiting with a bottle of chilled wine and some glasses.

"Hi, you must be Hugo. I'm Greg."

Hugo looked at Greg and thought staying in Cape Town might have some unexpected benefits after all. In some respects, Greg reminded him of Ben, but this was a slightly older version of Ben done to perfection. Greg and John couldn't fail to notice his lingering appraisal and smiled at each other.

"Oops, sorry, I was just taking in the view," said Hugo, blushing.

"Yes, the view has that effect on people," said John. "That's why he's such a popular doctor at the hospital." He grinned.

It was Greg's turn to blush. They sat down on the couch and John poured out the wine. Greg turned to look at Hugo.

"I'm sorry to hear about your partner going missing," he said. "How are you coping?"

"I'm not sure it's sunk in fully yet," replied Hugo. "He's only been gone for 24 hours, after all. I'm really just expecting him to turn up looking a bit sheepish and complaining of a sore dick. But I guess I'm probably clutching at straws."

"John's told me a bit about how the hotel has been dealing with it. I gather you met the delightful owner," said Greg.

"God, he was repellant. And he had the nerve to accuse me of leaking Ben's disappearance to the local paper."

"I know what you mean. Actually, he's just the sort of person I dread having to exam as a patient."

"What do you specialize in, Greg?"

"I'm an emergency department physician. It's shift work which suits us as we can get to the beach and gym during the day."

"That sounds interesting. What sorts of cases do you see?"

"Just about anything, really. It could be a giant, double-headed dildo stuck up some guy's rectum one minute and stabbings and gunshot wounds the next."

"You're joking!" said Hugo, looking amazed.

"No, it's true, although it's the ketchup bottle that's more of a problem."

All three of them laughed.

"And what do you do back in London?" asked Greg.

"Well, it probably sounds a bit boring, but I'm an assistant art curator. In fact, I'm meant to be giving a talk on a French artist called Nicolas Poussin in about 40 hours from now."

"That's very interesting. There's something I'd like to show you after we've eaten," said Greg mysteriously.

Hugo looked intrigued.

"And it's definitely not his dick," said John.

Greg turned to kiss his boyfriend and then got up to go to the kitchen. "There's more wine in the cooler," he called out from inside the apartment.

"He's really nice," said Hugo.

"One in a million, I think. Now, what about your predicament? Have there been any further developments?"

"Okay, you know about the buggy and that two men were seen driving it?" John nodded. "So it seems certain that Ben was taken with coercion unless he agreed to lie in the back under the waste, which seems unlikely. Martha mentioned that the police were looking for the buggy but there's been no further news on that. I spoke with a helpful guy in the British Consulate this afternoon and they'd already spoken with the police after seeing the piece in the Cape Argus. I've arranged to go to the consulate at 11:00 tomorrow, so there may be an update. I've also phoned both my mother and mother-in-law. My mother will catch a flight at the drop of a hat if we think it'll help. I've suggested we wait a day or so just in case Ben turns up. His mother wasn't so helpful, and to be honest I haven't told her the entire truth, as I don't think I could take a tirade about what he does or doesn't do with his dick. So that's it in a nutshell. What do you think?"

"First off, I think you're doing a good job of keeping your head together. Secondly, I agree about holding off your mother leaving the UK. It's the weekend coming up, so there'll be plenty of time to think about what to do next. And the hotel knows you're staying here, so there shouldn't be any problem with messages getting through. We've got Wi-Fi, so you can use your laptop."

"Thanks, John, I really can't thank you enough."

John bent forwards and brushed Hugo's cheek with his fingers.

"Dinner's served!" called Greg.

The three of them sat down for the simple but delicious meal that Greg had prepared. This included gazpacho that was smoky with paprika, a whole sea bass that he skilfully dissected in front of them, and a local dessert called Malva pudding that was accompanied by homemade vanilla ice cream. All this was washed down with more of the sauvignon blanc they'd had on the terrace. They returned to the terrace after the meal.

"So, Hugo, what's a handsome young art curator on his honeymoon doing having hot sex with one of my waiters while his husband is sunning himself by the pool?" asked John with a mischievous look.

"Oh Christ, I thought you'd bring that up. To be honest, I've been thinking a lot about it... I mean, about why I did it rather than what I did... Well, actually a lot of both, really." Hugo looked charmingly embarrassed. "I guess a bit of it was paying Ben back for having sex with his best man, but there was something else which I don't quite understand. Perhaps it was me wanting freedom to do something spontaneous. I'm not sure, really. But I do know it's left me feeling a strange combination of guilt and excitement."

"And what about now? Shouldn't you be the dutiful husband waiting by the phone for the next call from the police?" asked Greg, equally cheekily.

"Perhaps I should be, but it would drive me crazy. I think being with friends rather than being stuck on my own is the only way to get through this."

"Well, as both a friend and doctor concerned with your welfare, I'd agree with that, but be careful. You're very vulnerable." He looked earnestly at Hugo. "But now I'd like to show that 'something'." John gave Hugo a wink.

Hugo followed Greg back into the apartment, up some stairs to a mezzanine level, through a cozy lounge area with a large flat screen TV, and then left into an office space. Hanging on the wall directly ahead was the original of Nicolas Poussin's 'Self-Portrait: 1649' that Hugo had spent the last few months trying to track down. He stood rooted to the spot with his mouth open in amazement.

"I don't believe it!" he exclaimed. "I thought some Russian oligarch purchased it just a few weeks ago."

"Russian, yes; oligarch, no. Count Grigoriy Eduardovitsch Dobrygin at your service, Mr Hugo," he said in an exaggerated Russian accent and with a deep bow. "But generally known as Greg Edwards."

"But how did you manage to buy it? Its auction value is well into the millions."

"Let's say it was all down to a wealthy relative and knowing the right people."

"I'm impressed, Greg, really seriously impressed. Do you mind if I take a photo of it?"

"Be my guest. What's ours is yours while you're staying with us."

Without realizing what he was doing, Hugo turned and kissed Greg on the cheek. Greg looked momentarily surprised.

"Oh Christ, and I barely know you!" exclaimed Hugo.

"Think of it as your post-traumatic response to seek confirmation that you're being looked after. It's quite normal, I can assure you. But let's go back to the terrace before John thinks were up to no good."

Hugo laughed.

***

Hugo's bedroom was on the floor below the master bedroom and the open plan construction of the apartment meant that noises carried. That included the sounds of his hosts' lovemaking and he wondered whether they were putting on a display in the hope that he might join them. He concentrated on imagining everything resolved and him and Ben back in their one-bed apartment in London. But just thinking of the tiny apartment in its unprepossessing location was enough to make him realize that so much had changed. He thought of Greg and John in bed together and felt his dick stirring. He sighed. He badly needed to sleep. He closed his eyes and imagined himself back in front of Greg's Poussin, examining every brushstroke and interplay of color and texture, and he fell asleep within minutes.

Saturday, February 12, 2011

Ben awoke with a rather vague recollection of recent events. Various sensations in his pelvic region made him aware that he'd had sex but he couldn't recall with whom or how many men that might have involved. He was also aware of a lingering taste in his mouth that was definitely that of semen. He licked his lips. Of course the master had insisted that he should stay in the harness; after all, all good slaves needed to be constantly conditioned and reminded of their position. He felt proud to have been chosen by someone so powerful and felt sure that he we would be able to perform even the most exacting task required by his master.

***

Hugo woke early the following morning and pulled a bath towel around his waist. He walked across the open-plan expanse and out onto the balcony where he could see Greg naked, leaning over the balcony and looking at the expanse of Cape Town. He was as perfect from behind as from the front.

"Do you think he's somewhere out there?" asked Hugo.

"Oh hi, Hugo, I didn't realize you were awake," said Greg. It suddenly dawned on him that he was naked in front of their guest. "Oh jeez, let me go put something on!" he said in a camp, Brooklyn accent.

"You don't have to on my behalf. The view is still as enjoyable as it was last night."

Greg turned to him, smiling. "So did you sleep well,

young Poussin expert?"

"Surprisingly well, really. I imagined myself in front of the Poussin going over every detail and that sent me to sleep." He looked into Greg's dark eyes. "I am so very sorry, Monsieur Poussin," he said in a mock French accent.

Greg laughed and put his hand on Hugo's shoulder as they continued to look across the city. "It's good that you're still able to see the light side of things. I'm not sure I'd be able to do the same if I was in your position." He turned to look at Hugo and noticed the shape his dick was making in the towel. "And it looks as if your dick is still responding quite normally too."

"Oops, sorry." Hugo went red and rearranged the towel.

"There's no need to apologize. In any other situation we'd probably be leaping into bed together at about this stage of the proceedings."

"But as you pointed out, I'm very vulnerable, and also I'd never live with the guilt."

"Something like that." Greg turned back to looking across Cape Town. "You were asking whether I thought he was out there?"

"Yes."

"Well, those buggies can't go far, so that must limit where he could be."

"What do you think they're doing to him?"

"Well, if it's just the two men, probably just the usual and he'll be sent on his way. A ransom demand is the other possibility and we should hear about that pretty quickly. So I'd be surprised if we don't get some news soon."

Hugo digested what Greg said and sighed. "You know,

I heard you making love last night."

"Did you mind?"

"No, it was nice. You seem to care for each other in such an open and easy-going way. It's different to Ben and me."

"In what way?"

"Ben's a bit of a wham bam action man, if you know what I mean."

"In bed or out of bed?"

"Both, really. I guess I put up with it because I love him."

"That's relationships for you. I put up with John's growing collection of *bric*-à-*brac* and reproduction antiques but I still love him." Greg kissed Hugo lightly on the lips. "But now I think we should get showered and dressed for breakfast for when John returns from the gym."

Greg and Hugo were enjoying the morning sun on the terrace when John returned. He'd bought crusty bread and croissants from the local deli. He'd also dropped by the hotel to check whether there'd been any update on Ben's disappearance overnight. He pulled out a plastic envelope from the paper bag and put it on the table.

"This arrived for you last night, Hugo. It was dropped off at the security entrance and I put it in a plastic cover just in case. A boy delivered it, so security didn't think it was important."

The three of them peered at the object in the plastic cover. It appeared to be an entirely normal A5 envelope with some writing on the front, although the characters were poorly formed as if the writer was trying to avoid detection.

What was written was unambiguous:

MR HUGO BROWN
ROOM #202, NELSON LODGE HOTEL

"Shouldn't we call the police?" asked Hugo.

"I'll get some gloves," said Greg. He went inside and returned with their first aid kit and took out latex gloves, tweezers and a scalpel blade. After putting on the gloves, he opened the plastic cover and used the tweezers to extract carefully the envelope. Then after turning it over, he inserted the scalpel and cut along the top of the envelope, being careful not to damage the contents.

Hugo was impressed by this new skill of Greg's. "Where did you learn that from?" he asked.

"Oh it's just one of those things one picks up. Patients come to us with all sorts of weird things written down, and I once had a guy who handed me his hand-written murder confession. Watching CSI: Miami comes in handy too."

He eased the envelope open and the three of them peered inside. The small slip of paper measured no more than one inch by three and they all recognized the typed characters on it as a URL:

www.xstreamtube.net/watch/bbc1*4462

Greg and John had come across the website before and exchanged an uneasy look.

"Is that some sort of X-Files on YouTube?" asked Hugo naively.

"Not exactly," said John. "It's a porn site - gay, straight and bi - some of it's free but a lot you have to pay to watch." The significance of what he'd just said sank in for all three of them. John's crusty bread and croissants no longer seemed so appealing.

"Oh Christ, that's going to involve Ben, isn't it?" said Hugo, looking ashen.

"I suppose it might," said John, trying to think of how he'd break the news if the worst case scenario transpired when they saw whatever was on the link. "Look, Hugo, you stay here while Greg and I go upstairs and try the link." He copied the URL and Greg put the slip and the envelope back into the plastic cover.

Greg and John went up to the living room and connected a laptop to the flat screen TV. They entered the URL and a video clip started to play. There was no sound, so what they saw was strangely disembodied. The jerky camerawork and single overhead bulb added to the overall effect of a low budget movie. Apart from the overhead light, the room was dark and the shine on the walls made it look cold and damp. The clip started with a distant shot of someone naked strapped at an angle into a metal chair fixed to the ground. As the camera zoomed in on the figure's genital region it was clear that the figure was male. Shockingly, the camera showed him voiding urine onto the floor, the stream glistening under the light and the camera tracking the stream to the floor. The camera returned to tracking up the man's muscular abdomen and his well-defined chest. He was breathing heavily. The camera moved to his head. At first it appeared that he had no head, but then someone off-screen removed the black material covering his head and a hand slapped him on the right cheek. A gag had been forced into his mouth. The look of fear in his dark eyes was palpable. Another hand appeared and pulled the man's hair, forcing his head back. A large, erect penis was repeatedly hammered into the man's mouth and throat, forcing him to gag violently. The penis was abruptly pulled out and ejaculated all over the man's face, covering his eyes, nose and mouth. The clip finished with the penis being forced back into the man's mouth and the camera zoomed in on the man's terror-struck eyes.

As soon as the clip finished, a box came up onscreen inviting viewers to view the entire video for an extra $50 payable by all major credit cards. Beneath the video player, a counter showed that the clip had already been watched by 167 individuals, with comments such as "So hot!", "Luv u 2 cum on me 2" and "Def. worth $100+."

Greg and John looked at each other, feeling shaken to the core. Greg dabbed at the tears welling up. Just at that moment, they became aware of a movement to their right and saw that Hugo was standing a few feet away, transfixed by the image frozen on the screen.

"Oh no!" he screamed. "What are they doing to him?" He collapsed onto the chair next to Greg and started sobbing uncontrollably. Greg put his arm around him and gently rocked him from side to side. "It's okay, love, we're here to help you." Hugo looked up at Greg and John and they saw the terrified look of a rabbit caught in headlights.

John called the police and they agreed to dispatch a car immediately to collect the envelope and to get additional information about how it came to be in their possession. They weren't pleased that the evidence had been opened but John reassured them that Greg had done everything necessary to prevent contamination. John tried to dissuade Hugo from going to the consulate but Greg thought it best that he did go and agreed to accompany him. He was due to do a late shift in the emergency department from 4:00 p.m. and planned to go to the gym after leaving the consulate.

The consulate was eight blocks away in Riebeek Street,

so it was a fairly easy walk from their apartment. Greg looked at Hugo while they were walking and wished he'd met him years ago. John had many positive attributes but anything remotely artistic wasn't one of them. They reached the consulate, which turned out to be on the 15th floor of an unprepossessing tower block rather than the grand, colonial mansion the title had suggested. Mr Anderson was there to greet them as soon they stepped out of the elevator and Greg suggested that the two of them watch the video clip before Hugo joined them.

Ten minutes later, Mr Anderson came out of his office looking noticeably unnerved, but obviously trying to appear upbeat, and invited Hugo to join them. When Hugo walked in, he was surprised to see a fourth person of about Greg's age whose casual appearance seemed out of place in the official setting of the office, which was complete with a photo of the Queen and a Union Jack desktop flag.

"Please sit down, Mr Brown," greeted Mr Johnson. Let me introduce my colleague Martin Ziegler who's from the Rainbow Project. I thought it might be helpful to have him here as he has some expertise in the Cape Town scene." Martin smiled at Hugo but it was a somewhat pained look, suggesting that he'd found the video uncomfortable viewing.

"Hugo, I can't begin to imagine how dreadful this whole experience is for you," said Mr Johnson. "That video was certainly most unpleasant. However, as I was saying to Dr Edwards, I think it's essential that we remain objective whatever videos these people put on the internet. Ben is a handsome man and that's an asset worth a great deal to the people who abducted him. I also think they'd be foolish to milk the situation too far or to cause significant harm to him."

He looked at Hugo and Greg to see how they reacted to this. They seemed to be hanging on to every word.

"Would you like to continue, Martin?" asked Mr Johnson.

"Of course," said Martin. He turned to look at Hugo. "Sadly, the gay scene here has moved on to something darker where anything can be supplied if there is a demand, which includes prostitution and less mainstream sex. The Rainbow Project was set up both to monitor this and to help people who find themselves in trouble. I suspect this is what Ben has become involved in and undoubtedly under coercion. As Mr Johnson has hinted, I think there will be more videos and the content may well become more extreme. But I don't actually think Ben's life will be at risk. I also think a ransom demand is highly likely."

Mr Johnson looked at Greg and Hugo and wondered what their relationship was: clearly not exactly doctor and patient.

"Hugo, it would be helpful for us to know what you think about the situation and also about Ben himself," said Mr Johnson.

Hugo looked to Greg for support and he took hold of his hand. "Okay, but this is really difficult, and that video has totally thrown me. But I think you're right about what Ben has got involved in. Before I met him, he was involved in some heavy scene in Earls Court in London - I guess it what's now called BDSM - but he's never talked about it during all the time we've been together. Sex-wise, he's fundamentally dominant, so I'm not sure how he'd react to being forced to submit. But his alpha maleness might be enough to get him through it."

"Martin, have you come across this sort of thing before?" asked Greg.

"Well, there have been a few cases of women being abducted for sex, but it's usually opportunistic and for kicks rather than anything more organized. I haven't heard of anything involving gay men, though. The cases we generally come across involve vulnerable males being lured rather than forced into doing something. This situation feels very different and what Hugo said about Ben's past could be relevant. Some BDSM communities operate on a principle of master and slave, and once that relationship has been struck the bond is believed to exist for life - just as if the individual is in servitude, in fact."

"One thing I was wondering is the relevance of the BBC1 handle attached to the video upload," said Greg.

"I hadn't noticed that before, but it's clearly not the British Broadcasting Corporation," said Mr Johnson. "Someone is obviously having fun at our expense."

"I think I may have some idea about that," said Martin. "I've heard of something called the Bareback Club which guarantees safe but unprotected sex for men who are prepared to pay for it. But from what I've gathered, it's fairly tame stuff and just does what it says on the tin."

"But perhaps they're connected in some way. You know, like the Bareback Club being the point of access for other stuff," suggested Greg.

"Yes, that's possible," said Martin.

"So how can we find out more about it?" asked Hugo.

"Well, it's a bit off the beaten track, but there's a bar called Video which may have some connection with it, but you'll need to be very careful where you step," replied Martin.

"I agree," said Mr Johnson. "This is a delicate situation and it's sometimes easier to let things pan out for a bit rather than doing something precipitous, particularly if you're on your own in a place you don't know. And speaking of which, where will you be staying for the next few days?"

"Greg and his boyfriend are putting me up at 180 Bree Street. My mother will probably be flying out, so we might find a hotel together."

"I think I'd advise staying put for the time being, as things might get more difficult," said Mr Anderson. Greg nodded in agreement.

"Oh God, you mean more videos, ransom demands and that sort of thing?" asked Hugo.

"Quite possibly, I'm afraid," said Mr Anderson, "and I would strongly advise you to pass on anything you receive to the police. In fact, I insist on it, dear boy."

***

Following Greg and Hugo returning from the consulate, Greg gave John a quick account of what had been discussed and then went off to the gym, leaving John to take Hugo out for lunch at Bardelli's cafe on Kloof Street. Hugo was looking pensive when John returned with their food.

"What's on your mind? Is it something they said at the consulate?"

"Well, there is that, but I can't stop thinking of that image of Ben in the video clip."

"I'm not surprised. It's difficult to shake off."

"I wonder what's going through Ben's mind at the moment."

"I'd imagine he's thinking of someone who means a lot to him."

"You mean me."

"I'm sure of that."

Hugo looked thoughtful. "Have you heard of the expression 'sometimes good things fall apart so better things can fall together'?"

"That's Marilyn Monroe, isn't it?"

"Yes, but I don't think it was from a film. It's what I keep telling myself although it's hard to believe it at the moment."

"So what would you like to do this afternoon?"

"I think I just need to take my mind off things. And I'll also have to phone my mother sometime."

"Well, we could watch a DVD. How does 'Some Like It Hot' appeal to you?"

"That sounds perfect."

They ate their food absorbed in their own thoughts. John looked up at Hugo and watched his beautiful face as he ate, feeling drawn in by the limpid blue of his eyes.

"Greg mentioned that you might move out if your mother gets a flight. You really don't have to, you know."

"But I feel I'm just screwing things up for you."

"Hugo, our home is yours for as long as you need it."

"Thanks so much, John." They briefly held hands across the table.

***

Following lunch, Hugo rang his mother to update her on the current situation, although he didn't mention the video clip. If she needed to know, that would be best coming from Greg or John. She called back a few minutes later to say that she'd booked a flight and would be arriving first thing on Monday morning. John did offer for her to stay with them but she didn't want to impose on Greg and John's hospitality and insisted on staying in a hotel. John suggested the Cape Heritage Hotel at the other end of Bree Street and booked her in for an indefinite stay.

The Tony Curtis & Jack Lemmon farce made them laugh and John was relieved to see Hugo's spirits lifting. But inevitably the issue of the video clip came up again.

"John, I need to ask something: what was on the rest of the video?" asked Hugo.

"How much did you see?"

"Just the final shot of Ben's eyes and the, er, dick in his mouth. Was it worse than that?"

"Okay, I think you need to know, but I wish Greg was here as he'd be better at explaining." He took a deep breath and looked into Hugo's eyes. "I wouldn't say it was worse, but it was obviously building up to what was quite literally the money shot and the request for payment. The start of the video was a shot of Ben restrained in the chair, then tracking up his body to his head. He had a hood on at first and when it was removed we could see he had a gag in his mouth. That then got replaced by the dick and the guy came on his face. So a lot of it was run-of-the-mill porn but it was the restraint and coercion that made it so difficult to watch."

"How did Ben seem in the video? I mean, apart from being frightened, did he seem to be enjoying it?"

"It's difficult to be sure exactly, but I can't imagine

anyone in that position actually enjoying it. And he definitely didn't have an erection at the beginning." John omitted the voiding of his bladder. "How do you think he'd cope in that situation?"

"Well, as I mentioned at the consulate, Ben has always been the dominant one, so being submissive wouldn't come easy for him. I'm not sure that he'd put up a fight, though, so he might learn to cope. But I think the fear of being hurt would be pretty difficult for him."

John made a simple meal that evening with salad and plenty of the crusty bread he'd bought that morning. They watched a couple more DVDs sitting on the couch together. Greg returned from the hospital just after midnight.

"How was the shift?" asked John.

"Busy as hell," replied Greg, "No dildos but two shootings, three stabbings and a guy brought in DOA with his neck broken. I'm shattered."

John gave Greg a lingering hug; Hugo felt a little embarrassed but touched by the warmth of their relationship.

"Bed time, I think," said John.

***

Hugo tossed and turned trying to get to sleep. The light shining in off the street through gaps between the blind and the window frame cast shadows on the walls and added to the feeling of claustrophobia he felt in the small bedroom. He tried repeating the previous night's brush stroke analysis of the Poussin painting but found that the friendly face of the artist kept on being replaced by that of Ben from the video.

At about 3:00 a.m., Hugo realized that he'd never get to sleep, so he got out of bed with the sheet wrapped around him and went out into the living area. He was surprised to see Greg and John sitting on the couch with a bottle of wine and glasses on the table in front of them.

"I see that someone else couldn't sleep," said Greg. "Come and join us for a glass of wine - strictly for medicinal purposes, of course."

Hugo sat down between them, feeling strange to be wrapped up in a sheet when the two of them were naked.

"Penny for your thoughts," said John, looking at Hugo.

"More of the same, really," said Hugo. "Poussin's friendly face morphing into Ben's look of fear and generally feeling scared of what's going to happen next. What about you?"

John looked at Greg for confirmation. "Well, we were both thinking about you. It's not exactly usual for us to have someone quite like you staying with us."

"God, I'm sorry. I'll move out tomorrow." Hugo looked distraught.

"Don't be silly," said Greg. "They were good thoughts but a bit mixed up with everything else that's been going on."

They went to sleep on the couch with Hugo in the middle. By the time the morning came, the sheet was shared by all three of them. Greg awoke with the early rays of sun warming his face. He turned to look behind him and noticed tears drying on Hugo's face. He traced his fingers over Hugo's soft cheeks and wondered what he'd been crying about.

Sunday, February 13, 2011

Greg switched on the TV in the kitchen for an update on the news. He was taken aback by the image on the screen of Hugo and Ben shot at Frederick's after their civil partnership ceremony. He called out to Hugo and John: "Hey guys, come take a look at this!"

Hugo and John ran across the living area and crowded around the small TV on the counter top. A photo of Hugo and Ben was shown in the top left-hand corner of the screen and the BBC World Service newsreader was giving an account of Ben's disappearance:

"Benjamin Cavendish and Hugo Brown arrived in Cape Town nine days ago for their honeymoon after their civil partnership ceremony in Islington, London, and were staying in the world-famous Nelson Lodge Hotel. Hotel employees describe them as like any other newly married couple who were enjoying time together and sightseeing in Cape Town. The day before they were due to return to the UK, Benjamin Cavendish went missing." The screen switched to showing a brief clip of Ben at the poolside. "This video was taken from the hotel security cameras and seems to show him going off into the bushes with another man. He has not been seen since. Local police and the British Consulate are working jointly to determine his whereabouts but he is officially a missing person. Benjamin Cavendish is the son of the chairman of Cavendish Foods. Sir James and Lady Cavendish have declined to comment on their son's disappearance."

The three of them were taken aback. Greg was the first to say something. "Well, you certainly make a handsome couple. It's a shame they showed the clip of Ben disappearing into the bushes, although at least he was pulling his trunks up rather than down."

"I don't think the hotel owners will be too pleased," said John. "I mean, who were the "hotel employees" giving out that information? And how did they get hold of the video clip? I can see heads rolling come Monday."

"Ben's parents won't be happy, either," said Hugo. "They've never approved of him being gay and weren't too keen on our civil partnership, although they did attend the ceremony. I phoned his mother the day after he disappeared and she made all sorts of excuses about being too busy to fly to Cape Town. I didn't tell her about him going off into the bushes with that man, so being confronted with the video clip just before going to church on a Sunday morning won't have gone down well."

"Oh well," said Greg, "let's get showered and dressed and then we can make plans for the day."

Breakfast was warmed up croissants and strong black coffee. The Weekend Argus and Cape Times both had longer pieces on Ben's disappearance and showed stills from the security camera video. The hotel's security office was clearly as leaky as a sieve. Interestingly, Ben was referred to as 'The Honourable Benjamin Cavendish', a title which Hugo had never heard him use. DI van der Merwe and Steven Anderson from the British Consulate were both quoted in the pieces but leads seemed to be few and far between. The Xstreamtube video wasn't mentioned at all.

"Well, as my mother's arriving tomorrow," said Hugo, "I'm wondering whether today we could go around bars and see whether anyone recognizes Ben's photo."

"That sounds a decent idea," said John. "I'm surprised that the police haven't thought of doing that already."

"But as the guy at the consulate said, we should be careful in case we make things worse for Ben," said Greg. He turned to Hugo. "Most of the gay clubs are in De Waterkant, which is very near here. I'd say that Bronx and Amsterdam are worth trying, although they're a bit sleazy and unsophisticated. Crew Bar is a bit more discerning with younger, wealthier clientele. And we might want to try the club the guy from the project mentioned. I've looked up Video on the internet and it's down at Duncan Dock, which is a short drive from here. I suggest that the three of us split up and visit the three clubs in De Waterkant this evening and then go together to Video later on. What do you think?"

"Sounds good to me," said Hugo.

John nodded and turned to Hugo. "So what would you like to do for the rest of the day?" he asked.

"Well, I'd like to take you both out for lunch to thank you for your amazing hospitality and help," said Hugo.

"You really don't need to, Hugo. That's what friends are for," said Greg.

"Exactly," said John, reaching across and touching Hugo's cheek.

"No, I insist," said Hugo, looking bashful. "Where do you recommend?"

"Well, we could try for a table at Blues in Camps Bay," said John. "It's a bit touristy but the food is good and there's a nice balcony. Then perhaps we could go to Clifton 3."

"Is that the gay beach?" asked Hugo.

"Mainly gay but some straights, although unfortunately

it's not clothing optional," replied Greg.

"I'll go and phone Blues and see whether we can get a table on the balcony. I know the manager, so we might get lucky," said John.

Greg moved to sit next to Hugo. "I couldn't help notice that you'd been crying last night," he said. "Was that about Ben?"

Hugo looked into Greg's eyes. "I saw you looking at me this morning and felt your fingers on my face. I'd wanted to say "I love you" but it didn't seem right. I guess I was crying more because of that really."

Greg kissed Hugo gently and lingeringly on the lips.

John stood at the top of the stairs watching the two of them. He was absolutely right: threesomes never really work in reality. He'd also fallen in love with their guest, although he was the first to admit that it was mainly Hugo's physical attributes that he craved. He went to the phone to make the lunch reservation.

Miraculously, a last minute cancellation meant a table on the balcony was available, so they loaded the Mercedes with beach paraphernalia and made their way to Camps Bay for a walk along the beach before lunch. Hugo decided that walking along the warm, white sands arm in arm with two handsome friends was as good an aperitif as he could think of just at that moment. And just as John described, the food was good and the manager even brought a complimentary bottle of Methode Cap Classique to toast their handsome guest and to wish the early return of The Honourable Benjamin Cavendish.

Clifton 3 was surprisingly free of the usual south-easterly wind and gay men far outnumbered straight couples. Hugo was impressed by the bodies on show which proved how wrong fashionistas were to scorn budgie-smugglers. Mind you, as Greg, John and many others on the beach had noted, his own speedos seemed to be smuggling something more akin to a cockatoo.

Back at 180 Bree Street after a few hours of sun, the three of them went through their plan of action for the evening. Greg's advice was to dress like the average clubgoer in tight denim jeans and a vest, but John disagreed and opted for a fitted white shirt and chinos. Hugo went for tight jeans and a white shirt and looked like he'd just stepped off a plane from Milan. All three of them left the apartment just after 8:00 p.m. to head for their respective clubs and had copies of a photo of Ben that Hugo had printed out from his laptop. They agreed to rendezvous at 9:00 p.m. at a café on Napier Street.

Crew was already buzzing by the time Hugo got there. He decided not to show Ben's photo to the bouncers on the door in case that made them suspicious. The bartenders seemed a better bet and he was surprised to see how good-looking they were. Unfortunately, all of them seemed more interested in him than examining the photo. He thought the next, best tactic was to go around groups of men, so as to avoid being seen as using the photo as a perverse sort of chat-up line. It was after going to the second group that there was a tap on his shoulder. He turned to see one of the smartly dressed bouncers who made it clear that he wanted Hugo to come with him.

The bouncer took him to an area next to the bar and into an office. Hugo wished that Greg and John were with him. He took his cell phone out of his pocket but saw that the battery needed charging. An overweight man whom he took to be the manager was sitting at a desk and had a copy of the Cape Argus open at the page that included the account of Ben's disappearance. "Please sit down, Mr Brown," he said with barely a trace of a smile. Hugo felt as if he was being scrutinized from head to toe and didn't enjoy the experience. "You really should be more careful, Mr Brown. People might get the wrong impression if you persist in showing around photos of good looking men. I need to remind you that procurement is still a crime in South African law and our police officers are likely to be rather enamoured of your blond good looks."

"That sounds like a threat," said Hugo defiantly.

"Think of it as a warning, Mr Brown." He turned to the bouncer. "Please show our young friend out."

With his tail between his legs and feeling a little shaken, Hugo walked down Napier Street to Café Dijon and sat outside to wait for Greg and John. He ordered a glass of sauvignon blanc from a rather harassed but cute waiter who greeted him when he sat down: "I recognize you from the newspapers. You look as if you've seen a ghost."

"Something like that. I had a weird experience at Crew. I was showing around a photo of my missing partner and got taken into the manager's office where he threatened me."

"I'm not surprised. The gay mafia doesn't like anyone rocking the boat. You should be careful."

"Thanks for the advice. Ah, here are my friends. Can we have another two glasses of wine?"

"Coming up," replied the waiter with a warm smile.

Greg and John arrived, walking hand in hand. "How was Crew?" asked Greg.

"Not good. The bartenders were more interested in me than the photo. I then got taken into the manager's office where he made a veiled threat of calling the police. I got the impression that he'd enjoy seeing me being raped by South African police officers."

"Who are renowned for having huge truncheons," said John.

"Well, I told you we should be careful," said Greg. "It obviously wasn't a wise decision to send you there on your own."

"How did you and John get on?" asked Hugo.

"Well, no threats, but nothing useful either," replied Greg. "The guys at Bronx and Amsterdam seemed too drunk or stoned to think beyond what they'd be doing with their dicks later on. To be honest, I felt rather old and undesirable."

"Which you're definitely not, and particularly when you haven't shaved for a few days," said John, stroking Greg's beard.

The waiter arrived with the glasses of wine. "Can I give you some advice?" he asked.

"Please do," said Greg, pulling out a chair for the waiter.

"Your friend's had his first taste of the gay mafia and I'd guess the word is out that he's asking questions. If I were you, I'd leave this up to the police."

"You're probably right," said Greg. "We were planning to go to Video later on. What do you think about that?"

"Hmm, it's not on the Somerset Road circuit. I know it's in the docks area. It's said to be very upfront. There's no website, so I'd imagine it's by word of mouth. I suppose if the three of you were to go together you should be all right, but don't ask too many questions."

"Thanks for the advice," said Greg. "We really

appreciate it."

The three of them finished their wine and left a generous tip for the waiter. They returned briefly to 180 Bree Street to get the car to drive to Duncan Dock. The drive wasn't long but it took Greg and John to an area of Cape Town that felt very foreign and out of their comfort zone. At night time, the cranes of the docks cast ominous shadows over the cold storage containers and looked like giant praying mantises about to strike. As they entered Duncan Dock, they weren't exactly sure where Video was, but as soon as they saw the vast black wall displaying a Tom of Finland character with a large erection they knew they'd found their destination. They found a parking lot behind the building with about 30 cars already parked. Making their way back to where they'd seen the sign, they noticed some doors set into the wall with a TV camera mounted above. Greg thought they'd have to press a buzzer to gain entry but both doors suddenly opened to reveal a cavernous, brightly lit interior pounding with disco trance. Their senses overloaded, they tried to take in everything they saw. The interior was divided up by various gantries and scaffolding platforms at different heights, some dark and some lit by spotlights. In the middle of the dance floor there was a brightly illuminated platform, suspended about 10 feet above floor level, on which a well-oiled go-go dancer was gyrating languorously while idly stroking his semi-erect cock. To the left, there was a long bar area with naked bartenders serving from a counter top set at crotch level. As it was still early in the evening, there were only about 50 men occupying the dance floor, but every single one of them was naked. All along the far wall, on numerous gantries, there was a massive array of TV screens of different types and sizes, ranging from ancient black & white TVs to large flat screens. Without exception, all were showing non-stop gay porn, although from where they were standing, it was just a mind-blowing blur of bodies. A naked member of staff directed them through to a large locker room: "Keys are 10 rand each and please don't lose them. Here are some wallets to put around your necks for cards if you want drinks or anything else. There are two rules: no fucking on the dance floor and you need a test if you go behind the screens." He left them deciding what to do once he'd given Greg a lingering look.

"Well?" asked Greg, looking a bit shell-shocked.

"He definitely liked you," said John, "even with your clothes on. What do you think, Hugo?"

"Well, the place is certainly very upfront," replied Hugo.

"And probably in your face if you were standing under that dancer too long," said Greg. "I say let's give it a go."

John and Hugo agreed, so they took off their clothes, put credit cards in the wallets they'd been given and headed back to the dance floor, feeling rather self-conscious. Drawing the short straw by virtue of his less tumescent dick, John went across to the bar to get some drinks. Greg and Hugo stood looking at the video wall trying to take everything in. The nearest that Hugo had come to seeing gay porn in public was at a bar in Sitges, but that was just a single screen and the sex was distinctly mainstream. This video wall, on the other hand, seemed to cater for every variation on gay sex that either of them had ever imagined and the content on some of the screens considerably expanded on that.

Hugo felt someone touch him on the shoulder. He turned to see a young black guy, a couple of inches shorter than him, with close-cropped, bleached hair and a nice smile. His jaw dropped when he saw Hugo's dick.

"I'm guessing it's your first time here," he said helpfully. Hugo nodded. He pointed towards the video wall. "It's quite something, isn't it? The numbers at the bottom of the screens mean that it's a live feed. If you want to join in, you go behind the wall and pay according to what's on offer. But you'll need an HIV test first. The other screens are showing clips from the internet and elsewhere." He smiled expectantly and reached out to touch Hugo's dick. "Actually there's a spare cubicle if you're interested."

"Sorry," said Hugo, smiling, "but I'm here with a couple of friends and I need to take all of this in first."

"Okay, that's cool," said the black guy, looking a bit deflated, "Perhaps I'll catch you later."

Greg returned from the bar with some beers. They stood looking at the screens, drinking their beers. Hugo felt turned on by the surfeit of porn. He felt another tap on his shoulder. He turned to see the guy who'd shown them around the locker room. "I'm sorry to bother you, mate, but I'm wondering whether you'd like to stand in for our dancer. He wasn't up to it this evening. We'd pay well, particularly for that amazing dick."

John and Greg had been listening and watching with their mouths wide open and were barely able to suppress a chuckle.

"What do you think guys?" said Hugo.

"Darling, if you've got the equipment," said Greg, in a sexy Russian accent, "I'd say you jolly well ought to use it."

"In for a penny, in for a pound, as they say in the UK," said John, with a twinkle in his eye. "And it has to be a better way of getting attention than asking too many questions."

"Okay, I'm all yours," said Hugo to the guy. "Lead the way."

The guy led him to the stairs leading up to the platform. "When you get up there, just let yourself move with the music. You can touch yourself any way you want, but make it really sexy. Try and pace yourself for about 10 minutes. I'll be increasing the tempo and volume over the last few minutes. If you want to come, try to spray as many of the audience as you can, as they love catching drops of spunk."

Hugo made his way up to the platform and was relieved to see that there were some wires around it to stop the dancer from falling off. No one seemed to have noticed that he was on the platform, so he simply concentrated on getting used to moving his body in time with the beat. The spotlight above the platform was dimmed up and he could see his blown-up image from different directions appearing on TV screens dotted around the dance floor. Moving his pelvis sinuously, he traced his fingers over his chest and abdomen and then stroked his dick which by now was jutting up way past the horizontal. He touched the head of his dick and put his finger to his lips, savoring the pre-come and then sucking the length of his fingers, letting his other hand stroke his dick in time with the music. He turned around and bent over, pushing his butt over the edge of the platform and parting his buttocks with both hands. With one hand he slid his fingers up and down the cleft, teasing the opening, and with the other he continued stroking his dick. He sensed that the beat was starting to increase in tempo and stood up slowly, making snake-like movements of his hips and teasing his nipples. He licked the muskiness from his finger and concentrated on longer and faster strokes of his dick with his other hand. Looking at the audience below he could see he had their rapt attention with faces turned up and mouths open ready and waiting. Seeing his dick greatly magnified on screens all around added to the adulation that he experienced and he felt that wonderful, surging feeling of the moment of inevitability. At the point of ejaculation, he arched his back, shouted "Cock-a-doodle-doo!" and sprayed streams of spunk over the audience in an arc from right to left, using his dick like a pump-action shot gun. He continued stroking his dick, licking the spunk from his fingers and slowly letting himself down from the high. Wild applause broke out among the audience and he went to the front of the platform and bowed deeply, feeling just like a soloist in a concert hall. He walked down the stairs and back to Greg and John, aware of people shouting "Fucking amazing!" and feeling hands fleetingly but searchingly touching his dick, butt and torso.

"Well, how was it?" asked Hugo, breathlessly.

"Absolutely amazing," said Greg. "You certainly did away with any inhibitions you ever had. How do you feel?"

"Fucking exhilarated," said Hugo. "Bugger Nicolas Poussin and the Courtauld; I think I've found my true vocation."

"It was a bit like that scene in 'Perfume' where Grenouille controls the crowd with a wave of his perfumed handkerchief," said John. "I thought a mass orgy was going to start when you showed your butt."

The guy who'd asked him to do the stand-in came up to Hugo. "That was fucking brilliant, mate. Here's your 3000 rand. I've added a bonus for the amazing come shot. We'd like to book you for a weekly spot if you can make it."

"Sorry, I'm hoping to return to the UK any time soon, but thanks for the experience," said Hugo.

The guy shrugged his shoulders, said "Suit yourself, mate" and left the three of them in front of the video wall.

The black guy who'd been chatting up Hugo earlier came over, dabbing at the come on his face and licking his finger. "I told you I'd catch you later. That was really great."

"Thanks," said Hugo.

John added with a chuckle: "As Mr Spock said, 'the needs of the many outweigh the needs of the few… or the one.'"

"Hey, come and look at this," said Greg, pointing at one of the screens on the video wall.

Hugo and John looked at where he was pointing. Because many guys had emerged from cubicles to watch Hugo, fewer screens were active which made it easier to watch those that had something worth watching. Quite unmistakably, the Xstreamtube clip that Greg and John had watched only a few days ago was playing on one of the large flat screens. This time, they didn't try to stop Hugo watching it from start to finish.

***

"Yes, he appears to be watching it as we speak… And yes, it must be rather deflating for him after that Olympic performance... I agree that he would make an excellent candidate but logistically it would be problematic as he has his two friends with him. We also need his co-operation for the next stage with our other British subject. So, are we agreed to proceed as planned..? Excellent, I'll make the necessary arrangements. Goodnight."

***

Back home at 180 Bree Street, Hugo, Greg and John took stock of the evening's events over a meal of pasta with tomato sauce and a bottle of pinotage.

"Oh God, I can't believe I did that," said Hugo. "Ben would kill me if he knew what I just did."

"I'm sure he wouldn't," said Greg. "He'd hardly want to waste such a natural source of milk. Christ, Hugo, how do you produce that amount of spunk?"

"I don't know. Ben's always teasing me about that."

"You're an absolute natural, Hugo," said John. "That cock-a-doodle-do was amazing. You ought to take up porn professionally. You'd get top pay with your assets."

"You must be joking! It's all so sleazy and I don't think I'd cope with cameras peering up my ass and down my dick."

"And you'd be depriving the Courtauld Institute of your considerable curatorial assets too," said Greg, "although there'd be nothing to stop you from doing porn part time. In fact, one of my colleagues does it."

"I suppose I can see that working here where it's so liberal, but not in London where people don't want to be reminded of what we do in bed," said Hugo.

"Or quite so brazenly on a go-go dancing platform," said John, licking his lips and with a lecherous grin.

"I suppose my stage name could always be Johnny Deep," said Hugo, smiling coyly.

Greg and John laughed.

"So what about the video of Ben?" asked Hugo. "Do you think that was played because we were there?"

"That thought had crossed my mind," said Greg. "After all, there were cameras everywhere, and it wouldn't surprise me if we were tracked from the moment we entered. But I wonder what they expected us to do?"

"Well, we'll obviously have to inform the police first thing in the morning," said John. "It certainly suggests some sort of link between whoever abducted Ben and that club. From what we were told about HIV testing, it sounds as if the promise of barebacking is the way they lure their customers. But I think them showing the video means that we should also expect further developments."

"And what should I tell my mother who'll be arriving in…" He glanced at his watch. "…just under eight hours?" asked Hugo. "She doesn't know about the video, after all."

"I'd say she ought to know," said John. "All that's been released to the press so far is that Ben went missing after going behind the bushes. If in doubt, why not arrange for the two of you to see DI van der Merwe?"

"Thanks, I'll do that," said Hugo, pushing his seat back and standing up. "If it's okay with you, I think I'll turn in now. It's been a strange day and I need time alone to make sense of it all."

"That's fine, Hugo," said Greg. "We need some time together as well. John will take you to the airport at 6:30. We've both on duty from 8:00, so perhaps you could spend the day with your mother and then come back here for dinner."

"That sounds perfect and I'm just so grateful for everything you've done," said Hugo, his voice cracking with emotion. Greg and John stood up and hugged him.

"And you know where we are if you can't sleep and need company during the night," said Greg.

Monday, February 14, 2011

A teenage boy hand-delivered an A5 size envelope to 180 Bree Street just after 7:00 a.m. on Monday morning. Greg picked it up along with other mailbox contents after returning from a jog a few minutes later. As he sifted through the mail on the kitchen countertop, he saw the A5 envelope with the poorly formed characters and guessed what would be in it. The difference this time was that it was addressed to John and himself. Christ, these bastards were devious. He realized with a sinking feeling that their relationship with Hugo could never be the same. He picked up the phone and called DI van der Merwe's cell phone.

A sleepy voice answered: "Van der Merwe here."

"Good morning, Detective Inspector. It's Greg Edwards here. I'm sorry to ring you so early. I'm afraid there's been a development. An envelope similar to the one dropped off at the hotel has just been put through our mailbox at 180 Bree Street."

"Christ! Have you opened it?"

"No, I learned my lesson from last time. It's on our kitchen countertop: it has the same size envelope and the same poorly formed characters."

"Do you have any idea who delivered it?"

"No, but there's a coffee shop almost opposite and they may have seen something."

"Okay, don't touch anything. I'm on my way."

"Good. And I also need to tell you about something that happened yesterday."

While he was waiting for the DI to arrive, Greg phoned

the emergency department to let them know he was "unavoidably detained on police business", which was both true and unarguable, and he also texted John who was on his way to the airport with Hugo to collect his mother: "Anoth env arrd at 180. DTA. Called DI. X."

The DI arrived just after Greg had got out of the shower and dressed. He put on latex gloves and examined the envelope.

"I see it's addressed to you," the DI said. "How did they know Mr Brown was staying with you?"

"I'm not sure," said Greg, "but we may have been under some sort of surveillance."

"What makes you think that?" asked the DI, looking surprised.

"I'll tell you later," Greg replied. He pointed to what was written on the envelope. "As it's addressed to us, can I see what's inside?"

"I guess you have the right given that your names are on it," the DI replied. "Do you have something to open it with?"

Greg retrieved the first aid kit from a drawer and took out latex gloves, a specimen bag, tweezers and a scalpel blade. The DI opened the top of the envelope with the blade and extracted the slip of paper inside. As before, what was written on it was typed and there was more information this time:

www.xstreamtube.net/watch/bbc1*4463

R 1,000,000

-33.93127, 18.41109

2011-02-14T19:20:30+01:00

"Oh Christ!" exclaimed Greg.

"I'm afraid so," said DI van der Merwe, dragging his

hands through his hair. "Can we view that link here? If it's anything like the previous one, your expertise might come in handy. But if you'd rather not, I'd quite understand."

"Oh God, I guess I'll just have to engage my professional detachment. I can see myself becoming the expert witness, anyway," said Greg, regretfully.

Greg grabbed a laptop off the countertop and headed upstairs with DI van der Merwe. He connected the laptop to the flat screen TV and entered the URL into the internet browser. As soon as the video started, they could see that Ben was still in the same room, but this time he was restrained in a harness attached at various points to some sort of cage. As before, he was naked. His legs were held up into the lithotomy position and his head was enclosed in a black hood which had something keeping his mouth open. This time, there was a soundtrack accompanying the video, and they recognized the sounds of people undressing. The music gradually faded up.

"What's the music?" asked the DI.

"It's by a Russian composer called Stravinsky. The piece is the Rite of Spring and I think what we're hearing comes at the end just before..." He paused, aghast at the thought that had occurred to him.

"... the sacrifice," added the DI, looking equally shocked.

They continued looking at the screen. Ben had been tipped upside down. They saw a naked man wearing a mask thrust his erect penis into Ben's mouth. This was followed by another naked man forcing his penis into Ben's anus. Ben helplessly rocked backwards and forwards under the onslaught from both ends of his body.

"Is that what's called 'spit-roasting'?" asked the DI.

"Yes," replied Greg, not really wanting to add to the explanation.

After a few minutes, the two men were replaced by another pair who continued the relentless assault, and then they moved away for another pair to take over. It was impossible to tell exactly how many men were involved, but from the different body shapes and penis sizes, Greg judged that at least 10 men were involved. All were wearing black masks. As the minutes went by, the pairs were replaced with greater frequency, the rocking became more violent and the music grew louder and more aggressive. Quite abruptly, the video stopped, leaving just the final dissonant chord of the sacrificial dance echoing around the apartment.

"That poor guy," said the DI. "I'm going to get those bastards if it's the last thing I do."

"What about the rest of the note?" asked Greg.

The DI peered at the scrap of paper. "Well, it looks like a ransom demand for one million rand, and it's fair to assume that the message is that he'll be killed if it's not paid. We generally have a policy of not paying ransom demands but there may be no choice this time. The rows of numbers are interesting: the bottom one is obviously the date and time – in fact, today at 19:20 and 31 seconds – and the one above it looks like a map reference. Can you get Google maps up on your laptop?"

"I should be able to," replied Greg. He entered the numbers and watched with amazement as the grounds of the Nelson Lodge Hotel appeared on the screen. Zooming in, they could see a green arrow pointing to a horizontal black object on the grass with something white at the end of it.

"God, it's the sun lounger that Mr Cavendish was lying on before he disappeared!" exclaimed the DI.

"How are we going to get a million rand by this evening?" asked Greg despairingly.

"I'll sort it out with the consulate. They were expecting something like this to happen. It's not exactly common in South Africa, but it's a fairly frequent occurrence in Central Africa. We'll need to get the hotel to co-operate, though."

"I don't think they'll have any choice," said Greg. "I'll speak with John when he gets back. In the meantime, I'll text him to take Hugo and his mother direct to the Cape Heritage. Can you see them sometime today?"

"I suppose so," replied the DI. "What does she know?"

"Just about the disappearance, I think," replied Greg. "And nothing about the first video yet. It'd probably be helpful if she did know as we might need her to speak to Ben's family. You know they're Sir James and Lady Cavendish, don't you?"

"I'd gathered that from the consulate. It does make things a little delicate. You can tell them I'll come round to their hotel at 3:00 p.m."

"Actually, Hugo is still staying here."

"I don't think he should. He may have your support here, but you're both working and there'll be more security at the Cape Heritage. But it's your call. What was the other thing you wanted to mention?"

"Oh, we went out last night to various bars on Somerset Road to see whether anyone had seen Ben. I know it wasn't wise but we felt we had to do something. Hugo got called into the manager's office at Crew Bar and felt quite threatened. After that, we went to a club called

Video down at Duncan Dock. They have this video wall playing all sorts of live and internet feeds and we noticed they were showing that first video on one of the screens. With all the cameras in the place, I'm pretty sure they knew we were there."

"I haven't heard of it. What sort of place is it?"

"Well, lack of clothing isn't exactly optional and there's live sex on and off the dance floor. We think the Bareback Club is a front for heavier stuff, and the fact that they were showing the video leads us to think they're behind Ben's disappearance."

"So it's not somewhere you'd visit in your lunch hour for a drink and a chat."

"Not exactly."

"Well, it's certainly a lead, but I hope your visit hasn't ruffled too many feathers."

"I think it might have." He was going to tell the DI about Hugo's spectacular performance but thought better of it.

"And it was just showing the video as we saw it? No sound or words on the screen?"

"No, exactly as we saw it, and looping over and over again."

"Interesting." The DI looked at his watch. "Look, I must go, Dr Edwards. Thanks for your assistance. I'll be in touch."

The DI carefully put the envelope into the specimen bag that Greg had produced, shook hands and left the apartment.

After the DI had departed, Greg sent a further text to John: "Chng of plan. Take H dir to hotel. Tell H DI will C at hotel at 3. CU at 180. X."

***

As DI van der Merwe walked along Bree Street to his car, he contemplated the many things he'd need to put in place for Ben to be returned in one piece later today. His first phone call would be to the consulate and then he'd have to clear everything with the Chief Superintendent. He'd been impressed by Greg and thought that he would make an excellent expert witness if anything came to trial. He also found him very attractive, which isn't something that he'd admit to his wife or any of his colleagues back in the police station. And he'd found watching the video both disturbing and arousing. He might have to pay Video a visit one evening this week, but obviously only to assist with the investigation.

***

The flight landed on time, although Hugo's mother had to endure the usual wait to get through immigration. Fortunately, she'd packed light with carry-on luggage, so Hugo caught a glimpse of her about 30 minutes after she'd disembarked. John had to wait a good minute before they disengaged from their tearful hug just outside the exit from customs. Mother and son certainly made a striking couple and John could see where his good looks had come from. John's cell phone alerted him to a text and he was staring at it when Hugo's mother finally drew John back into the greeting party.

"Are you Greg or John?" she asked, smiling broadly with her hand extended.

"Sorry, John," said Hugo, blushing. "I didn't mean to leave you out. Mum, this is my friend, John; John, this is my mother, Joanna."

"It's very good to meet you, Mrs Brown," said John, shaking her hand but looking distracted.

"Is there anything wrong?" asked Hugo.

"Just a text from Greg," replied John. "There's been a change of plan. He's asked me to take both of you to the hotel. The Detective Inspector will be coming to see you at the hotel at 3 p.m."

"That sounds ominous," said Hugo, looking concerned.

"Yes, I'm not sure what to make of it. Let's get the two of you back into town for some breakfast," said John, trying to be upbeat but not making a very good job of it.

***

After dropping off Hugo and his mother at the Cape Heritage Hotel, John drove to 180 Bree Street and parked. He found Greg on the balcony, staring across the city and looking worried. "I got your texts. What's up?"

"Oh Jesus," said Greg tearfully, "it's all going from bad to worse."

"Let's sit down," said John. "Take a deep breath and focus."

"Okay…," said Greg, "as I said in the text, an envelope was dropped off early this morning. It was addressed to the two of us." John looked shocked. "I phoned the DI and we opened it here. It was a link to another video and a ransom demand for one million rand. There was also a map reference for the ransom drop. You won't believe it, but it's the sun lounger that Ben was using at the hotel and they want the money at just after 7:20 p.m. today!"

"Christ! What's on the video?"

"Do you really want to know?"

"Not really. I take it was worse than the first."

"Much, much worse, I'm afraid. And the message was pretty clear: pay up or he dies."

"What did the DI say?"

"Well, he thinks he can organize the ransom with the consulate. He wants to talk with you about making arrangements with the hotel."

"That could be difficult."

"Is there an alternative?"

"I guess not. Was there anything else?"

"Yes. He thinks Hugo should move out to the hotel with his mother."

"Oh God."

***

Hugo and his mother dropped off her bags at the hotel and went for a walk up Kloof Street to kill time until she could check-in. They walked past Studio 91 where there was the usual queue of people waiting for early morning auditions. Some of the men looked at Hugo but he didn't really take much notice. They went into the same deli that Hugo and Ben had visited when they arrived after their flight. The waitress took their order and they sat looking at each other, holding hands across the table top. Hugo started crying and she reached across to wipe away his tears.

"It's more complicated than I thought, isn't it?" she said.

"What do you know?" asked Hugo, blinking away tears.

"Just that Ben went missing last Thursday and was seen going into bushes with another man. And that Sir James and Lady Cavendish weren't available for comment. A storm in a teacup, in other words."

"If only it was."

"I'd guessed that."

"I suppose I should tell you everything."

"It might help." She held onto his hands tightly.

"Well, on the day of his disappearance he flirted outrageously with the waiter who brought us breakfast and actually tried to get him to join us in bed. That made me really pissed off. After breakfast, he went off to get some sun and I stayed in the room to work on a talk for the Courtauld. The waiter returned and I'm afraid to say I got my own back and had sex with him. I know that was stupid but it just sort of happened." Hugo looked embarrassed. "When I went down to the pool to fetch Hugo for some lunch he'd vanished. Later that day, the hotel showed me the recording from the security camera at the poolside. The police arrived but didn't find anything significant. The following day, I was called into the office and was told by the owner that I'd have to leave. That's when John offered for me to stay with him and his boyfriend and I moved in with our bags that evening. On the Saturday, John came back from the hotel with an envelope that was addressed to me. We opened it and found a slip of paper with a link on it for a website. Greg and John put that into their laptop and I caught the end of it. It was very hardcore and showed Ben naked in restraints. We saw a guy at the British Consulate that morning and he's been in contact with the local police. That's the person who's coming to the hotel this afternoon. Yesterday we went around some bars with a photo of Ben to see whether anyone had seen him. My questions obviously weren't welcome and I got threatened at one bar. We then went on to another, rather... er... explicit club which was showing lots of videos, and one of them was the video of Ben."

"Oh darling, I'm so sorry for you," said Hugo's mother, looking earnest and concerned. "I really had no idea it'd become that complicated. But having sex with the waiter was hardly sensible, darling."

"I know. I feel such an idiot."

"What do you think Ben would say if he knew?"

"I'm not sure, but knowing him he'd probably have wanted to join in."

"You've never been unfaithful to Ben before, have you?"

"No, that was the first time."

"And what about now?"

"You mean, with Greg and John?"

"Yes, I could see the way John looked at you."

"Well, nothing's happened yet, although we did end up sleeping on the couch together, but that was only because we were thinking too much and couldn't get to sleep in our beds. But I have to admit I like them a lot."

"Please be careful, darling. You're very vulnerable at the moment."

"That's what Greg said." He looked thoughtful and then blushed. "I guess I should tell you what happened at the last club we went to as you'll probably hear sooner or later."

"Tell me, darling."

"Well, I did a turn as a go-go dancer and I was naked."

"Hugo!"

"I'm sorry, Mum."

***

DI van der Merwe was trying to decide what to tell Hugo and his mother. He'd figured that she must know by now about the first video, so the revelation of a second video and the ransom demand wouldn't be that unexpected. He wasn't so sure how Hugo would take it. He was a young man with many things on his mind and clearly they weren't just related to his partner's disappearance. He'd attempted to contact Sir James Cavendish in relation to the ransom but was given short shrift by his officious secretary. Fortunately, Steven Anderson in the consulate was helpful and efficient and had assured him that the one million rand in large denomination notes would be couriered to the hotel by 4:00 p.m. Greg's partner, John Bredenkamp, had cleared it with the hotel for the money to be left on the designated sun lounger at precisely 7:20 p.m. and 31 seconds and he'd courageously agreed to take on that task himself. But for the life of him, the DI couldn't understand why the perpetrators had chosen such a visible spot in the middle of the city to collect the money and return the victim. A helicopter might be one way of facilitating a rapid exchange, so he'd alerted air traffic control to be on the lookout for any unauthorized activity above the City Bowl. Various armed police officers were to be stationed at strategic points throughout the hotel gardens, although they were under strict instructions to keep a low profile and not to speak to guests. The hotel had decided to put on a special buffet of South African cuisine, with traditional dancing included, in the hope that this would keep guests indoors throughout the duration of the operation. The DI had agreed to co-ordinate the proceedings and had permission to use the hotel's security office as his base. He'd decided to head for the hotel as soon as he had confirmation that the money had arrived, but now it was time to see Hugo and his mother at their hotel.

***

After checking-in at the hotel, Hugo and his mother went off in search of an early lunch. It didn't take them long to find another restaurant just up Kloof Street from the deli and they surveyed the lunch menu.

"How do you think Ben's coping with the situation he's in?" asked Hugo's mother.

"It's difficult to say," replied Hugo. "He's got a murky past that involved a rather heavy scene when he was living in Earls Court but he's never talked about it. I suspect it's not too far off what's happening to him at the moment. So that could be in his favor, but he's also terrified of being in enclosed spaces, and he almost freaked out when we visited Robben Island and saw the cell that Nelson Mandela was imprisoned in."

"But there must be more to it than abducting him for some sort of perverse sexual pleasure. Why was *he* taken in particular?"

"There was something that a guy at the consulate said about the past catching up with him and that someone may still believe that Ben owes him something; the idea of the bond between the master and slave is the way that he put it."

"But that sounds positively medieval!"

"Which is when they had torture chambers, of course."

"Darling, it doesn't bear thinking about! Let's order

lunch and I'll tell you what's been happening at home."

***

DI van der Merwe arrived at the Cape Heritage Hotel with time to spare. This was a hotel he wouldn't mind staying in: more boutique than multi-national, and with a friendly sociable feel that fitted with the history of Heritage Square. He found the manager and explained the reason for his visit. The manager had already been brought up to speed by John Bredenkamp and willingly offered his office to the DI for the meeting with Hugo and his mother. He explained that the room adjacent to the one occupied by Hugo's mother was free and generously offered 50 percent off the second room. He also had a pleasing twinkle to his eyes.

"Please come in," said DI van der Merwe to Hugo and his mother. "The manager has very kindly vacated his office so that I could see you in some privacy." He turned to Hugo's mother. "Let me introduce myself. My name is Jim van der Merwe and I'm the Detective Inspector leading the investigation into the disappearance of Benjamin Cavendish." The DI shook hands with her and then with Hugo.

"Hugo has said good things about you, Detective Inspector," said his mother, smiling warmly.

The DI was momentarily lost for words when he noticed the similarity in appearance between mother and son: good looks like that definitely don't grow on trees, he thought.

"I really hope I'm going to deserve them, Mrs Brown," he said with a serious expression. "I'm afraid things have moved on and we don't have much time." He noticed

Hugo and his mother sharing a concerned look. "There's no easy way to say this: there's been another video with a ransom demand attached."

"Oh Christ!" exclaimed Hugo. His mother looked equally shocked.

"This time an envelope was hand delivered to where Hugo has been staying with Greg and John for the last few days. As well as the link for the video, there was also the demand for one million rand and the map reference and time for the ransom drop."

"What was on the video?" asked Hugo, looking petrified.

"You really don't want to know, Hugo, but I can assure you he's still very much alive."

"How much is one million rand?" asked his mother.

"Not as much as it sounds," the DI replied. "It's about 75,000 pounds sterling at the current exchange rate."

"But there's no way we can come up with that sum," said Hugo's mother, looking panicked.

"Mrs Brown, please don't worry about that. I've sorted something out with the British Consulate," the DI reassured her.

"And if the ransom is paid, does that mean Ben will be returned?" asked Hugo.

"Well, that's the normal way things happen with kidnappings, but one can never know for sure," replied the DI. "The strange thing is that they've specified the hotel for the ransom drop, and in fact exactly the same sun lounger that Ben was last seen using. The time for the drop is just after 7:20 this evening. Usually kidnappers would specify somewhere remote and in the middle of the night. This time, it's almost as if they want to be seen."

"Can we wait at the hotel for when he's returned?" asked Hugo.

"I wouldn't recommend it," replied the DI. "We don't know exactly what's going to happen or the condition he'll be in. I've arranged for an ambulance to be there to take him to the emergency department at the Groote Schuur Hospital and Dr Edwards is alerting his colleagues to expect him sometime this evening."

"Is there anything else we can do?" asked Hugo's mother.

"Well, one thing you could try is to get through to his parents, Mrs Brown. So far, we've met with a total block when we've tried to speak to either Sir James or Lady Cavendish, which seems very strange given that it's their son who's been abducted. I'm also worried that this may not be the end of the matter, as his abductors seem to be making it too easy. And as far as your son is concerned…" He turned to look at Hugo. "…I'm afraid I must insist that Hugo stays here as I think it's too risky for him to return back to 180 Bree Street."

Hugo looked forlorn and buried his head in his hands. His mother bent over to comfort him and noticed he was sobbing.

"I really wish I could make this easier for the two of you," said the DI, "but kidnapping and extortion is never straightforward. In the meantime, here's my cell phone number in case you need to contact me." He handed Hugo's mother his card. "I suggest you stay in the hotel for the rest of the day and I'll phone you as soon as I know anything. I'll ask Hugo's friends to drop off his bags at the hotel."

The DI stood up, shook both their hands and opened

the door for them. Hugo turned to him, looking very scared: "What if he isn't returned tonight?"

"Let's pray he is, Hugo. But let's cross one bridge at a time. I'm not going to let go of this. You've got my promise on that." He touched Hugo on his shoulder and felt him wince.

***

DI van der Merwe arrived at the hotel at 6:00 p.m. and found John Bredenkamp in his office. He looked exhausted and was staring at a photo on his desk. He looked up as the DI came in and it was obvious he'd been crying.

"Are you all right?" asked the DI. "You don't look good."

"Well, apart from my life being totally torn apart, I guess I'm okay," replied John. "I can see that the biggest mistake was allowing Hugo to stay with us, but then he's also been the best thing that's ever happened to us, so I'm sure you can understand why it's all been a bit too much."

"He seems to have that effect on people," said the DI.

"You should have seen him at the club yesterday. He had guys eating out of his hand when he was dancing. Having that sort of presence is a rare thing. And now it's all been destroyed by that fucking envelope." He banged his fist on the desktop.

"If you don't mind me asking, why did you volunteer to do the ransom drop?"

"Oh God, I'm not sure. I suppose after everything that's happened I felt I owed something to Hugo to get him back together with his partner."

"Are you sure you still want to go through with it?"

"Yes, I'm not going to back out now. What do you want me to do?"

"Well, I've got plain clothes officers out in the grounds already. They should be dressed just like other guests. They've all got earpieces so I can stay in contact. I've no idea who will collect the ransom or how Ben will be returned, and for all I know they could already be in the hotel. I reckon that it will take you 30 seconds to walk from your office to the poolside, so I suggest you walk out with the money at 7:19 p.m. sharp. Once you've made the drop, walk straight back inside and don't get involved if anything unusual happens."

"Like what?"

"I've no idea but it's best to expect the unexpected."

***

At 7:10 p.m., DI van der Merwe went into the security office ready to co-ordinate the drop and exchange. His officers reported in one by one. Apart from a few gardeners doing their usual clear-up at the end of day, the grounds were quiet and there'd been so sign of unexpected traffic through the main entrance. The hotel guests were busy enjoying the buffet and entertainment. The security cameras showed nothing unusual. At 7:19 p.m., the DI noticed John Bredenkamp walking at a normal pace towards the pool area carrying a bag with the money in it. By 7:20 p.m., John had placed the bag on the sun lounger and was walking back to the hotel. All of a sudden, the DI was aware of loud popping noises coming from the grounds which were also being relayed through his officers' radios. "Down! Down!" he shouted. Pandemonium broke out in the grounds, with officers diving for cover wherever they could, including into the swimming pool. At 7:22 p.m., the officers cautiously raised themselves from wherever they'd taken cover. The popping sounds had stopped. They looked towards the sun lounger and saw that the money had vanished. In its place, there was an A5 size envelope addressed to DI van der Merwe. There was no sign of Ben.

***

"A remarkably efficient operation, I think. The firecrackers were very effective and it was a stroke of genius to dress up the boy as a gardener's assistant. I trust he was able to leave without any hindrance… Very good. And following behind a family as they left the hotel premises was a really excellent idea. Many congratulations. Now we await Sir James Cavendish's response. I'm sure he'll find the video most impressive…"

***

It was 8:30 p.m. and DI van der Merwe was sitting in his office staring at the third envelope and wishing that he'd never answered the early morning call from Dr Edwards. He dreaded making the call to Hugo and his mother. Today was clearly going to be the worst day of his life. His department would have hell to pay for losing one million rand and he'd be lucky if he escaped without an inquiry and disciplinary action. His officers had found the burnt-out firecrackers and uniform of a rather short gardener when they searched the grounds. Hotel security had seen a small framed, teenage boy leaving the grounds carrying something in a supermarket bag, but he was smartly dressed and looked just like one of a family going out for dinner.

He realized that he couldn't put off opening the envelope any longer, so he put on gloves and reached for the letter opener. His hands trembled when he extracted the slip of paper and saw what was typed on it:

www.xstreamtube.net/watch/bbc1*4464

R 10,000,000

-34.089186, 18.352404

2011-02-15T22:10:30+03:00

c.c. Sir James Cavendish

DI van der Merwe simply couldn't face seeing where that link took him this evening. And 10 million rand by tomorrow night was well-nigh impossible, even for someone as obviously wealthy and connected as Sir James Cavendish. The DI put the co-ordinates into Google maps and saw a stretch of Chapman's Peak Drive appear on the screen of his PC. That particular co-ordinate related to a look-out point that was popular with tourists and would probably make as good a ransom drop as anywhere. But before he decided what to do about it, he needed to speak to Hugo and his mother. He dialed the number for the Cape Heritage Hotel and asked to be put through to Mrs Joanna Brown.

"Mrs Brown? It's Jim van der Merwe here. Are you able to talk?"

"Yes, of course, Detective Inspector. We've been waiting for your call. Is Ben back safely?"

"Is Hugo with you?"

"No, he's next door having a shower before we go out to eat. I take it that it's not exactly good news, then."

"Not exactly, Mrs Brown. In fact, to be brutally honest with you, it was an unmitigated disaster and you'll probably read all about in the local press tomorrow."

"What happened, then, Detective Inspector?"

"Well, it's a long story, but basically they pulled a fast one and used a child to snatch the money without returning Hugo's partner. And I'm afraid there's more: they left another envelope which was addressed to me this time."

"Oh dear. What was in the envelope?"

"Unfortunately, a link to another video and another ransom demand, but this time for 10 million rand. And copies of the link and the demand will probably be in Sir James's in-tray already."

There was a brief silence from the other end of the phone. "What do you think they're up to, Detective Inspector? This seems more like a game they're playing with us."

"I'm not sure, Mrs Brown, and I agree that it looks as if they're taunting us. But they now seem to want to bring Ben's parents into the picture. Do you know whether they have the money to pay the ransom?"

"I've no idea, Detective Inspector. That's not something I've ever discussed with Ben's parents. When do they want it by?"

"Tomorrow evening."

"Dear God!" She paused. "What would you like me to do, Detective Inspector?"

"It would help if you could phone Lady Cavendish. Ben's parents may have a good reason for not getting involved but I think it's gone past that point now. I'll try to get through to Sir James at his office in the morning. Hugo obviously needs to know what's happening but perhaps you could do your best to make it appear that we're on top of things."

"That's a tall order, Detective Inspector, but I'll try."

***

Hugo's mother mentally checked time differences and came to the conclusion that Lady Cavendish would just be starting her third gin & tonic of the evening. Her cell phone picked up on the first ring, almost as if she'd been expecting the call.

"Barbara Cavendish here."

"Barbara, it's Joanna, Hugo's mother."

"Oh, Barbara. How nice of you to call. How are you?"

"Oh, I'm fine. I'm in Cape Town."

"Ah. You know that Hugo called me last week?"

"Yes, he told me. You must be worried about Ben."

"Joanna, there's never been a day when I haven't been concerned about Benjamin. Why do you think there's so much white hair on my head?"

"But aren't you even more concerned now?"

"Joanna, as far as I'm concerned, if he's fallen into a cesspit of perversion, it's up to him to crawl out of it."

"Barbara, I don't think it's up to him."

"I don't understand. What do you mean?"

"Don't you know? He's been kidnapped. There've been videos and ransom demands."

"Dear God! How much are they demanding this time?"

"What do you mean by 'this time'?"

"It's happened before. It was about five years ago, before Benjamin met your son. He got involved with some low life and demands were made. They threatened to send some sort of sordid video to the press. We paid up, of course, but the demands kept on coming. Then the

130

demands stopped, so we thought it was all over."

"Did you tell the police?"

"Goodness no: noblesse oblige and that sort of thing. So how much this time?"

"It started with one million rand, or about 75 thousand pounds."

"But we don't have anything like that amount." She paused. "In fact, we're virtually bankrupt."

"But I thought…"

"Oh the titles mean nothing, particularly when it's all been gambled away on investments."

"I'm so sorry. Did Ben know?"

"Benjamin? Oh no…"

"That explains why he was always saying you were mean."

"Did he? Oh dear…"

"You know the British Consulate was trying to get hold of you?"

"Were they? I didn't know."

"I believe your husband's secretary refused to put them through."

"Yes, she can be rather overprotective. So what's happened about the ransom?"

"It got paid by the consulate."

"So has Benjamin been returned?"

"I'm afraid not, Barbara. And the ransom has gone up to 10 million rand, which they want by tomorrow evening. Sir James should have received a copy of the demand already."

"Ah, that explains why he sounded so preoccupied on the phone earlier. So what will happen if the ransom isn't paid?"

"I really don't know, Barbara. The police here think whoever's behind this is taunting us or playing some sort of game."

"But Joanna, this is my son we're talking about!" Hugo's mother heard a glass put down forcibly. "Oh dear God. Poor, poor Benjamin." She started sobbing.

"I'll call you tomorrow, Barbara," said Hugo's mother softly and she started crying too.

Tuesday, February 15, 2011

DI van der Merwe had a restless night, with dreams that perversely combined spit-roasting, the images of Hugo and his mother naked, and the sound of firecrackers exploding. His wife eventually kicked him out of bed and he'd tried to sleep on the couch in the living room. Failing at this, he'd gone for a run in the hope that this would clear his head and equip him to cope with yet another dreadful day. He also had to complete writing up his report on the debacle at the hotel. But at least no shots were fired; shooting at firecrackers really would have been a public relations disaster.

The first thing that confronted him when he opened his office door at just after 8:00 a.m. was the slip from the third envelope in its protective plastic. He was waiting for fingerprint analysis on the envelope itself but didn't anticipate anything helpful. Sighing, he booted up his PC and entered the latest URL into the internet browser. He thought at first he was watching the same video as before but then noticed that the lighting was better, which had the effect of making Ben's incarceration seem even more visceral: the sweat on his skin glistening in the light and merging with the dank wetness of the walls. He couldn't avoid letting rip an expletive when he saw a black man walk towards Ben and slap his face with the largest penis he'd ever seen in his life. When the man started his jackhammer action on Ben's anus, the DI simply couldn't believe that anyone could survive such ferocity and wondered whether a red-hot poker might in fact be preferable. But the tidal wave of semen that ensued from the massive penis was undeniably impressive.

***

Hugo and his mother sat down for breakfast at the Cape Heritage Hotel.

"How did you sleep, dear?"

"Badly, although I'm sure it would have been worse if I'd spoken with the Detective Inspector. The build-up yesterday was bad enough but the let-down was the final straw. I just can't believe that they allowed a kid to escape with all that money."

"Do you trust him?"

"I'm not sure. He seems sincere enough but his eyes are a little too close together. It's as if he's peering inside you and trying to find your weak spot."

"I got the same feeling. Do you think he's gay?"

"In the closet, I think."

"Where you surprised by the revelation about the Cavendish's financial situation?"

"Totally. I just had no idea. And to think I used to refer to her as a stingebag."

"And what Barbara said about Ben's past might go some way to explaining why he was abducted."

"It certainly looks that way."

"I suppose we just have to wait and see what happens next."

"I guess so."

"If there's no ransom paid, do you think they'll release him anyway?"

"It was the guy at the consulate who said he thought Ben was worth more to them alive than dead and I think he's probably right." Hugo ate some muesli, chewing thoughtfully. "What would you like to do for the rest of the day?"

"Can we go up Table Mountain? Everyone says that's the one thing one must do if you visit Cape Town."

"I'll ask reception to arrange a taxi."

***

DI van der Merwe was sitting opposite the Chief Superintendent and the atmosphere was tense. There was a copy of the DI's report in front of him. The events of yesterday had already earned the sobriquet of 'Nelsongate' and colleagues had been coming up to him and whispering "Kiss me Hardy". His wife had also texted him to ask why his laptop was showing a pornographic video and he wasn't sure she'd believe his explanation. He sighed.

"It doesn't look good, Jim," said the Chief Superintendent, pushing across the early edition of the Cape Argus. 'POP POP WENT NELSON'S WEASEL' and 'THE NELSON'S WATERLOO' were the headlines that stood out in particular. "I've got the British Consulate shouting in one ear and the Nelson Lodge Hotel in the other. Why the drop there, for Christ's sake?"

"With all due respect, sir, I don't think I had any choice. I mean, if you were handed map references and a drop time that was down to the nearest second, would you have done anything different?"

"But didn't it seem a bit fishy that the perpetrators behind this fiasco had specified a sun lounger in the hotel gardens for the drop? I mean, that's really taking the piss."

"Actually, I thought it seemed quite appropriate, although I couldn't quite see how the victim could end up back on the lounger unless he was dropped on it from a height."

"Very funny." The Chief Superintendent wasn't amused. "So what do we have on the envelopes?"

"Well, the envelopes are the sort you'd get anywhere: cheap stuff, 10 for one rand. The writing is identical on all three and seems to have been made using the same ballpoint pen. We could try chasing stationary suppliers but it'd take forever. As you can imagine, there are lots of fingerprints, and there are some that are common to all three. But they're unusual."

"Meaning what?"

"They're not from an adult."

"The mystery boy who walked off with the one million rand?"

"It seems so. I've checked with juvenile and he's not ringing any bells. We're circulating his photo to social services in case he's on their register but it's probably a long shot."

"Do we have any other leads?"

"Just what we've learned about Video."

"Yes, that sounds worth following up. For all we know, that's where they may be holding him. I'd like you to get down there now, but please take someone with you, Jim."

"After what I've seen in those videos I don't think I'd want to go there on my own, sir."

***

Hugo and his mother stood on the observation deck at the top of Table Mountain looking out across the impressive vista of Cape Town and Table Bay.

"He's out there somewhere," she said.

"Yes, but I don't think he'll be the same."

"Will you still love him?"

"I hope so but I can't be sure."

"Oh dear. Have you fallen in love with someone else, darling?"

"Yes, Greg."

"Ah, that's complicated." She paused. "I noticed the cable car attendant looking at you."

"I know."

"You enjoyed the attention?"

"Yes, a lot."

"Cape Town has changed you, Hugo."

"I know."

"Perhaps we didn't give you enough freedom."

"It's not just you."

"We'll still love you whatever happens, darling."

"Thanks Mum."

They hugged each other and just stood staring at the vista, trying to take in everything that had happened over the last few days.

***

DI van der Merwe allowed his colleague to drive the squad car to Duncan Dock. He wanted to be able to devote all his attention to where they were going in case he picked up something that seemed out of kilter. At this time in the morning, the dockside seemed deserted and the cranes stood motionless but ominously ready to pounce. It didn't take them long to find Video, although it was hard to make out the Tom of Finland character without the back illumination at night.

"Is that what I think it is?" asked his rookie Sergeant, pointing roughly in the direction of the erect penis. "It seems rather big."

The DI thought of mentioning what he'd seen in the latest video but decided that might provoke uncomfortable questions. "I suppose it must be."

They checked the parking lot but it was empty. The DI's colleague suggested knocking on the door.

"Well, you can, but I'm staying in the car."

He undid his seat belt and opened the car door.

"They like fresh young meat, you know."

His colleague got back in and buckled up in double time. They continued to look around the area. Video stood separate from any other buildings and consisted of a large square building painted black with the parking lot at the back. On the other side of the access road, there were rows of cold storage containers and a larger building which the DI took to be the cold storage facility itself. There were a number of cars parked outside and the DI thought it looked safe enough to ask whether they'd seen anything suspicious. They parked alongside the other cars and went in the main entrance where they showed their ID badges to the receptionist.

A young guy wearing protective white overalls came out to greet them: "I'm Frank Dresden, the manager. How can I help?"

"Good morning, Mr Dresden. I'm Detective Inspector Jim van der Merwe from the Central Police Station and this is my colleague Sergeant Peters. We're investigating the disappearance of a young man who went missing from the Nelson Lodge Hotel five days ago. You might have heard about it."

"Hard to miss it, Detective Inspector. It's been all over the news. But what brings you down to the docks?"

"We're wondering whether you might have seen him. We've reason to believe that he may be held somewhere in the docks."

"Do you have a photo to refresh my memory of what he looks like?"

The Sergeant produced a blown up copy of the photo of Hugo and Ben from the Cape Argus and handed it to Mr Dresden. He pointed out Ben: "That's him on the right."

DI van der Merwe watched his reaction to looking at the photo and thought he detected a slight flicker of his eyes but it was probably just a trick of the light.

"They're a good looking couple, I'll say that, but I don't recall seeing either of them around here."

"We're also pursuing a possible sighting at Video a few days ago. Do you know anything about what goes on there?"

"I can't say I do, Detective Inspector. We're open in the day, they're open at night. I know it's gay, but that's not my thing."

"Okay, Mr Dresden, thank you for your time. If anything does occur to you, please contact me on this number." The DI handed him his card.

DI van der Merwe and his Sergeant left and got into the squad car.

"Did you notice anything, Sergeant?"

"He was pretty cool, I'll give him that, but his eyes flickered when he looked at the photo."

"That's very good. Anything else?"

"He was lying about not being gay. His pupils dilated when he looked at the photo, particularly when he looked at the guy on the left."

"That's quite remarkable, Sergeant. We'll make a detective of you yet."

Frank Dresden watched the two police officers talking in their car from his office. If he concentrated hard enough, he could just about remember the savory but sweet taste of the come as it landed in his mouth. He'd give a month's salary to spend some time on his own with the blond guy in the photo. He needed to alert someone. He reached in his pocket for his cell phone and punched a speed dial number.

**

DI van der Merwe finally managed to persuade Sir James Cavendish's secretary to put him through on his direct line. He'd assumed that he might be on high alert for a phone call from South Africa but thus far that didn't seem to be the case.

"Cavendish here."

"Sir James, you won't know me, but I'm Detective Inspector van der Merwe calling from Cape Town in South Africa."

"Ah, I wondered whether you might phone, Detective Inspector."

"It's about your son, Ben."

"Indeed. All very unfortunate. It would seem that he's been up to his old tricks again."

"You received the video link and the ransom details, then?"

"Of course. Utterly disgusting and I didn't watch more than a few seconds."

"And the ransom?"

"Well, there's absolutely no question of us paying it and

I'm sure whoever's behind this sordid business knows that. I'm a bit too long in the tooth to be caught out again. Do you play poker, Detective Inspector?"

"Sometimes."

"Well, you'll know about upping the ante. It may be Benjamin's life at stake but I'm sticking to the game I know and I won't give in to some petty blackmailer."

"I see, sir. Those are high stakes and I can only pray that you know the game better than Ben's kidnapper. Goodbye, Sir James."

The DI was shocked by Sir James's callousness and started to appreciate rather better why Ben had gone off the rails as a teenager.

***

Greg and John were sitting down for dinner after their shifts at the hospital and hotel but were barely touching the food.

"Have you heard from Hugo?" asked John.

"Nothing," replied Greg. "I guess his mind must be on other things after what happened at the hotel. Did you find out anything more?"

"Only that a smartly dressed teenage boy was seen coming in with one family late afternoon and then left with a different family after the firecrackers went off."

"Could this be the same boy that's been delivering the envelopes?"

"It certainly seems likely."

"Did you find out what was in the third envelope?"

"Another video link and a new ransom demand."

"Did you watch it?"

"Absolutely not."

"And the ransom?"

"10 million rand."

"Jesus!"

They returned to playing with their plates of food. Greg looked up at John.

"I'm really missing him, you know."

"Me too."

***

Just before he left the office to go on the stakeout at Chapman's Peak Drive, DI van der Merwe's PC pinged to alert him to a new e-mail in his inbox. The sender wasn't someone he recognized. He didn't know how they'd managed to get his police e-mail address but there was no doubt that the file attached to the e-mail had been sent for his personal attention. He saved the avi file to his desktop and tried running it. His PC complained that the file needed QuickTime to run it, so he wasted a good few minutes finding the right installer on the internet. Finally, he was able to watch the video. But when he heard the resounding snap of the cervical vertebra, he really wished he hadn't bothered opening the e-mail. He'd definitely opened something considerable more unpleasant than a can of worms.

***

The t-shirt man watched the stakeout proceeding down below at the lookout point with night vision goggles. The Detective Inspector had been interfering rather too much and it was fortunate that his plans had already reached fruition. He knew there'd never been the slightest likelihood of Sir James and Lady Cavendish coming up with the ransom, but he wanted them to feel the anguish of being powerless to help their son. He also wanted to pay Sir James back for all the losses he'd made over the years investing in his company.

To cover all eventualities, he'd brought Ben along for the ride and could hear him making sounds in the trunk. He'd need more sedation sometime soon. He also needed to make a final collection before he sent Ben on his way with the surprise package. And perhaps he'd enjoy his body one last time before bidding him farewell. Then there was the final video, which he was sure would interest the Detective Inspector and the National Prosecution Service. And if that didn't work, he still had another trick up his sleeve.

Wednesday, February 16, 2011

The gardener was doing his usual daily clear-up of fronds that had fallen from the palm trees. This was something he enjoyed: a simple act that restored the pristine beauty of the Nelson Lodge Hotel gardens for the guests to enjoy until he repeated the process the following day. What made the act special for him is that all the palms stood out as individuals: some growing proudly upright, some leaning to the right, some to the left, and some so bent over that they needed propping up with stakes. His wife joked that that was a bit like penises, but he thought that was demeaning the majesty of the trees.

He came to the end of his round and maneuvered the barrow of fronds to the spot where they'd be taken away by one of the head gardeners in a buggy. He was surprised to see that the buggy that had disappeared a week ago was back on its spot looking none the worse for wear. Perhaps it was just a joyrider after all, he thought. He reached the side of the buggy, ready to load the garden waste, when he noticed that someone seemed to be in the passenger seat. He looked closer and saw a white man, sitting upright, with many days of beard growth and a glazed expression on his face, and wearing nothing more than swimming trunks and flip-flops. He dropped what he was carrying and ran into the hotel lobby, looking for assistance.

"Mr John, Mr John!" he called out, seeing John Bredenkamp coming out of his office.

"Yes, Alberto, how can I help?"

"Must come quick, must come quick!"

John ran after the gardener not exactly knowing what

to expect, but thinking there must have been a minor catastrophe involving a palm tree that wasn't behaving itself. He did a double-take when he saw the figure sitting upright in the buggy: from a distance, the figure was the spitting image of Greg after a week of not shaving. Closer up, there was still the resemblance, but there was now no doubt that this was Benjamin Cavendish returned to the site of his abduction. As the gardener had noticed, Ben was wearing speedos and flip-flops but nothing else. There were red marks around his ankles and wrists that matched the restraints that John had seen in the video clip. Ben was looking straight ahead and seemed oblivious to their presence. John gently opened the buggy's door and crouched by Ben's side.

"Ben, I'm John," he said softly. "I work here and I'm also a friend of Hugo. We've been very worried about you."

Ben slowly turned his head to look at John but then turned back, looking straight ahead again. He seemed unable to speak. The gardener handed John a cup of water and he held it in front of Ben's mouth.

Ben slowly looked down at the cup but didn't take hold of it. He opened his mouth wide as if expecting to be fed something. John gently poured some water into his mouth but Ben didn't make any attempt to swallow and the water dribbled down his chin.

"Okay, Ben, you're perfectly safe now and no one is going to harm you. I'm just going to make a phone call so that we can get you somewhere warm and safe. Do you understand, Ben?"

Ben continued to stare ahead with his mouth wide open.

Leaving the gardener to watch over him, John walked back to the pool area and called Greg on his cell phone.

"Greg, it's John. Ben's turned up in the gardens at the hotel. He's just been dumped in the buggy still in his trunks. He's not saying anything and just staring straight ahead with his mouth open."

"Okay, love. It sounds as if he's in shock and may be catatonic. Can you call for an ambulance and get him to the emergency department? I'll see him as soon as he gets here."

"Should I do anything else in the meantime? I mean, like holding his hand or something?"

"I wouldn't advise that. Any sort of physical contact could trigger a violent response after all that he's been through. But can you call Hugo and DI van der Merwe?"

"Will do. I'll come to the hospital later when I get off duty. Thanks, love."

John called the ambulance service which wasn't busy at that early hour on a Wednesday morning and they said they'd be at the hotel within minutes. He didn't have the phone number for the Cape Heritage Hotel on his phone, so that call would have to wait until he was back in the office. He called the police department and got through to DI van de Merwe just as the ambulance pulled up outside the hotel with its blue light flashing.

"Van der Merwe here."

"It's John Bredenkamp at the Nelson Lodge Hotel. Ben Cavendish has just turned up. He's been dropped off in a garden buggy and he seems in a bad way. The ambulance has just arrived."

"I'm on my way. Don't touch anything."

The paramedics managed to get Ben into the

ambulance although his retarded state made the process rather touch and go and they'd had to consider sedating him at one point just so they could move him. The ambulance reached the emergency bay at the Groote Schuur Hospital at just after 9:00 a.m. with the police not far behind. Following John's call, Greg had wrestled with the ethics of examining the partner of someone he'd fallen in love with but rationalized that Ben's needs were too acute to be managed by someone with less experience. He took the precaution of asking two female nurses to act as both chaperones and to cover any unexpected complications. But when he drew back the curtains to the assessment cubicle, he saw that this wasn't going to be an easy case with a simple resolution. His patient was also extremely handsome.

Ben had been transferred to a trolley, and at some point his trunks had been removed, but he wasn't in a state of repose. He resembled a textbook case of catatonia, with his head held a few centimeters above the pillow, still staring dead ahead and with his mouth wide open. Having seen the first two videos, Greg could well imagine what his mouth had been conditioned to expect.

Commencing with a superficial exam, Greg saw that he was malnourished with a loss of abdominal fat, which paradoxically gave him the appearance of having a healthy six pack. His body had a variety of contusions, including on his wrists and ankles, which were consistent with prolonged restraint and other forms of coercion. He was generally covered with dirt and grime.

"Ben, can you hear me? My name is Greg and I'm a doctor in the emergency department. I'm a friend of Hugo and he's going to be here very soon. You're safe now and no one is going to hurt you. But I'm going to need to examine you to make sure you're well enough to go home. Can you nod if you understand?"

Ben showed no response, and if anything his head rose a further centimeter or two. His mouth remained wide open. Greg gently raised Ben's right arm and noticed the increased tone. It remained up in the air until he lowered it back to the trolley.

"Now, Ben, I'm going to need to run some tests but I'm going to check with you each time I do anything. I'm going to start with your temperature and blood pressure and then I'll need to take some blood for some tests. Can you nod if you understand?"

As before, Ben didn't respond. Greg checked his axillary temperature as he thought sticking a thermometer in his mouth could be potentially dangerous. He took a quick set of swabs from inside and around Ben's mouth. His blood pressure and pulse were normal, and listening to his chest with a stethoscope didn't indicate any problems with his heart or lungs. His external genitalia looked normal, with no obvious contusions to his penis or scrotum. He put a tourniquet around Ben's upper arm and filled some vacutainer tubes, including for HIV serology and an urgent toxicology screen. Throughout, Ben remained in a bizarre, frozen state which reminded Greg of nothing less than a rather battered but anatomically correct sex doll.

"Now, Ben, I'm going to need to examine your bottom to see whether you've been hurt. Do you think you could turn over on your side?"

Ben's response was totally unexpected, as he immediately raised his legs in the air into the lithotomy position. Greg anticipated that he'd lower his legs almost immediately but they remained elevated. Greg bent down to examine his anus and perineum and was surprised to see that his anal opening was already dilated as if something very large had just been forced into his rectum. He took a swab and collected a specimen of what he thought must be dried semen from around the opening. As he did so, Ben's anal sphincter dilated more and he could see something glassy descending down the rectum. What had this poor boy been subjected to all this time? Greg shook his head in disbelief.

While performing this exam, Greg had been aware that Ben's penis was stirring and he'd heard the nurses exchanging a jokey comment about 'the Greg effect'. Greg was well aware of this and requesting a chaperone was really more for his protection than that of the patient. What happened next took all three of them by surprise. The glass object emerged at speed and with an explosive plop onto the trolley. At the same, Ben arched his trunk, reached down with both hands and frantically stroked his penis which then ejaculated spurts of semen onto his chest and into his open mouth. He frenziedly scooped up the ejaculate with his fingers, licking and sucking his fingers as if dying of thirst. Suddenly, he flopped back onto the trolley with his hands by his side, as if all the air had been sucked out of his body. His mouth was now closed but his eyes remained wide open, staring into space.

Greg and the nurses looked at each other and were momentarily lost for words. Greg thought it best to conclude his assessment with the minimum of delay.

"Okay, Ben, I've finished examining you. Are you able to tell me anything about what's been happening to you for the past week?"

Ben showed no response for about twenty seconds and then abruptly went into his previous rigid posture with his mouth wide open again.

"Er, ladies," asked Greg bashfully, "would you mind cleaning him up? I think I should keep my distance." He tossed them a box of wipes and they got to work, casting wary glances at his penis in case another eruption occurred.

Greg examined the glass object that had been forcefully expelled just a few minutes before. It was exactly the same size and shape as a coke bottle, measuring about 10 inches in length and 2 inches in diameter at the base. This sort of old-style bottle sometimes found service as a butt plug, as the inward curve towards the base meant that it stayed in. The screw-top bottle was full of something milky. Greg thought it highly likely that the contents were semen but his mind boggled at the idea of someone collecting 50 or more ejaculates to fill the 12 ounce volume. He considered opening the bottle to check but decided that should definitely be left to forensics. He sealed the bottle in a plastic bag and marked it with Ben's details and the date. The nurses finished their clean up job and one of them remained behind to keep a watch on Ben's condition.

As Greg pulled the curtain back around the cubicle, he turned to the other nurse and said: "I think it'd be best not to say too much about that. I'm just wondering what the hell I'm going to put on the card."

"I'd say it's proof positive of the Greg effect."

"One to tell your gay nephew, perhaps?"

"Too dangerous: he'd be around here in a flash to try it out."

Greg grinned and blushed in the bashful way they all loved.

The blood results came back from the lab and confirmed that Ben was mildly dehydrated with slightly low serum sodium. He'd therefore need intravenous fluids and admission to the clinical decisions unit at least overnight. The other chemistry and hematology was normal. HIV serology was negative but Greg was going to start him on prophylaxis anyway to reduce the risk of conversion if he'd been exposed. He'd also charted high dose diazepam in the hope that the drug might release him from the catatonic state.

At around mid-day, three people arrived in the emergency department: Hugo and his mother to see Ben; and DI van der Merwe to see Greg, with the intention of finding out whether Ben was fit to be interviewed. Hugo was looking ashen.

"Christ, Greg, how is he? Can I see him?"

"One thing at a time, Hugo. Let's go and have a talk. Perhaps your mother could join us afterwards." Hugo's mother nodded. Greg took Hugo into a room reserved for relatives.

They sat down opposite each other and Greg took Hugo's hands in his. "Look, Hugo, the first thing I should say is that I tried to find someone else to see him, as I'm worried that our friendship might create a conflict of interest. But nobody else was around, so I assessed him with two female nurses as chaperones when he was brought in by the ambulance. If you'd prefer for me to get someone else to take over, I'd totally understand that."

"No, Greg, I think I'd trust you more than anyone else. How is he?"

"Well, in a nutshell, he's not his normal self. He's obviously been through a very traumatic time. Physically, he's not too bad: a few cuts and bruises, he's lost some weight and he's a bit dehydrated. All that will heal quickly. Psychologically, it's not that straightforward. He seems to be in a state of what's called catatonia. That can be caused by extreme stress. So he's not talking at the moment and his behaviors are quite strange. To be honest, I'd be surprised if he responds to you, but we'll see. If he doesn't, he might need a short admission to a psychiatric ward until he's ready to fly back with you to the UK. For the time being, though, he'll be in our clinical decisions unit and I've started him on intravenous fluids and some medication. You ought to know that we've tested him for HIV and that came back negative. But because seroconversion can take months after exposure, I've started him on prophylactic medication."

"Did he tell you any more about what happened or who did those things to him?"

"Absolutely nothing at the moment, and it may take some time for him to say anything at all. I've started him on some medication to try to release him from the catatonic state but it doesn't work for everyone. I think it'll be crucial to see how he reacts to you."

"Can you go through that with my mother? She's said she'll phone Ben's mother later today."

"Of course. I'll bring her in."

Greg went off to find Hugo's mother, leaving Hugo feeling uncertain about almost everything in his life. Having gone through a rapid adjustment to not having Ben around and then forming the growing friendship with Greg and John, he was now having to process Ben's return in a condition that was clearly so very different to when they first arrived in Cape Town. And what if he'd changed so much that he was a different person? Would he still love him? Hugo's thoughts were interrupted by Greg returning with his mother. She sat down next to him and grasped his hands.

"Dr Edwards - I mean, Greg - thanks for seeing me. I hadn't expected to see you again in these circumstances."

"Well, Joanna, as I was explaining to Hugo, I'd ideally have asked a colleague to see Ben but there simply wasn't anyone else in the department. I checked with Hugo and he's happy for my still being involved in Ben's care." He looked at Hugo who nodded. "What about you, Joanna?"

"Well, I can't begin to understand what's been happening to poor Ben, but if Hugo trusts you, then that's good enough for me. But obviously we want to get him back to the UK as soon as we can. I've spoken to Mr Anderson at the consulate and they're ready to do whatever is needed. Can you take us through his current condition? I was a nurse, so I've got some medical knowledge."

"Okay. Physically he's not too bad and he's on fluids for mild dehydration. As you've gathered, he's likely to have been sexually abused by multiple men on numerous occasions. As is usual after potential exposure to HIV, I've started him on acyclovir. Psychologically, he's in a state of profound shock and isn't speaking, but that isn't so unusual when someone has been exposed to prolonged stress."

"Greg, you mentioned about 'strange behaviors'. Can you explain what you mean by that?" asked Hugo.

"Well, to start with, he's unable to relax, so when he's

lying on the couch his head is held just above the pillow. We call that 'the psychological pillow'. Most of the time, he's just staring into space, sometimes with his mouth open. With this sort of catatonia, patients can suddenly flip into an excited state without any warning and we've already seen that happen once in Ben's case."

"What happened?" asked Hugo.

"I'm not sure whether it'd be right to say in front of your mother," replied Greg, looking embarrassed.

"Greg, I really don't think anything could shock me now," said Hugo's mother, holding his hands tighter.

"Okay... Well, I was bending down to examine him, when suddenly he arched his back, reached down for his penis and ejaculated. He then just flopped back onto the couch."

Hugo and his mother looked equally shocked but Hugo was the first to find his voice.

"And that was without you touching him or anything?"

"Well, I was taking a swab, so I guess that could have stimulated him. But I had gloves on, of course."

"Er... Greg, he used to have a thing about latex."

"Ah, that probably explains it." Greg looked sheepish.

"Was that the only strange thing that happened?" asked Hugo.

"Well, there is one other thing, but I think I should tell you that in private as you're his next of kin."

"Can we see him now, Greg?" asked Hugo's mother.

"Sure. But if you don't mind, I'll just have a quick word with Hugo before I take you to see him."

Greg opened the door for Hugo's mother and pointed to an area where she could wait.

"What did happen then, Greg?" asked Hugo.

"Well, this is really weird, but when I was examining his anus for injuries I noticed that it was quite dilated, and the next thing that happened was that he expelled a coke bottle onto the trolley."

"Jesus! But why would someone put a coke bottle up his ass?"

"There's more to it: the bottle was full of something milky and I'm guessing it was semen."

"What the fuck?" exclaimed Hugo.

"I know it's bizarre," said Greg. "I'm wondering whether that was a message to us: like the number of men who've ejaculated into him."

"Oh Christ, it doesn't bear thinking about. I think I'm giving up sex for good," said Hugo.

Greg squeezed Hugo's arm. "Let's go find your mother and see Ben."

By now, Ben had been moved into a side room in the clinical decisions unit. He was still on an emergency department trolley and the sides had been pulled up in case he started thrashing around. He was wearing the standard, undignified hospital gown that closes at the back. The side room was chosen for a couple of reasons: the first being his propensity for sudden changes in behavior; the second because it was anticipated that relatives and the police would want to see him. A nurse was sitting in a chair next to the bed reading a magazine.

As Hugo entered behind Greg, he drew a sharp intake of breath and looked shocked. He stood in the doorway looking at Ben and then turned to Greg with a helpless look on his face.

"That's Ben but he looks so different. Why's he just staring into space?"

"That's what happens with catatonia. Let's see how Ben reacts when you get closer. Just walk nearer to him and try telling him you're here."

Hugo walked slowly towards Ben and stopped when he was about three feet away. Ben seemed oblivious to Hugo's presence. He crouched down to be on the same level as Ben. He could see the side of Ben's face with his aquiline nose and strong jaw, his eyes still staring up towards the ceiling.

"Ben, darling, it's me, Hugo," he said softly, his voice almost cracking with emotion. "Ben, can you hear me?"

Very slowly, Ben turned to look in the direction of Hugo's voice but he showed no recognition and turned his face to look upwards again.

"Ben, I want to touch you, but I don't want to do anything in case you think it'll hurt you."

All of a sudden, Ben opened his mouth wide and they could see that he was holding his head just above the pillow. He remained like that for several minutes and then suddenly went floppy on the bed and his mouth closed. His eyes remained staring into space. Hugo tried again to get some response.

"Ben, I've been so worried about you. Can you just say my name so that I know you've recognized me?"

Ben slowly turned his face again towards Hugo, but rather than saying anything opened his mouth wide. He remained in that position as Hugo stood up sobbing and went to hug his mother for support.

Greg sent Hugo and his mother to the hospital canteen for coffees and to help them take stock. He took DI van der Merwe into his office.

"Thank you for seeing me, Dr Edwards. What can you

tell me about Mr Cavendish's current condition?"

"As I've said to his relatives, he's in reasonable physical shape apart from bruising. He's a bit dehydrated and malnourished, which is to be expected if he's been held captive. My big concern is post-traumatic stress. He's currently in a state of catatonic shock and isn't able to communicate."

"What about when he was with his partner?"

"Nothing, I'm afraid. He just stares and opens his mouth. But a few strange things did happen before his partner arrived."

"Like what?"

"Firstly, he arched his back and ejaculated when I started to examine him. Secondly, he expelled a bottle from his rectum which I'm pretty sure contains semen. I've put it in a bag for your forensic people."

"Jesus Christ!" said the DI, looking shocked, "But I can't say I'm that surprised. You probably don't know this but there've been two more videos."

"Oh God. What do they show?"

"More of the same, but also much worse."

"How much worse?"

"I'm afraid as bad as it gets. Mr Cavendish seems to have been party to what's called a 'snuff movie'"

"You mean where someone gets killed when they're having sex?" asked Greg, looking horrified.

"That's what it looks like. I guess it could have been staged but there was a snap which definitely sounded like some guy's neck being broken."

"Shit."

"Absolutely. And Mr Cavendish is right up to his neck in it, if you'll pardon the expression."

Greg handed the DI the bag containing the bottle. The DI handled it rather cautiously and asked for another, thicker bag as if needing additional protection from the contents. Greg didn't blame him and would probably have done exactly the same in his position. The thought of three billion spermatozoa from multiple donors swimming around in the bottle was truly bizarre and conjured up images of a Woody Allen-type sperm party.

Greg's train of thought suddenly switched. "Christ! I've just remembered: we had a patient brought in DOA late Saturday with a fractured vertebra. I can't remember all the details but he was a John Doe in a smart suit. We thought he'd just slipped on the sidewalk after drinking too much. Your guys were in the department most of the night dealing with some stabbings and shootings, so you may have a report already. His body should still be in the morgue if you want to take a look."

"Lead the way, Dr Edwards."

Greg turned to look at the DI as they were walking to the morgue and thought that he wasn't actually that bad looking, although he wasn't his type.

"Well, you're certainly getting a crash course in gay sex, Detective Inspector."

The DI looked uncomfortable. "Actually, it's not that new to me."

"Ah." Greg paused. "Are you in a relationship?"

"Only with my wife. Although I'm not sure how much longer that will be after she found one of the videos on my laptop."

"Oops. If you don't mind me asking, Detective Inspector, how did those videos make you feel?"

"Off the record?"

"Of course."

"Well, with the exception of the last, pretty horny, but I'd definitely prefer rather more consensuality and less restraint."

"Agreed. I think you've passed the gayness test. Welcome to the wonderful world of homosexuality, Detective Inspector."

The DI chuckled. He was about to describe the generous contents of the third video, which Greg hadn't seen, but opening the door to the morgue called a halt to further banter.

"Now, let's see," said the morgue technician, "I remember that John Doe but more for the fact that he came with a suit than for any other reason." He found the relevant drawer and pulled it out for their inspection. As soon as Greg pulled back the sheet covering the body, it was apparent that his neck had been broken as his head was lolling to one side. He found the emergency department card in the pocket at the front of the drawer. There was a complete lack of information from when he was brought into the emergency department apart from the fact that he'd been found quite literally in the gutter at the bottom of Long Street outside one of Cape Town's more notorious drinking holes. What didn't quite fit was the lack of any sort of ID on him, but the emergency department staff had assumed that anything of any value had been stolen while he was lying on the ground. The police officers in the department were too busy with other cases to give him anything other than a passing glance. Although Greg had been the senior doctor on duty that night, John Doe had been assessed by someone with limited experience who'd simply put two and two together and had attributed the C2 fracture to falling while under the influence of alcohol. And while his blood alcohol had measured at 0.51, which was barely compatible with life, his physical exam was woefully inadequate. Greg turned him over on the gurney with the technician's assistance and it was clear that there was more to the case than falling into the gutter, as there were streaks of dried semen all over his buttocks and back.

"Are you thinking what I'm thinking, Detective Inspector?" asked Greg.

"Mr Cavendish's work," replied the DI.

***

Hugo and his mother returned from the canteen and sat waiting for Greg to return to the emergency department. They were debating whether to stay with Ben overnight or to return in the morning. When Greg finally arrived back with DI van der Merwe, he told them that it was extremely unlikely that Ben's condition would change that quickly, so they decided to return to the hotel and phone for updates. He didn't tell them that Ben was now implicated in someone's death. John turned up shortly thereafter and found Greg in his office writing up notes.

"Hi, love. How are Hugo and Ben?"

"Hugo's bearing up but he's obviously finding it pretty difficult. It's good that his mother is here, because it's her support he really needs right now. Ben, on the other hand, isn't so good. I mean, he's a striking looking guy, but whatever those bastards did to him isn't something that'll be cured overnight. And there's some pretty weird stuff, too, although I probably shouldn't really be telling you."

"Come on, you can tell me."

"Well, he ejaculated just after I started to examine him."

John showed a look of disbelief. "You mean he just came in your hands, so to speak?"

Greg looked uncomfortable. "Not exactly. I was just doing my routine physical exam and said I needed to examine his bottom. The next thing I knew, he'd drawn up his knees as if expecting to be fucked and then he reached down to wank his dick and came just seconds later."

"That fast? And that's without even seeing your dick? Wow, you must have really turned him on."

Greg looked even more uncomfortable. "I guess it must have something like that, although I promise I was only doing the professional thing and had gloves on. Actually, Hugo mentioned that he used to have a thing about latex. But how he did it seemed so strange: in fact, more as if he'd been conditioned to perform."

"So what was the next part of this performance?"

"Well, it got weirder. When I was taking swabs for semen from around his anus, I noticed something glassy descending his rectum. The next thing I knew he'd ejected a coke bottle onto the trolley."

"You must be joking!"

"Absolutely not. And more than that, I'm pretty sure the bottle was full of semen."

"No way!" exclaimed John.

Greg's professional reserve collapsed. "Come here, love. I need a hug very, very badly."

***

That night, after Greg went off duty and returned home with John to 180 Bree Street, all hell broke loose on the clinical decisions unit. This seemed to coincide with Ben being given the first dose of the diazepam charted by Greg. A problem with the supply of police officers unfortunately coincided with Ben's nurse taking a bathroom break. Within minutes, and for reasons no-one would fully understand, Ben morphed into an animatronic sex machine. Nurses had a difficult time trying to extract him from compromising positions with a number of other patients and he eventually required intramuscular sedation to manage his bizarre, indiscriminate sexual behavior. This episode wasn't mentioned to Hugo when he phoned for an update: "Ben's sleeping" is what he was told, which was certainly technically correct after the hefty dose of medication he'd received.

Thursday, February 17, 2011

DI van der Merwe removed the evidence bag containing the coke bottle from the fridge in his office and placed it on his desktop. It wasn't the usual sort of bottle he was accustomed to viewing at 8:00 in the morning. The forensic lab had been alerted to its presence but they were still trying to decide how to deal with it: the most complex and most plausible scenario was that the bottle contained many donations, which meant multiple DNA analyses that would take their departmental budget well into the red; the simpler but clearly least plausible scenario was a single donor with the bizarre habit of collecting his semen for posterity.

Coupled with the incontrovertible video evidence of male rape, there'd clearly be ample opportunity for multiple prosecutions, but DI van der Merwe thought somehow that it'd never stick and just be too complicated for the National Prosecution Service to want to pursue. He suspected that whoever was behind Ben's abduction was adept at covering their tracks and quite probably out of the country by now. The very audible evidence of a death was another matter, though, particularly when coupled with the copious forensic evidence left behind. He reached for the phone to call the direct line at the British Consulate.

"Good morning, Mr Anderson. It's Jim van der Merwe here."

"Ah, good morning, Detective Inspector. I gather there have been all manner of developments in the Cavendish case. The media seems to be indulging in a most unwholesome frenzy of speculation. It would be helpful to have an accurate update on the situation."

"Well, it's complicated. The good news is that Mr Cavendish is in one piece but he's not quite all there. Dr Edwards describes his condition as catatonia, and most of the time he's just staring and not saying anything, so it's been impossible to interview him. However, from time to time, he almost literally explodes, and that's included ejaculating while Dr Edwards was examining him and expelling a bottle from his rectum that appears to contain a large quantity of semen."

"Dear God." The DI heard a leathery squeak from the other end of the phone as Mr Anderson sat down rather heavily.

"And I'm afraid there's more," said the DI apologetically. "I had a fourth video clip sent to me direct at the station which shows Mr Cavendish having anal sex with a man whose neck was then broken. This man was brought into the Groote Schuur Hospital last Saturday evening as a John Doe. When Dr Edwards examined his body in the morgue yesterday, his back appeared covered with dried semen, which presumably was deposited by Mr Cavendish. In other words, Mr Cavendish appears to be at least a witness to murder and possibly even an accessory."

"Dear me, that is quite dreadful. You're sure about this, Detective Inspector?"

"That's how it appears, although it'll need forensic analysis to prove it."

"What does his young friend Hugo know?"

"Only about his current condition in the hospital."

"And his family?"

"I believe Hugo's mother was intending to call Lady Cavendish last night."

"Yes, I spoke with her yesterday. I think it's best that we keep the latest developments to ourselves. I'll need to speak with the Foreign & Commonwealth Office. By the way, has anyone else seen the video?"

"No."

"Good. Please keep it that way. We'll talk again, Detective Inspector."

***

Greg had just reached his office in the emergency department when his cell phone rang. He didn't recognize the caller.

"Greg Edwards here."

"Greg, it's Hugo. I'm sorry to call you at work but I just wanted to say something: I'll always love you." Greg could hear the raw emotion in Hugo's voice and hoped his voice wouldn't crack as well.

"Hugo love, that sounds so final," he said softly.

"I just had to say it now in case anything else happens."

"Oh Hugo, I'll always love you too."

Greg ended the call, wondering how he'd explain his red eyes to John.

***

By the time Hugo and his mother reached the Groote Schuur Hospital just before 11:00 a.m., Ben's intravenous line had been removed and he'd been transferred to ward C23, which they gathered was Cape Town's psychiatric assessment unit. He was still under the influence of the sedation given the previous night but he had two police officers and a nurse keeping their wary eyes on him.

The C23 designation to the ward reminded Hugo of

departure gates in an airport but that was the only similarity to anything enjoyable that they saw once they'd gained access through the locked doors. The brusqueness of the nurse who first addressed Hugo and his mother surprised them, although she softened her attitude when she realized who they were. The ward itself seemed a maelstrom of distress, with some patients desperate for human contact, some doing anything they could to avoid it and a number of others doing their best to escape by the way they entered. The nurse took them into a small room where a young doctor was busy writing in a patient's notes. Hugo could see Ben's name on the top of the page.

"Dr Coetzee, would you mind seeing Mr Brown and his mother? He's the partner of the patient who's just been transferred from the emergency department."

Dr Coetzee looked up smiling. "I'd be happy to. Please grab a pew." He motioned to a couple of cheap-looking plastic chairs to his right and Hugo and his mother sat down. "How can I help?"

Hugo spoke first. "Can you tell us how Ben's doing? We saw him last night but he didn't seem to recognize me."

"Well, he's only just arrived on the ward, so he's settling in. He needed rather a lot of medication last night after he went a little crazy in the clinical decisions unit but we think that was probably a reaction to the diazepam he was given. So we've reduced the dose and we'll see how he goes today."

"Have you been told the whole story?" asked Hugo's mother.

"As far as anyone knows it, I think so. To be honest, it's beyond me that anything like that can happen in Cape

Town." He turned to Hugo and looked at him earnestly. "It must have been so dreadful for you in particular. I think I'd have gone to pieces if a similar thing had happened to my partner."

"I don't think I could have done it without the support from Greg and John."

"That's Dr Edwards and his partner is it?"

Hugo nodded. Dr Coetzee glanced at Ben's notes.

"Now, one thing I wanted to check with you is whether Ben has got any past psychiatric history or any medical problems we should know about."

"Nothing as far as I know but we've only been together for a couple of years."

"And he's not on any regular medication?"

"No, nothing."

"What about alcohol or drugs?"

"Well, we occasionally share a bottle of wine, but that's about it. He's a bit of a gym bunny, so he looks after his figure. And I've never known him to use drugs, not even a spliff."

"That's interesting, because his toxicology screen came back positive for quite a number of drugs, including benzodiazepines, cocaine and amphetamines. He must have been given all that when he was held captive. That's quite a cocktail for someone who isn't used to drugs, so I'm not surprised that his behavior has been so strange."

"You heard about what happened in the emergency department, then?"

"Yes, I'm afraid they're referring to it as 'the Greg effect'." Some patients do tend to go a little wobbly at the knees when they're examined by Dr Edwards but we haven't had quite that reaction before. Actually, with a wash and a shave, Ben would look rather like Dr Edwards."

Hugo blushed, hoping that Dr Coetzee hadn't noticed. "Is it possible for us to see him briefly?"

"Yes, I don't see why not, although I should warn you he'll still be a bit drowsy."

Dr Coetzee escorted them out of his office up one of the corridors to a room that had a couple of police officers stationed outside.

"Why the police?" asked Hugo.

"I'm guessing it's for his own protection," replied Dr Coetzee, opening the door.

Hugo saw that Ben was lying on his bed, still with the same gown on that he had on in the emergency department, but he looked relaxed and his eyes and mouth were closed.

"Is it okay for me to touch him or try talking to him?" asked Hugo.

"Be my guest," said Dr Coetzee, "but try to avoid doing anything sudden in case it frightens him."

Hugo bent down by the bedside and put his fingers gently on Ben's right hand. "Ben darling, it's me. Can you hear me?"

Almost imperceptibly, Ben turned his head slightly to the right and Hugo felt Ben's fingers respond to his touch. His eyelids flickered and he slowly opened his eyes. "Hugo, it's you," he said hoarsely, as if trying to force words out through a damaged throat.

"Yes, darling, it's me, and Joanna's here too."

Hugo's mother came across and knelt by his side. "Dear Ben, we've been so worried about you," she said softly.

"Where am I?" Ben asked, again struggling to make meaningful sounds.

"You're in hospital and you're safe now," said Hugo. "No one is going to hurt you again and I promise that. I'll look after you, my darling."

"I love you," Ben said croakily. Hugo kissed him softly on the lips and held onto his hand, not wanting to let go.

"Darling, I think we ought to let Ben get some rest," said his mother, who'd been prompted by Dr Coetzee.

"Can we come and see him later?" asked Hugo, still reluctant to let go of Ben's hand.

"Absolutely," replied Dr Coetzee. "The usual visiting hours are from 7:00 p.m. and I'll make sure that the ward knows to expect you this time. Do you think you could bring some clothes and toilet things?"

***

Driving his passengers back from the hospital to central Cape Town, the taxi driver didn't really know what to make of the handsome duo of mother and son in the back seat. Half the time they seemed to be in tears and half the time they were laughing and smiling. Tourists were a strange lot, he decided.

***

Lunch for Hugo and his mother was a very different affair to previous days. Both had been subsisting on little more than hotel breakfasts and the rest of the time it had been adrenaline that kept them going.

"Do you really think it's all over now, Mum?"

"I don't know, darling, but I can't tell you how glad I was to see him looking so much better."

"I wonder whether he'll have changed in some way."

"It's difficult to say. I remember looking after some patients who'd had the most dreadful things happen to them and they remained right as rain, whereas others who had little more than a scratch totally went to pieces. As you've said, Ben has a lot of strength and hopefully that will get him through the ordeal."

"I really hope you're right, Mum. I can't wait for us to get back home."

***

DI van der Merwe phoned ward C23 at around 2:00 p.m. and gathered from both ward staff and his own officers that there'd been a considerable improvement in Mr Cavendish's condition, which they were now attributing to his body clearing the cocktail of drugs he'd been administered during his period of captivity. He'd already received a phone call from Steven Anderson at the consulate indicating that plans were being made to expedite Mr Cavendish's repatriation back to the UK, as there was a danger that prolonging his stay any longer in South Africa could both seriously harm the tourist industry and further destabilize the political situation. Although Sir James Cavendish wasn't the multimillionaire many had assumed and clearly played a risky game of poker, he certainly proved he had influence in the highest echelons of the UK government. And given the appalling abuse Mr Cavendish had suffered while on his honeymoon, the Chief Superintendent's view was that his being a witness to murder should be overlooked. The toxicology results also made it unlikely that he was in a fit state to know what he was doing at the time the crime was committed by an unknown third party. The National Prosecution Service concurred with the Chief Superintendent's view, although suggested that the investigation should be kept open pending further examination of the video evidence and forensic analysis of the contents of the coke bottle.

DI van der Merwe decided to visit the ward later that afternoon to tidy up his own lines of inquiry and particularly to find out whether Mr Cavendish had any recollection of what had happened to him. He almost did a double take when he saw him sitting up in bed reading a magazine. Although he was younger and had several days of beard growth, he could have sworn that it was Greg Edwards who was smiling at him so warmly.

"Hello, you must be the police officer I've heard about."

The DI was momentarily lost for words, as he was trying to reconcile the sight of this healthy young man with the appalling and relentless abuse he'd seen inflicted on him in all four videos. Could it really be that he had no recollection whatsoever?

"Ben, we haven't met before, I'm Detective Inspector Jim van der Merwe. If it's all right with you, I'd like to ask you a few questions. Would that be okay?"

"Of course, Detective Inspector."

"Good. I'd like to start with some very simple questions. Do you know where you are at the moment?"

"In hospital." He looked around. "And this is my room."

"Do you know where the hospital is?"

He looked puzzled. "I'm not sure. I don't think it's in London."

"It's in Cape Town."

"Ah. That's where we had our honeymoon." He smiled.

"What do you remember about your honeymoon, Ben?"

"The hotel was nice and we had lots of sex." He blushed.

"Do you have any bad memories about the honeymoon, Ben?"

"No, why should I have?"

"Do you remember going off into the bushes at the hotel with another man?"

"No. Did I?"

"Do you think you might have had sex with anyone other than Hugo?"

He looked surprised by the question. "No, why would I? We're married now and I love Hugo."

"Do you remember staying anywhere other than the hotel?"

"No, we were in the hotel the whole time, Detective Inspector."

"You don't remember being somewhere cold and wet?"

"Oh no, it was nice and warm in the hotel."

"Thank you, Ben. That's all I needed to ask. Goodbye, Ben."

"Goodbye, Detective Inspector."

DI van der Merwe closed the door behind him and turned to the police officer sitting outside. "He doesn't remember a thing, not a bloody thing. It's almost as if those bastards have wiped his mind clean." He walked away shaking his head and then turned around. "You can go off duty now. I don't think you'll be needed here anymore."

***

Hugo and his mother returned to ward C23 at just after 7:00 p.m. and were astonished to see the transformation when they entered Ben's room. Ben had obviously had a shower and someone had lent him a shaver and some clothes to use. He was eating supper and it was clear from the way he was attacking his food that he was ravenous. He looked up from his food, smiling, said "Hi sweetie, hi Joanna" and then continued eating.

Hugo's mother whispered: "I think the two of you need some time on your own." She left Ben's room to find the canteen to get something to eat.

Hugo sat opposite Ben and let him finish his food. Ben pushed the plate to one side and said: "Gosh, I was so hungry." He put his arms out to Hugo and they snuggled up on the institutional armchair, lips to lips and letting their fingers get reacquainted with each other's bodies. Tentatively, they unbuttoned their shirts and traced fingers over their chests. Before long, all their clothes were on the floor and their fingers and tongues were doing what lovers' fingers and tongues do so well. But when Hugo looked into Ben's eyes, he thought he seemed to be focusing on something in the distance. Surprisingly, Ben's approach remained soft and gentle and they continued making love side by side on the bed, touching and stroking, and ultimately coming on each other's abdomens in an unusually old-fashioned but delightfully sexy way.

Ben traced his fingers through their combined streaks of come and let Hugo suck on the goodness. "Nice?" he asked.

"Wonderful. Welcome back, lover."

Friday, February 18, 2011

Hugo and his mother arrived back at 10:00 a.m. for the ward round. They were shown into a room with about half-a-dozen people already sitting down. They recognized Dr Coetzee and assumed that the handsome middle-aged man in a suit sitting opposite was another psychiatrist.

"Please come in and sit down," he said, looking at Hugo. "You must be Ben's partner." He extended his right hand. "I'm Dr Jacobson, the chief psychiatrist in the unit. I gather that you've already met my registrar, Dr Coetzee." Dr Coetzee nodded and smiled at Hugo.

Dr Jacobson turned to Hugo's mother. "And you're Hugo's mother, I believe. Welcome to both of you. It would be helpful to talk briefly about Ben before we bring him in. I gather that you visited him yesterday, Hugo. How did you find him?"

"Pretty much back to normal really," Hugo replied. "He's lost weight but he seems to have a good appetite now. We talked a bit but he doesn't seem to remember anything about what happened."

"That's what the Detective Inspector found when he visited him yesterday. What about when you interviewed him, Dr Coetzee?"

"Exactly the same. I obviously didn't want to probe too hard, but as far as he was concerned, he'd been at the hotel the entire time."

"Was he able to describe what he'd been doing during their time at the hotel?"

"He said they'd enjoyed plenty of sun and, er, lots of sex."

"Which I suppose is what any couple would do on their honeymoon. But I'd imagine if pushed, he wouldn't be able to describe any particular event during their week at the hotel."

"It would seem so."

Dr Jacobson turned to Hugo and his mother. "This makes us think that Ben is in a state of what we call psychogenic amnesia. In some ways, that's a good thing, as it's a sort of mental sticking plaster that protects the mind from having to deal with too much too soon, but it can lead on to full-blown post-traumatic stress disorder."

"Do you think the memories of what happened to him will come back?" asked Hugo.

"That's difficult to say. Certain things – like having sex, for instance – might trigger flashbacks or other reactions, so it's important to tread carefully. So, if you don't mind me saying, I'd suggest avoiding anything penetrative."

"He seemed fine when I spent time with him yesterday evening," said Hugo, blushing.

"Ah really. A little unorthodox perhaps but I suppose that's the advantage of a single room. So he responded normally to you, then?"

"Yes, but he was different: unusually gentle, in fact. We only touched though. One thing I noticed is that he seemed to be focusing on something in the distance rather than me, which seemed strange."

"I think that's to be expected. People with psychogenic amnesia can appear quite detached from the world around them. It's a bit as if the important parts of the brain are on autopilot while other parts are trying to catch up with reality, including whatever happened to cause the amnesia in the first place."

"What happens when he's back in London? Can he get help there to deal with the amnesia?" asked Hugo's mother.

"Ah yes," said Dr Jacobson. "That brings me to the other issue. The fact is that he's now fit to travel, so we don't need for him to stay here any longer. The consulate has been in contact with British Airways and there are seats for the three of you on a flight that leaves for Heathrow at 8:45 p.m. today. I believe you've got seats in first class too. Now, because of what happened to Ben and the unusually dramatic improvement we've seen in the last 24 hours, the consulate has taken the precaution of arranging a transfer from Heathrow to a private psychiatric unit which specializes in psychological trauma. Ben's parents have also been informed about this and are broadly in agreement, although they're naturally concerned about costs. I really don't think this stay would need to be for very long, but it should give everyone the reassurance that he is back to his normal self. And it might also be an opportunity to start some psychological therapy, although this would have to be done very carefully. Now, do either of you have any questions before we bring Ben in?"

Hugo and his mother shook their heads, smiling, but almost in tears and delighted to hear the good news.

"Good. Let's bring Ben in."

Ben walked into the room dressed in the same clothes that he'd been wearing on the flight out to Cape Town. There was thinness to his face and his jeans hung a bit loosely but he looked surprisingly fit and healthy. Dr Jacobson motioned him to sit down next to him.

"How are you doing this morning, Ben?"

"I'm feeling good, doctor."

"I gather that you spent time together with Hugo yesterday evening."

"Yes, it was nice." He blushed. "We love each other, you know."

"I'd imagine so, Ben, particularly as you've just had your wedding. Where did you have your wedding?"

"It was in London. It was nice."

"And when you came to Cape Town, where did you stay?"

"The Nelson Lodge Hotel."

"And were you staying there the entire time you've been in South Africa?"

"Yes. We had plenty of sun and lots of sex. It was nice." He smiled.

"And there wasn't a single day when you weren't staying in the hotel?"

"Oh no."

"Thank you, Ben. As I've just been explaining to Hugo and his mother, you won't need to stay here any longer and in fact you'll be flying back to London with them this evening. What do you think about that?"

"I'd like that. Thank you, doctor."

Dr Jacobson turned to Hugo and his mother. "Dr Coetzee will prepare a summary for you to take to the hospital in London and we'll give you a few diazepam tablets for Ben to take on the flight. Do you have any questions?"

"No, doctor, we're really grateful for everything you've done for Ben," replied Hugo. "Thanks so much."

"Well, best of luck to you all, and particularly to Ben, and have a good flight."

Ben left the room with Hugo and his mother. Dr

Jacobson turned to his registrar.

"Did you notice how bland his responses were? It was almost as if he'd been programmed to say the bare minimum."

"Yes, he was almost robotic. What do you think would happen if the memories of his abuse came back?"

"I really don't know but I wouldn't want to be in his partner's shoes when they do."

***

Hugo phoned Greg on his cell phone from the ward.

"Greg Edwards here."

"Greg, it's Hugo. Can we meet?"

"Where are you?"

"I'm on the ward with Ben."

"It's my lunch break, so I can meet you in the canteen in five minutes."

When Hugo arrived in the canteen he saw Greg sitting with an untouched plate of food in front of him. He looked up and smiled when he saw Hugo but it was more a smile of resignation than one usually shared between lovers.

"I'm glad to hear he's so much better."

"I can't begin to thank you for everything you've done. It's hard to believe that I've actually got Ben back." He reached out and held Greg's hand but it was only a fleeting contact.

"I'm really pleased for you."

"It's funny, really. For a time, I thought I'd never be able to leave you and Cape Town. So much seems to have happened since we met." He looked down at the table. "You know we're flying back to the UK this evening?"

"I'd gathered that."

"I suppose this is when we have to say goodbye."

"I guess so."

"Oh, Greg, I wish it wasn't like this." Hugo started sobbing and reached out again for Greg's hands but this time didn't let go.

"Did you mean what you said before?"

"That I'll always love you? Oh yes, that hasn't changed."

"Me too."

They leant across the table and kissed, not wanting to let go but knowing that that would probably be their last physical contact ever.

***

Hugo's mother arrived back at the hospital at 5:00 p.m. in a taxi with the trunk full to the brim with their luggage. Ben left the ward holding hands with Hugo. By the time they arrived at the airport to check-in, Steven Anderson from the consulate was already there and ready to whisk them through diplomatic channels and into the first class lounge.

"So this is the young man I've been hearing so much about," he said, smiling in an avuncular sort of way. "We've been very worried about you, dear boy."

"Why's that?"

"You went missing, dear boy."

"Did I?" Ben momentarily looked puzzled but then his expression relaxed. "We were staying at the hotel. We had plenty of sun and lots of sex. It was nice." He smiled.

"Ah, I see. Never mind, dear boy. Let's get you back home."

***

The three of them were virtually the only passengers in first class and it was clear from all the attention they received that the flight crew had been well briefed on the circumstances of their flight back home. Hugo made sure that Ben was within eyesight at all times and didn't leave his seat until he'd fallen asleep after being given a diazepam tablet. As he went up to the galley to go to the lavatory, one of the stewards tapped him on the shoulder.

"Mr Brown, I was on the flight when you came out for your honeymoon. I've been keeping an eye on the news. I can't believe what you've had to go through. How is your partner now?"

"It's difficult to say really. At least he's in one piece physically. And I really appreciate all the attention you're giving us."

"You deserve it. Oh, by the way, I saw a video of you. It was an amazing performance. I've even started going cock-a-doodle-do with my boyfriend although I fall short a bit."

Hugo blushed. "Oh God, I didn't know it was on the internet as well. I feel so silly for having done that now; it was just a spur of the moment thing and I was egged on by friends."

"Well, if I had that in me, I'd give this up and go pro. I can give you the name of a producer in the UK, if you'd like."

"Thanks but I've got my hands rather full now."

"I can see that. Actually, my boyfriend and I have our honeymoon in Cape Town next week."

"You're not staying at the Nelson Lodge Hotel, then?"

"Definitely not!"

Hugo returned to his seat wondering how far his impromptu turn at Video had spread.

Hugo's mother leaned over from her seat.

"What was he saying, dear? Something about cock-a-doodle-do?"

"Oh, it was just one of those silly trolley-dolly jokes, Mum."

Saturday, February 19, 2011

When the plane landed at Heathrow Terminal 5, the three of them were surprised to receive the same VIP treatment as on their departure from Cape Town. So, within 30 minutes of landing, Hugo's mother had departed for Islington in Ben's car with the keys to their apartment and their luggage; and Hugo and Ben were in a private ambulance heading for the Florence Nightingale Hospital in central London. Hugo felt immense relief to be back on familiar territory although he knew that the hunger pangs for Greg and an alternative life in Cape Town wouldn't be that far behind. He could see Ben staring out of the window as the landscape went past and wondered what was going through his mind.

The hospital entrance had 'Florence Nightingale' reassuringly emblazoned above the main door but there was nothing remotely Victorian about the contemporary clinical interior. Once the admission formalities had been completed, Hugo and Ben were escorted to the assessment ward, which looked rather more like a four star hotel than what they'd experienced at the Groote Schuur Hospital. While Ben was being given a guided tour of the facilities, Hugo was shown into an office and he handed over Ben's notes and summary to a female doctor. Hugo sat patiently while she glanced through the contents.

"So it looks as if their final diagnosis was of psychogenic amnesia following abduction, although there was some unusual behavior in the emergency department which they've attributed to the drugs he was administered while in captivity. They were also concerned that he might go on to develop post-traumatic stress disorder. Do you think that's a fair summing up?"

"I think that's more or less what we were told. Everything else you need should be in that pack," Hugo explained. "I'm afraid Ben himself still isn't able to remember anything about what happened, which may not be a bad thing given what was in the videos."

"Did you see any of them?"

"I only saw the first and that was enough. I caught a glimpse of the end of it when I was staying with a couple of friends and then saw the whole thing when it was shown in a gay bar. The links to the videos should be in the notes but I'm afraid they won't make for easy viewing."

"What are the police back in South Africa doing about the abduction?"

"Well, it was a Detective Inspector van der Merwe whom I was dealing with but I think even he felt a bit out of his depth. He thought linking the videos with the forensic evidence would take too long and that the case might get dropped because it was too expensive and too complicated."

"What sort of forensic evidence?"

"I'm not sure you'd want to know."

"Try me, I'm not that easily shocked."

"Would you believe a coke bottle inserted into Ben's rectum which probably contained semen from as many as 50 different men?"

"Oh my goodness! That is shocking." She looked down at the notes briefly and then gave Hugo a caring look. "What about you? How have you coped with all of this happening on your honeymoon?"

"It's been hellish but at least he's back with me now.

It'll probably hit me soon enough but I'm just trying to take one day at a time. Can you tell me what happens next?"

"Well, I'll complete my assessment and we'll think about any medication that he might need. He was on some diazepam but he might not need it anymore and we obviously don't want him to become dependent on the drug. There's an occupational therapy session this morning and it'd be good to see how he interacts with other patients and copes with some simple tasks. Our psychologist is in this afternoon to run a group and I'll ask her to see him with a view to starting psychological therapy. Then there's a ward round on Monday which starts at 9:00 a.m. and you're welcome to attend that."

"Thanks, I'll be there. I'd also like to visit him tomorrow if that's okay."

"No problem, Mr Brown."

***

It was strange being back in the apartment without Ben but at least it gave him a chance to clear his head and deal with practical issues. His mother had left a bag of groceries and a note asking him to phone her later. She mentioned that she'd phoned Ben's parents and that they'd be visiting him that evening. He hadn't touched the pile of wedding presents taking up a significant part of their living room and decided to leave that until Ben was back home.

Checking through their mail, he found two cards from the Courtauld Institute: one wishing the two of them felicitations for their wedding and the other a speedy return to work once his personal issues had been resolved. He wondered how the Courtauld had coped in his absence. He booted his laptop and found the number for Alexander Zutic, a friend from university and a work colleague.

"Hi, Alexander, it's Hugo. I'm sorry to ring you on a Saturday but I've just got back from South Africa."

"Hugo? Gosh, I don't believe it. We've all been going frantic not knowing what's been happening to you."

"It's complicated. Did you see the news reports?"

"Yes but they needed some reading between the lines. Am I right in thinking Ben was abducted for 'immoral purposes', as they say?"

"Very immoral. Come round for supper this evening and I'll tell you the full story. In fact, I badly need to share the whole fucking mess with someone before I go a bit crazy myself."

***

The psychologist took Ben into her office. She'd read his notes, and like everyone else who'd come into contact with him, she found herself struck by the disparity between his bland, almost emotionless countenance and the grisly account of the horrific abuse he'd endured. She hadn't tried any of the video links herself but was aware that one of the male staff nurses had and felt physically sick. She almost felt sick on his behalf.

"Please sit down, Ben. My name is Joy and I'm a clinical psychologist. Is it okay if we talk a bit?"

"Thank you, Joy, I'd like that." Ben smiled blankly.

"Ben, do you know why you're here?"

"No, not really."

"Do you remember being in South Africa?"

"Yes, we had plenty of sun and lots of sex. It was nice."

"Ben, I'd like to take you back in time a bit and I want you to close your eyes so you can think more easily about the things I'm going to ask you. Do you understand that, Ben?"

"Yes, Joy. Thank you." He closed his eyes.

"Now, Ben, I want you to think back to when you stepped off the plane after arriving in Cape Town. Can you remember what you saw and felt?"

"Yes, it was warm. There was some wind. I could see a funny shaped mountain. I felt very happy."

"That's good, Ben. Now, after you arrived at the hotel in a taxi, did you go straight to your room or somewhere else?"

"No, the room wasn't ready. We went for some coffee. Both of us got erections and felt horny." He giggled.

"That's very good, Ben, you're doing well remembering those memories. So, when you went to your room, what did you do?"

"We had a shower and then we had sex. Hugo fucked me. That was nice."

The psychologist wondered how much more explicit Ben's memories might become but she pressed on.

"Ben, I'd like you to fast forward to the day before you and Hugo were due to return to London. That was the Thursday. Can you tell me what happened that morning?"

He licked his lips. "We had breakfast in bed. I wanted the waiter to join us."

"Ben, do you mean you wanted the waiter to have breakfast with you?"

"No, Joy, I wanted him to have sex with us. I wanted to fuck him."

"Thank you for telling me that, Ben. Now, after

breakfast, what did you do?"

"I went to the pool. I wanted the sun."

"And what were you wearing when you went to the pool?"

"Speedos. Hugo likes me in speedos. He says they make my balls looks big."

She took a deep breath. "Now, this is very important, Ben, do you remember leaving the pool at any time?"

"Oh no."

"Are you absolutely sure about that, Ben?"

"Oh yes."

"Okay, Ben, I want you to imagine yourself lying in the sun near the pool. What do you remember feeling?"

"It was warm and nice. My dick was getting hard."

"Thank you for telling me that, Ben. Now, I want you to imagine looking around from where you're lying by the pool. You can see the bushes and they're nice and green. Can you see anyone looking at you?"

"Man... green eyes... t-shirt... cold... very cold." He started shivering, his teeth chattering, and hugged himself for warmth.

"Okay, Ben, now it's very important that we take you back to somewhere that's warm and where you're happy again. I want you to imagine yourself back on the steps leaving the plane and you can feel the warmth of the sun, the wind in your hair and you can see the funny shaped mountain. You're feeling really warm and happy and you're with Hugo."

Ben stopped shivering and hugging himself and slowed his breathing. "Yes, Joy, I'm feeling warm and happy."

The psychologist breathed a sigh of relief. "That's excellent, Ben, we've had a good talk today. I'd like to see you again. Would that be okay with you, Ben?"

"Thank you, Joy. I'd like that." Ben smiled.

The psychologist escorted Ben back to his room and concluded that she'd been lucky to get away without a complete meltdown of his psyche; the primitive drive of his libido seemed to be the only thing really keeping him going at the moment. His mother clearly had a lot to answer for.

***

Alexander was dressed in a canary yellow mohair jumper, tight pink jeans and green, tasseled loafers. The garish ensemble seemed out of keeping with the Buddhist appearance of his entirely hairless head, which he said was due to childhood alopecia. He sat on the edge of the couch in the living room of Hugo and Ben's apartment with his mouth wide open and an untouched gin & tonic in his right hand. "So that's what really happened to him. How come none of that was released to the press?"

"From what I've gathered, too many people were worried about the effect on tourism and the political situation in general. Also, gay tourism is big business in South Africa and the gay mafia may have played a part in keeping a lid on things," explained Hugo.

"I just can't believe how anyone could do anything so awful to another human being. It's enough to put one off sex for good."

"I agree, but even though the videos are horrifying, they're also close to being a turn-on. It's a bit like watching porn where's there's an element of restraint involved and you don't how much is real and how much is acting. It's a bit like WWF wrestling, if you've ever seen that on TV."

Alexander laughed. "I do my best to avoid it but I know what you mean. How does Ben seem now? Does he remember anything?"

"In some ways, he's better than I thought he would be, particularly given his dramatic reappearance in the hotel gardens and his bizarre behavior in the hospital. But he's not back to normal: it's as if his body is back but his mind is still somewhere else. He's also unusually soft and gentle – submissive, in fact – which is actually quite nice but very different. And he still doesn't remember much. So, if you ask him where he's been staying, he just says he's been in the hotel getting plenty of sun and having lots of sex. The explanation given by the doctors in the Cape Town hospital is that he has amnesia but they couldn't say how long it would last or whether any memories of his abduction would return."

"So how did you manage when he was being held captive for all those days? You must have almost gone crazy waiting by the phone all day long."

"I wondered when you'd ask that. It's tricky."

"Try me."

"Well, after he went off to sun himself by the pool, I had sex with a waiter. Ben had been flirting with him when he brought us breakfast and that pissed me off. And I was still annoyed with him for fucking Jonathan on his stag night."

"That sounds more or less forgivable, I suppose. I hope he was good."

"He was and very cute, although I felt guilty for cheating on Ben."

"Would you have told him?"

"I'm not sure. Probably, I guess. Actually, I gave the

waiter my card and invited him to look us up if he was in London."

"Wow, this really is a new you. So what happened after that?"

"Well, after Ben went off into the bushes and disappeared, the police got involved and then the local press got wind of the situation. I was asked to leave the hotel because the situation was getting too embarrassing for the owner. I moved in with two guys: John, a manager at the hotel, and Greg, a doctor at the Cape Town hospital. One thing led to another and we ended up sleeping on the couch together although nothing really happened. The trouble is I also fell in love with Greg."

"Oops."

"I'm afraid there's more. On the Sunday, we went to a club called Video at the docks and I got persuaded to do a turn as a naked go-go dancer, which culminated in me wanking over 50 naked mens' expectant mouths."

"What?" Alexander's mouth dropped further towards the carpet and he took a quick slurp of his drink. "Well, I wish I could have been there to witness your performance. My mouth would have been well and truly wide open."

"Actually, I think it's already on the internet somewhere."

"Oops. And Ben knows nothing of this?"

"He's been rather too occupied in one way or another." Hugo put his head in his hands. "Oh God, Alexander, I'm such an idiot. And to think it was me who was criticizing him for what he did with his dick."

Alexander's expression morphed rapidly from thoughtful to lascivious. "You know, Hugo, I've never forgotten that drunken fumble in our first term at

Oxford."

"Ah."

"You wouldn't like to repeat it, would you?"

"No, sweetie, we go too far back for that; we're like sisters. Also, your color scheme is making me feel nauseous. Let's have some supper."

Sunday, February 20, 2011

When Hugo arrived at reception in the Florence Nightingale Hospital on Sunday morning, he was surprised to see Ben's mother already waiting to be escorted to visit him. If he'd had a choice, he'd probably have wanted to continue trying to speak with her on the phone rather than in person but he wondered whether she'd softened up a bit since the conversation with his mother, which seemed to show a softer, more compassionate person beneath the stiff carapace of dignity and breeding.

"Good morning, Hugo, I didn't know you'd be here as well," she said, looking surprised.

Hugo looked at her face and noticed dark circles under her eyes and an attempt to disguise her exhaustion with make-up. "I'm trying to get to get to see him every day. How are you doing, Barbara?"

"Oh, muddling along really. This whole business has worn me down and Sir James doesn't want to talk about it. The ransom demand was the final straw. To be honest, it's all been a bit too much…"

She turned her head away from Hugo and he could see tears welling up. He went up to her and took hold of her hands. "It's okay, Barbara, at least he's back now and we're both here to support him."

"Thank you, Hugo." She smiled tearfully. "I've always known that you were the right person for Benjamin. I'm just so sorry I couldn't say it. You know how it is."

A staff nurse arrived and breezily introduced herself. She led them down the corridor and into the wing where Ben had his room. She knocked on his door and opened it.

"Ben, I've got a couple of visitors for you: Hugo and your…"

The sight that stopped her introduction mid-flow was that of Ben stark bollock naked, standing in front of the window and evidently on the point of ejaculating onto the Axminster carpet. She swiftly closed the door, hoping that Ben's visitors hadn't seen too much.

"I'm sorry but Ben doesn't seem quite ready to receive visitors. Let's give it a few minutes and then come back."

Hugo thought he'd caught sight of Ben naked although he couldn't be sure, so he guessed what the nurse might have been embarrassed by. Sex on a Sunday morning was always part of their routine. Ben's mother was behind him, so she wouldn't have seen anything anyway.

They returned ten minutes later and saw the nurse coming out of the room with some gloves on and holding some industrial strength tissues. "Sorry, just a bit of a spill. It's fine for you to go in now."

Ben was sitting in a chair, dressed in pressed jeans and a white shirt, and barefoot. Hugo noticed a damp patch on the carpet near the window. He sniffed and caught the unmistakable aroma of Ben's spunk.

"What's that strange smell?" asked Ben's mother, looking puzzled.

"Oh, I think it's some sort of cleaning product," said Hugo, extemporizing wildly.

Ben's mother went over and bent down to kiss her son on his right cheek. She sat down on the bed to look at him. "Darling, you've lost weight. You can't have been eating properly." She suddenly gave a start, realizing how ridiculous that statement was when applied to someone who'd been held captive for a week. "How was your honeymoon, darling?"

Ben turned to smile at her blankly. "Hello, Mother. We had plenty of sun and lots of sex. It was nice."

"That's good, dear. Did you do anything else?"

"We went up the mountain in a cable car. I wanted to have sex with the attendant. He was very sexy." Ben smiled again and put his hand against his crotch.

"I'm sure you did, dear." She turned to look imploringly at Hugo and he noticed that tears were forming again.

"Ben, darling, I'll be back later," said Hugo. "I'm going to take your mother for a bit of lunch now." He went over and kissed Ben and stroked his face.

**

Hugo and Ben's mother were sitting in the restaurant on the ground floor of the hospital. Hugo was hungrily devouring his salade niçoise but Lady Barbara was playing with her mixed leaves and vinaigrette.

"Hugo dear, I know he's been through an awful lot but why is he so obsessed with sex? It's not very nice to listen to."

"That's just him. He likes sex. In fact, we both like sex. And I think at the moment he's just hanging onto something that's an important part of his identity."

She looked out of the window. "I think he's always been rather highly sexed."

Hugo was surprised by this unexpected revelation. "What makes you say that, Barbara?"

"Did your mother tell you about our conversation to do with Ben's past?"

"Not in particular. I think she was more concerned

about letting you know about the ransom demand."

"Well, perhaps she thought you had too much on your plate already."

"Perhaps. What did you tell her?"

"Many years ago, before you'd even met Benjamin, we used to live in Fulham. Benjamin started to go to a club called Backdoor in Earls Court. We didn't approve of it, of course, but we kept quiet and let him do whatever he felt he had to do. One day, we received a letter with an Earls Court postmark. It was unsigned and there was no address but whoever sent it threatened to give the press a video showing Benjamin having sex with other men unless we paid them money. We paid up, of course; Cavendish Foods was going through a difficult time and we simply couldn't afford that sort of bad publicity. Unfortunately, the threats and demands continued."

Hugo's jaw had well and truly dropped hearing this account. "But didn't you go to the police to stop it? I mean, this wasn't the 1950s when gay sex was illegal, after all."

"Oh we thought about it, Hugo, but James's financial and legal advisors convinced us otherwise. We lost a lot of money, of course, but eventually the threats and demands stopped and we just got on with our lives."

"Did you find out the name of the person blackmailing you or where they lived?"

"Oh no, we were asked to leave the money in different locations each time and we never stayed behind to see who took the money."

"Did you keep the letters or the envelopes?"

"No, they all got thrown away when we moved from Fulham."

Hugo was astonished by the naivety of Ben's parents and couldn't believe that Victorian prudery had blinkered them to this extent. "Did Ben ever learn about this?" he asked.

"I don't think so, or at least we never told him and he never raised it with us."

"If you don't mind me saying so, Barbara, it does explain quite a lot about your attitude towards his sexuality and towards us."

"I suppose it must and I'm sorry now that we didn't do anything about it at the time." She looked pensive. "Do you think it's got something to do with what happened in Cape Town?"

"That's the 64,000 dollars question. I think I should e-mail the Detective Inspector who was dealing with the case back in Cape Town."

"I do hope Benjamin will be all right."

"So do I, Barbara, I really do."

***

Hugo spent some time on Sunday afternoon trying to decide what to put in and what to leave out of the e-mail to DI van der Merwe, as he didn't want to implicate Ben's parents too much as being complicit in perpetuating blackmail. However, he realized that his concerns were likely to be largely irrelevant given that the DI was 6,000 miles away and it all happened five years ago. His final e-mail went as follows:

"Dear Detective Inspector,

I thought it might be useful for you to have some background information on what my partner Benjamin Cavendish seems to have been involved with before we met, in case this has some bearing on his abduction.

According to his mother, he started going to a club called Backdoor in Earls Court sometime in 2006. His parents then started receiving blackmail letters with an Earls Court postmark threatening to send a video to the press of him having sex with other men if they didn't pay up. They didn't inform the police and they continued paying up at different locations and without ever finding who was making the threats. The demands suddenly stopped for no obvious explanation and they thought the blackmail was over. They threw away the blackmail letters when they moved. Perhaps the person behind these demands still believes Ben owes him something.

One other thing I forgot to mention is that when we first went into our room in the hotel, there was a message on the TV saying "I hope your enjoy your room upgrade. I'll see you later. M." Our first thought was that it was my mother who'd sent the message but she denied it. Ben seemed a bit perturbed by the initial 'M', so perhaps that's significant as well.

If you think I should report any of this to a London police station, please let me know.

Yours sincerely,
Hugo Brown"

Monday, February 21, 2011

Having been to the ward round at the Groote Schuur Hospital, Hugo thought that attending a ward round at the Florence Nightingale Hospital would simply be a continuation of the assessment process already started back in South Africa. The beginning of the ward round was fine, as everyone introduced themselves and then the key elements of Ben's abduction and its sequelae were well explained by the doctor he'd met on Saturday. Unfortunately, nobody mentioned that Ben had been seen shivering in bed during the routine observation of patients that night and had continued to shiver despite being given an extra blanket.

The ward round rapidly descended into a rather prurient farce when the consultant psychiatrist picked upon some poor, but rather cute looking, medical student and asked him to tell everyone in the room what he knew about Xstreamtube. Hugo tried to interrupt at one point, but by then, the nurse who'd watched the second video was being asked to describe what he saw together with his nauseated reaction to it. Judging by the way things were heading, he thought the next revelation would be the nurse spilling the beans on Ben spilling his spunk, so he left for a breath of fresh air that wasn't so tainted by thinly veiled homophobia. He returned to the ward round just as the rather stern-looking psychologist was being asked to describe her initial attempt at commencing therapy.

"So, Joy, perhaps you could tell us what happened when you saw Mr Cavendish in your office on Saturday?" asked the consultant.

"Well, first off, I was struck by how dissociated he was. His language was regressive and childlike and his libido seemed to be governing his memories and behavior. I asked him about going off into the bushes with another man and he quite literally froze on the spot, which I think represents memories of maternal disapprobation for over-sexualized behavior and possibly even being made to have a cold shower."

"Excuse me, doctor," said Hugo, looking at the consultant and urgently trying to interject, "but don't you think that's jumping to conclusions without really knowing the patient." He stared pointedly at the psychologist who looked in the other direction.

"Thank you for your view, Mr Brown, but I think our clinical psychologist's account is relevant and could make for an interesting thesis. Let's ask Mr Cavendish to come in."

Ben came in, smiled wanly at Hugo, and sat down. He seemed anxious about something and was drumming his fingers against the sides of the chair.

"Good morning, Mr Cavendish. My name is Dr Michaels. How are you today?"

"I'm fine."

"Do you know why you're here?"

"No."

"I believe you met Joy, our psychologist, last Saturday."

"Yes, we had a talk."

"How did that make you feel?"

"I felt cold, so very cold." He started shivering and hugged himself.

"Could it be that it felt as if your mother was telling

you off for being naughty?"

Ben didn't answer and continued to shiver. Everyone in the room seemed to be watching and enjoying his discomfort. Hugo went across the room and put his arms around Ben. "I'll take him back to his room," he said, without waiting for anyone's approval.

Hugo returned to the ward round after making sure Ben was okay back in his room. He felt he was back in the spotlight and being made to pay for his intervention. The ward round continued as if he wasn't present. Unlike the psychiatrist at the Groote Schuur Hospital who'd used sensible language and had been clear about what he thought had happened to Ben, the Florence Nightingale doctors insisted on using expressions like 'psychotic regression' and 'id dominant personality', which Hugo thought was of no use to anyone and certainly unlikely to help Ben out of his current state. The medical student who'd been asked about Xstreamtube did actually pipe up and try to put the discussion back onto a more conventional and meaningful track but no one seemed interested in his opinion.

When Hugo left the hospital, he noticed the medical student hovering by the entrance and wondered whether he'd been waiting for him.

"Christ, that doctor was a bastard," said Hugo.

"Yeah, he's got a reputation for doing that. He's such a fucking homophobe," said the medical student.

"Actually, you coped quite well with the question about Xstreamtube."

"Thanks. The problem was not saying too much, if you know what I mean." The student's cheeks turned rather pink.

"Does that mean you've seen the videos of Ben?"

"A couple of them. I can't say I felt sick but they weren't primetime viewing either. Poor guy. And poor you for having to cope with it all."

"I'm getting by somehow."

"So I noticed: that was a fucking hot video of you."

"Oh no, not you as well!"

"What do you think that psychologist would make of it?" asked the medical student.

"I think she'd point at my id and send me for a cold shower. And then she'd be sick." replied Hugo.

They both laughed.

***

Following the rather dispiriting ward round, Hugo headed over to the Courtauld Institute for his first day back at work. Alexander was the first person he saw and he was surprised to note his toned-down ensemble of a blue suit, pink shirt and crimson bowtie.

"Welcome back, sweetie." He lunged at Hugo and deposited wet lips on both his cheeks.

"Are you going to a funeral?" asked Hugo.

"No, dear, we've got a visitation – from the Royal Household, would you believe?"

"Are you sure you're not getting confused with Mr Sewell? His presence is rather all over the place, after all."

"No, silly, this is the real thing: perhaps not quite Her Majesty herself but the next best thing. There's talk about a position going for assistant curator of the Queen's Collection."

"Is there a short list?"

"I don't know but it wouldn't surprise me if you're

already on it."

"Me? No way Jose."

"Oh, by the way, Hugo, you're down to do your talk on Poussin tomorrow lunchtime."

"You're joking!"

"Sorry, I postponed it for as long as I could, but the powers that be insist that it goes ahead tomorrow."

"Oh Christ!"

***

When he returned home, Hugo looked in his inbox and was surprised to see a response from the Detective Inspector's @saps.org.za e-mail account quite so quickly:

"Dear Hugo,

Thank you for the information. This actually fits with some intelligence I've received from a colleague at New Scotland Yard. It's obviously before your time but there was a case in 1990 involving a group of men having consensual sadomasochistic sex who were found guilty of malicious wounding and ABH. The investigation went under the heading of 'Operation Spanner', and although the operation is officially closed, this colleague has continued to follow up the more extreme, non-consensual end of the BDSM spectrum. He knew that Earls Court had a certain reputation for this sort of thing but he wasn't aware of the involvement of the Backdoor club. I've passed on your details and he should be in contact with you shortly.

The information about Ben's parents being blackmailed is particularly helpful, although we and our New Scotland Yard colleagues would need to be cautious about how this is pursued.

As far as investigations in South Africa are concerned, I can confirm that the forensic evidence is now being fully evaluated and I am also arranging for the videos to be examined frame by frame in the hope that potential suspects can be identified.

I hope your partner is recovering from his ordeal and I wish both of you a happy life together.

Kind regards,

Detective Inspector Jim van der Merwe"

Tuesday, February 22, 2011

Hugo wasn't quite sure how he achieved it, but somehow he pulled himself and his PowerPoint presentation together sufficiently to give the lecture on Nicolas Poussin the day after he returned to work. He'd changed the title to 'Poussin le Caméléon' and pride of place went to the photo he'd taken of 'Self-Portrait: 1649' hanging on the wall above Greg's desk at 180 Bree Street. His particular thesis, which he thought was quite an original one, was that artists like Poussin felt compelled to alter their persona due to market forces, and his talk went on to draw parallels with other commercially-savvy artists like Warhol who lived out his reinvented self until his premature death.

As he walked into the half-full lecture theatre, steeply raked and redolent of many decades of burnished scholarship, he couldn't help but notice a rather frail looking man tottering along the back row, supporting himself on a silver cane, who sank his corduroyed bottom into the poorly upholstered seat with an audible and exaggerated sigh of resignation. He wasn't 100 percent sure, but he had more than a sneaking suspicion that it was Brian Sewell, particularly when the aforesaid raised a pince-nez to his rheumy eyes through which Hugo felt he was being scrutinized and systematically undressed throughout the lecture.

Hugo started his lecture with a real coup de théâtre gesture by showing his own photo of 'Self-Portrait: 1649', which drew particular attention to the fact that it was hanging up in someone's apartment rather than in some dehumidified, hypoallergenic, cold war vault. The look and sound of astonishment displayed by his audience was palpable and Mr Sewell's pince-nez momentarily dropped a foot, accompanied by a richly resounding "Ooooh".

For the rest of the 45 minutes, Hugo had his audience eating out of his lap and he relished every minute of it. In fact, it was really almost as good as his 10 minutes of fame as a naked go-go dancer.

When he returned to his desk after lunch, he noticed that someone had left a postcard with a naked youth of the 60s decorously posed on the front and spidery writing on the back: "Simply loved your talk. Bella eiaculazione. Please come round for tea and crumpet. B.S."

Hugo realized he'd made it: his true vocation was confirmed.

***

Later that evening, Hugo rang Lady Cavendish to see what she thought about the care Ben was receiving.

"Hello, Barbara, it's Hugo. I was hoping to have a word with you about how Ben is getting on in the hospital."

"Oh, Hugo, I'm glad you've called. I saw him today and he didn't seem himself at all."

"In what way?"

"Well, he's complaining of the cold so much of the time. Seeing that psychologist seems to be making things worse. And he isn't masturbating anymore."

"Excuse me, Barbara, but did you say "masturbating"?"

"Of course I did, Hugo. I wasn't born yesterday. The smell is rather identifiable, after all."

"Oh." Hugo paused for thought. "Barbara, I was thinking about bringing Ben home to look after him myself. What would you think about that?"

"I think it'd be a splendid idea, Hugo. We'd be happy to have him stay during the week if that'd help. I'm sure some walks in the countryside would do him no end of good."

"That's just what I wanted to hear, Barbara. I'll let the hospital know tomorrow."

Wednesday, February 23, 2011

There was a knock on the door to DI van der Merwe's office. A Sergeant who'd been seconded from another station, and whom he'd only met briefly, put his rather handsome head around the door. "Is it okay if I come in, Detective Inspector?"

"Yes, please come in, Sergeant…?"

"It's Sergeant Michelson, James Michelson."

"What can I do for you, Sergeant?"

"Well, you know you asked me to do some frame by frame analysis of those videos from the Cavendish case?"

"Oh yes. It can't have been easy for you with all that sex and stuff going on."

"Well, it wasn't exactly that bad." He paused, looking sheepish. "The thing is I think I recognize one of the men."

"What?"

The Sergeant looked uncertain whether to continue. "Erm, you must promise that you'll keep this to yourself but I sometimes go to a place called Hothouse in Jarvis Street. One of the men in the video has unusual tattoos and they're the same as on the man I've seen at Hothouse. When I asked him what they were, he said they're called 'Yin Yang'. One's above the cleft of his buttocks and the other is above his dick and to the right. They're quite unique and I was thinking of having the same done myself."

"Does he have any other distinguishing features?"

"Yes, his dick bends upwards and to the left. He said it's because of a condition called Peyronie's Disease. He's very popular at Hothouse because of it. And you can see the bend in the video."

"You don't know his name by any chance?"

"Yes, his name is Frank and he said he works down at the docks."

The DI leapt out of his chair and planted a sloppy wet kiss on the Sergeant's lips. "That's fucking brilliant, Sergeant Michelson! You've just made my day! I owe you a drink."

The Sergeant looked momentarily taken back and then smiled. "I'd like that, Detective Inspector. I'd really like that."

***

Hugo phoned the Florence Nightingale Hospital first thing on Wednesday to announce his intention to discharge Ben and take him home. The officious person he spoke to seemed ignorant of the law when it came to civil partnerships and his legal responsibility as Ben's next of kin. But by the time it came for Hugo to collect Ben and his belongings in a taxi, the way seemed to have been paved for a relatively straightforward discharge. Before leaving, Hugo met up with the doctor he'd talked to when Ben was admitted.

"I'm sorry it's come to this, Mr Brown. To be frank with you, I think the wrong approach has been taken with Ben's care. Joy is fine with some patients but Ben's preoccupation with sex has gotten in the way of her clinical judgment. He's had a couple more sessions with her and all it seems to have done is to reinforce his fear of the cold. I've no doubt that's all very relevant but I don't think she's the person to get him to take the next step. If you're interested, I can give you the details of a psychologist who sees patients privately and might be more suitable for what Ben needs. He's gay as well, so you wouldn't have to endure all that homophobic stuff which should have gone out with the ark."

"What does your consultant think about Ben's condition?"

"I'm afraid he'd side with the psychologist rather than me. I think the psychiatrist back in Cape Town had the right idea and it's a shame he didn't spend longer there. Still, I think Ben is over the worst in terms of anything unexpected happening, and as long as he's got your support and some therapy going, I don't see why he shouldn't gradually improve with time."

"Is there anything I should be careful about?"

"That's a good question. Wherever he was and whatever was done to him, his circadian rhythms have been shot to pieces. So, as part of normalizing him back to the real world, he needs his usual activities like sleeping and eating put back into place. I think a low-key structure of getting up in the morning, having breakfast, watching TV, going for walks and that sort of thing would do a lot of good. And there's also a place for sex as long as he perceives it as loving rather than threatening. But that's a lot to put on your plate and you need to consider whether you can cope with all that at the same time as going to work."

"Thanks, that's really helpful." Hugo leant forward to touch her arm. "Ben's mother has offered to have him stay during the week and she's definitely keen on the walks side of things. I think she's also starting to put his needs ahead of hers, so hopefully both of them will benefit."

***

So, by 6:00 p.m., Ben was back home in their apartment. He padded around bare foot, reorienting himself, and from time to time he'd pick up a book or some other object, look at it and then replace it. Hugo had made sure that the central heating was turned up full and he was relieved to see that Ben seemed comfortable and wasn't complaining of feeling cold.

"How are you feeling, lover?"

"Good. It's nice to be home again."

"Are you glad to have left the hospital?"

"Yes, I didn't like the room. It was too small. And Joy made me feel uncomfortable."

"I'm sorry about that, darling, but I think she was only doing what she thought was best for you. Do you want to talk about what made you feel uncomfortable?"

"Not now. Can we have sex? That would make me feel good."

Hugo took hold of Ben's hand and led him into the bedroom. Ben stood still as if waiting for something to happen. Hugo gently and unhurriedly undressed him. He noticed how much weight he'd lost, although this had the advantage of making his dick look bigger. He lifted Ben's hands and kissed the red marks on his wrists where he'd been restrained. He ran his fingers over Ben's chest and down his back, sliding his fingers into the cleft between his still tanned buttocks. He knelt on the floor and let his lips envelop the head of Ben's dick while tonguing the opening. He felt the blood pulsing in Ben's dick and started stroking the shaft, allowing his mouth to mold around the head and suck at the pre-come. He looked up at Ben and noticed a faraway look and tears in the corners of his eyes. Hugo increased the frequency of his strokes and then took the full length of Ben's cock into his throat. Hugo looked up again and saw that Ben had closed his eyes. All of a sudden, Ben reached down to frantically stroke his dick and came, deliciously and messily, all over Hugo's face, covering him with spurts of creamy spunk. Hugo stood up and let Ben lick at his face, and then they used their tongues to share the taste.

"Nice," he said.

"Nice," agreed Hugo.

***

Later in the evening, after Ben had gone to bed, Hugo rang his mother to update her on his progress since their return from Cape Town.

"Hi, Mum, a lot seems to have happened since we got back."

"I've gathered some of that from talking to Barbara."

"Yes, it's good that she's involved. I saw her at the hospital on Sunday."

"She mentioned that – and Ben's accident."

"Well, as I said to her, he was just doing what comes naturally."

"I'm sure he was but it was a bit in her face. She mentioned that you were planning to take Ben home."

"Actually, he's back already."

"You didn't think the hospital was helping him, then?"

"No, the psychiatrist seemed homophobic and hung up on sex. He was seeing a psychologist but she was making things worse."

"How is he now that he's back home?"

"Better, I think, but we'll take each day as it comes."

"I gather that Barbara has offered to have Ben stay with her during the week."

"Yes, that'll be good. We'll try that next week. Oh, by the way, I finally gave my Poussin talk yesterday."

"Really? How did it go?"

"Mum, it was absolutely brilliant. I used the photo I took in Greg's apartment of 'Self-Portrait: 1649' and that seemed to win everyone over. And Brian Sewell was in the audience and left a card to congratulate me."

"That's wonderful, darling. So what happens next?"

"Well, Alexander says that they're looking for an assistant curator for the Queen's Collection but I don't think I have a chance in hell of getting that."

"You're very good with dogs."

"But not corgis, Mum."

"You'll learn, dear. You're so very adaptable."

Thursday, February 24, 2011

As Hugo entered the office he shared with Alexander at the Courtauld Institute, he could see that today was going to be special. Alexander's outfit du jour consisted of a fitted pink-spotted top, Little Lord Fauntleroy yellow breaches, long purple socks and his favorite green tasseled loafers. He'd also added a blond bobbed wig to complete the ensemble.

"Is that to frighten the corgis?" asked Hugo.

"No, dear, I just thought I needed a change from all that drab stuff," he replied. "And I also wanted to make a special effort for our assistant curator-in-waiting."

"You are joking, aren't you?"

"No, darling, it's as good as yours now that Mr Sewell has cast his beady eyes over you."

"You know he invited me for tea and crumpet?"

"Isn't it crumpets in the plural, unless he's being very mean in his dotage?"

"No, crumpet is what it said and crumpet is what I'm sure he means."

"Ooh, how decadent. Perhaps you should go in your industrial strength chastity belt."

"Actually, I think that's what Ben used to specialize in."

"Really? Do tell more."

***

Hugo phoned Lady Cavendish later that evening after Ben had gone to bed.

"Good evening, Hugo. Actually, I was about to call you to find out how Benjamin was getting on."

"I think he's doing okay really, although it's early days. He certainly seems happier than he was in the hospital. We've got a routine going now. I've also got contact details for a private psychologist and I'll try to get an appointment soon. And we'd like to take you up on your offer of having Ben stay with you. Would Monday or Tuesday next week suit you and Sir James?"

"Yes, that should be fine. I'll ring you at the weekend to make arrangements."

"One other thing, Barbara. I've heard back from the Detective Inspector back in Cape Town and he found the information you gave me very useful. He mentioned a colleague at New Scotland Yard who's been following up groups similar to the one that Ben got involved with and he should be contacting me soon. Another bit of news is that they're working hard on investigating Ben's abduction, so perhaps something will come out of that as well."

"That is encouraging, Hugo. Let's talk more about that at the weekend. Goodnight, Hugo."

"Goodnight, Barbara."

Hugo was surprised how cold Lady Cavendish had sounded. Perhaps Sir James had been in the vicinity. She was so hard to fathom.

Saturday, February 26, 2011

The week had settled into a comfortable routine of Ben getting up and having breakfast at the same time as Hugo and then going into the living room to watch daytime TV until Hugo returned at lunchtime and made lunch. Hugo then usually put on some non-violent, family-friendly DVD for Ben to watch in the afternoon, although he was invariably asleep on the couch by the time Hugo returned home from work.

Hugo had contacted the psychologist mentioned by the doctor at the hospital and Ben had an appointment in a few days' time. Hugo had considered inviting Alexander back for dinner one evening to get Ben back in the habit of socializing but then decided that his lack of color co-ordination might be too much for Ben to process at the moment.

Friday evening had been pizzas in front of the TV, although Ben's appetite hadn't been good and he'd slipped off to bed early. He seemed restless during the night and had pulled the duvet rather forcibly over to his side of the bed. Come the morning, Ben seemed to be sleeping soundly, so Hugo got out of bed without disturbing him, put on some clothes and went out to buy the Saturday newspapers. As he came back into the living room, he heard Ben say "Yes" and then the sound of the phone being put down on the table. He noticed that Ben was naked and his dick was pointing rather impressively towards the ceiling.

"Who was that, Ben?"

"Wrong number."

"It must have turned you on, though."

"Let's have sex."

Hugo dropped the newspapers on the table, took off his clothes and followed Ben back into the bedroom. Ben was standing at the end of the bed with his dick as erect as Hugo had ever seen it. Hugo recognized the expectant look and lay on the bed with his ass in the air. He parted his buttocks with his hands.

"Fuck me, Ben."

Ben lost no time in responding to Hugo's request and soon he was fucking him with a passion and intensity that seemed to Hugo to be just like the old days. His pelvic thrusts were smooth and fluid like some well-oiled machine. Ben glanced up without breaking the rhythm of his thrusts and saw the glassy eyes of the camcorders watching his every move. He smiled softly at his old friends. He reached down and gently teased Hugo's hair. Hugo moaned as he stretched his head back against his lover's caressing fingers. Ben increased the tempo and depth of his thrusting until he felt absolutely at one with Hugo's body. More moans from Hugo reassured Ben that this was exactly what he wanted. At exactly the point that he was about to come, he firmly clasped his hands on either side of Hugo's head and simultaneously twisted it and pulled it back until his C2 vertebra snapped. The master had taught him well. He dropped his partner's head, withdrew and ejaculated over Hugo's buttocks and back. He smiled at the cameras and lent down and licked at the come. He turned Hugo over and was pleased to see that he'd also ejaculated at the point of death. He looked long and hard into Hugo's dimming eyes and then traced his tongue down the white skin of his chest, lingering over the well-trimmed hairs of his crotch, and then took into his mouth for the last time the full length of his dick. He stood, briefly surveyed Hugo's body and walked to the bedroom door, smiling at the cameras as he left. He wondered how the master would reward him this time and licked his lips in anticipation of a visit from the Milkman.

Ben sat down on the couch in the living room he and Hugo had shared for the last two years. He reached for the phone and dialed 999.

"I've killed Hugo."

"Which service do you require?"

"I've killed Hugo."

"Sir, can you repeat that?"

"I've killed Hugo."

"Can you give me your name and address?"

"I've killed Hugo."

"Please don't hang up, sir. I'll get someone to you as soon as possible."

Within hours, Popham Street was taken over by the Metropolitan Police's CSI team. A white tent was erected on the sidewalk outside the front door and the immediate vicinity taped off. Hugo and Ben's neighbors were annoyed by the invasion of their privacy and the temporary restriction on their movements. Twitching of net curtains in the houses opposite reached fever pitch, and from time to time occupants would emerge to gaze at the proceedings and gossip.

"I'd never have believed it, you know, Doris. They always seemed such nice boys. And didn't they make such a lovely couple on their wedding day? Not that I really approve of what the gays do in bed, of course. I mean, God gave us certain things to use as man and woman, not like what the gays get up to. I mean, it's just not natural, is it?"

A short time later, the press got wind of the crime and fleets of news crews descended on Popham Street with their roving reporters and cameramen eager to boost ratings on a slow news day. The likes of Doris and her gossiping friend were quick to seize the opportunity for five seconds of fame and happily reiterated their story with more and more embellishments as the day went on.

"Well, I always thought there was something strange about the dark haired one. It was the look in his eyes, you know, almost as if he had something to hide. The blond one was lovely, though. He always had a smile for us. He was a male model, you know."

***

The detectives looked at each other. Their preliminary interview with Ben had been very unsettling.

"I don't get it. He kills his boyfriend while they're having sex, calmly dials 999 and sits with a smile all over his face just as if he was having tea with the vicar."

"And what about the stuff about waiting for the milkman? He's weird, that one."

"Yes, the way he licked his lips was right creepy. Personally, I'd prefer to sink a pint of John Smiths." He looked at his watch. "Shall we?"

"Okay, the first round's on you."

Monday, February 28, 2011

The pathologist looked down at the body laid out on the mortuary table. The combination of the olive-white torso with a dusting of downy hair and the beautiful face topped by wavy blond hair gave the body the appearance of an angel who'd crash landed onto a world that no longer cared for such beauty. This was going to be one of those cases where keeping a professional distance would be the only way of getting through the day. He sighed and prepared himself for the autopsy. Out of the corner of his eye, he noticed two police officers walk in hesitantly, clearly not sure of the protocol for observing an autopsy.

"Come in, gentlemen, and make yourselves at home. I'm just about to start."

The pathologist pulled the overhead microphone towards him and commenced the autopsy: "The body is of a white male in his mid-20s, who appears well nourished and with defined musculature of the chest and abdomen." He examined Hugo's penis and shone an ultraviolet light up and down its length, demonstrating fluorescing, yellow-green patches. "External genitalia are of abnormal appearance apart from unusual length of the flaccid penis, which I would estimate to be approximately seven inches. The subject appears to have ejaculated before death." He heard one of the police officers mutter "Well, at least he had a good time" and his colleague laughed. He briefly switched off the microphone and admonished them for disrespecting the dead. He switched the microphone back on and continued: "The subject's head is lolling to the left, which is suggestive of damage to the vertebral column."

He reached behind the head and palpated the cervical vertebrae. "External palpation of the vertebral processes indicates a fracture at the level of C2." He examined the rest of the head. "I find no evidence of laceration to the head or of any blunt instrument being used. The rest of the anterior surface is similarly intact." He motioned to the mortuary assistants to turn Hugo's body onto his front. The pathologist couldn't help but catch his breath when he saw the alabaster-like whiteness of Hugo's buttocks. "With the exception of deviation of the spinal column at the level of C2, I find no evidence of trauma to the dorsal surface." He peered closely at Hugo's back and at the top of the intergluteal cleft. One of the mortuary assistants handed him the ultraviolet light which cast an eerie glow on Hugo's skin. As he moved it up and down Hugo's back and into the cleft, he could see the tell-tale fluorescence of semen, particularly around the anal opening. "However, examination under ultraviolet light indicates the remains of semen deposited on the subject's back, along the intergluteal cleft and around the anal opening." An assistant handed him swabs which he pressed at various points and into the anal opening. "I have taken specimens of what is likely to be semen ejaculated during or after anal intercourse." The assistants turned the body onto its back. "In conclusion, my external exam is consistent with death from a manually applied rotational-stress fracture at the level of C2 that occurred in close temporal association with the deposition of semen as a result of anal intercourse and also the subject's own ejaculation."

Following completing the rest of Hugo's autopsy, the pathologist stripped off his gloves and apron and retreated to his office to compile his report. He was a handsome man in his late 40s with doe eyes that belied the horror of his specialty, although the worry lines starting to appear on his forehead gave the game away. He put his head in his hands and sobbed, unable to believe that such beauty could be destroyed so easily. Sometimes he hated his job and today was definitely one of those days.

***

The Chief Superintendent came into DI van der Merwe's office just after he'd returned from lunch. He looked more morose than usual and had a copy of the afternoon edition of the Cape Argus in his hand.

"Sorry, Jim, but I think you should see this." He put the paper on the DI's desk and started walking towards the door. "I'll be in my office if you want to talk."

The DI pulled the paper towards him fearing the worst. The headline, 'NELSON KIDNAP VICTIM KILLS PARTNER', bored into his eyes and wouldn't let go of its hideous grip. He buried his head in his hands and sobbed the tears of someone who'd just lost the love of their life. He resolved to make someone pay and he wouldn't be waiting for the forensic report to come back.

Tuesday, February 29, 2011

Two police squad cars and a van pulled up outside Frank Dresden's apartment at 5:00 a.m. The main door to the block had been helpfully left open and a battering ram was used to gain entrance to the apartment itself. Frank's surprised face greeted DI van der Merwe and the other officers from the bedroom door and a frightened, young male voice from inside could be heard saying "What's happening, uncle?" Frank himself was naked and a substantial amount of the evidence that had placed him at the scene of the crime was conveniently visible.

"It's a shame you didn't get your tattoos removed before you decided to rape your victim, Frank," said the DI.

"I don't know what you're talking about," he said defiantly.

"Oh I think you do. You should be more careful about where you stick your dick in the future, Frank. And to think you said that the gay scene wasn't your thing."

Frank said nothing and covered his crotch with his hands.

"Frank Dresden, I'm arresting you on suspicion of the rape of Benjamin Cavendish and the abduction and false imprisonment of the aforesaid. You have the right to remain silent. Anything you say will be used against you in a court of law. You have the right to an attorney during interrogation; if you cannot afford an attorney, one will be appointed to you."

"Okay, cuff him and let's get him to Central."

With their suspect on his way to the custody suite, the

remaining police officers searched his apartment. They allowed the under-age boy in his bed to flee for his life. It didn't take them long to discovered a stash of BDSM porn and accoutrements hidden in the attic space. The boy was probably lucky to have escaped from Frank's bed relatively unmolested.

***

24 hours in police custody in close proximity to other rapists, with nothing more than a blanket to protect his modesty, did much to loosen Frank's tongue. As far as his fellow prisoners were concerned, Frank's orifices were open season for them to enjoy. By the time Wednesday morning came around, Frank was ready to tell DI van der Merwe everything he knew about the operation that had led to Ben's abduction and his subsequent enjoyment of Ben's body.

The DI watched the naked suspect through the two-way mirror. The air conditioning had been deliberately set low and he was shivering. He turned the temperature up and went in with a blanket and a mug of coffee.

The DI slipped the blanket over his shoulders. "It looks as if you'd benefit from this, Frank." He passed him the coffee which he took gratefully and sipped the warmth.

Frank looked at the DI, trying to size him up. "What do you want?"

"Everything, Frank. And I mean by that absolutely fucking everything - unless you'd like to go back to your friends in the holding cell, of course."

"What do I get?"

"That's up to you, Frank. The more you give, the more you get. I can't say fairer than that, can I?"

And that opened the floodgates.

***

Later that afternoon, a fully clothed Frank Dresden accompanied DI van der Merwe and a couple of other officers to Duncan Dock. The forensic team wasn't far behind. Although it was now clear that Frank only knew the bare bones of how Ben had been abducted, he certainly knew everything about where he'd been held captive, and it was an old cold storage building across the way from Video that they were about to enter.

 Donning gloves, the DI switched on the single overhead bulb and saw that this was the room that Ben had been held captive in. The odor that hit them was an unpleasant combination of damp, sweat and semen. The suspension harness they'd used to restrain Ben was a complex, cage-like affair attached to both the ceiling and floor and it had clearly been designed for ease of access by a number of participants at the same time. Over to the left of the room, the DI could make out a bench which he guessed had been used for the final video.

The DI called out to the forensic team: "Does anyone have a UV light?"

One of the technicians in white overalls handed him the portable UV unit which he shone around the room. Yellow-green fluorescing patches shone on the floor in the vicinity of the BDSM equipment and there were also patches on the wall behind where Ben's head had been. The DI also noticed something glowing in the far left-hand corner of the room near the table. He bent down and picked up something made of rubber which he immediately recognized as the hood Ben had been forced to wear. The yellow-green fluorescing was unusually vivid when he shone the UV light on the mouthpiece.

"Okay, take Frank back," commanded the DI. "He's been a good boy and can have a cell to himself. And I want everything in here photographed, fingerprinted, swabbed, sampled and bagged. There should be enough evidence here to nail the whole fucking lot of them."

Friday, March 4, 2011

Hugo's funeral was a somber affair. His parents had bravely chosen an open coffin, but the sight of his beauty even in death was simply too poignant and compounded by him being dressed in the outfit that he'd worn for the civil partnership ceremony. Greg and John had flown to London for the funeral and the depth of the grief etched into their handsome faces made the other mourners wonder what they'd shared with him. The only sour note in the proceedings was when the presiding vicar referred to "such a young life being snuffed out like a candle." Unfortunately, he hadn't been briefed as to the cause of death. Ben wasn't present, of course, and he hadn't even gone through the process of seeking special dispensation from the Secretary of State for Justice to attend his partner and victim's funeral. In fact, even if he had, the request would have been rejected given the appalling circumstances of the case.

Choosing someone to deliver the eulogy hadn't been straightforward, and in the end a friend and colleague at the Courtauld Institute had agreed. Alexander walked up to the lectern feeling very vulnerable in his dark suit and aware of a hundred pairs of eyes watching him. He consulted his notes for a second, took a deep breath, and then started: "I remember when I first met Hugo at university. He was one of those rare people who really did turn heads and I think all of us were a little in love with him. What was so endearing was his lack of awareness of how he affected people. Ben of course was the one who was particularly struck by his beauty and I think anyone who'd been at their civil partnership ceremony couldn't help but have been in awe of the love in their relationship. And whatever transpired that led to Hugo's death, I want to hang onto that memory. I'd also like to share one other memory about Hugo, which is about his considerable expertise in fine art. Hugo would have gone very, very far and I can share the confidence with you today that he was being considered for appointment as assistant curator of Her Majesty's art collection. And between you and me, he was the only one on the short list, although he'd have had to pass the corgi test, of course. Sadly, Her Majesty will now have to find someone else to advise on her paintings and the corgis will need an alternative source of tummy rubs. But knowing Hugo and his obsessional generosity, I suspect he's keeping a curator's eye on that, wherever he might be now. So, dearest Hugo, we offer you our love and we'll never forget a single inch or atom of you."

The wake was held in Hugo's parents' mews house which was within walking distance of the church. As he was walking back, Alexander saw the tall figures of Greg and John leaning against each other for comfort. He wanted to say something to them without the entire congregation of mourners present so he walked faster until he caught up with them.

"I'm really sorry to bother you but I'm guessing you must be Greg and John. I'm Alexander."

The two of them looked surprised to be stopped in the street but recognition quickly kicked in. Greg was the first to speak.

"I'm Greg. Christ, I don't know how you were able to do that eulogy. I'd have gone to pieces. What you said seemed just so right and sincere. You must have loved him too."

"Didn't we all?" replied Alexander. "There wasn't a day at the Courtauld when I didn't look forward to seeing him. But what I really wanted to say without everyone else around is how much the two of you meant to him. I think if it wasn't for you he really would have gone to pieces after Ben went missing."

"And the bitter irony is that it's us who are going to pieces now," said John. "Like you, Alexander, we both thought that he was the best thing that'd ever happened to us but I guess I'd realized almost as soon as it started that our friendship couldn't last. But not in a million years would I have thought it'd come to this."

"And I can't stop thinking that there must have been more I could've done when Ben was at the hospital," said Greg. "You know, like insisting that he stays longer or finding out more about what was going through his mind."

"But perhaps sometimes it is just fate," said Alexander, "and there's simply nothing you can do about that."

***

Hugo's parents had sensibly kept numbers down for the wake and in any case their small house wasn't designed for crowds. A photo of Hugo was prominently displayed on the sideboard. This showed him on some beach coming out of the waves, his hair all over the place, smiling broadly at the photographer and his wet speedos struggling to contain their contents. Hugo's sister noticed Greg and John staring at the photo and appearing transfixed.

"I took that, you know. It was just after he'd got his degree and we all went on some bucket price holiday to Greece. He was in his element, flouncing around and generally being carefree. I never really saw that again." She paused, looking closely at the photo. "You'd never guess from that photo that he had a problem with self-esteem. Perhaps we were a bit over-protective but with Hugo it was difficult to avoid feeling one had to look after him."

Greg and John turned to look at Hugo's sister and were briefly lost for words when they noticed the similarity with her late brother. "You must be Helen," Greg said. "I'm Greg and this is my partner, John." They shook hands and Greg couldn't help noticing how similar her hands were to those of Hugo.

"It's a wonderful photo, Helen," said John, "and I'm not surprised you chose it. Hugo in a stuffy suit wouldn't be the way anyone would want to remember him."

"Did you know about Hugo's turn as a go-go dancer?" she asked.

Greg and John looked surprised. "How did you hear about that?" asked Greg.

"Oh, Hugo told Mum. I think he was actually quite chuffed that he'd done it."

"We were there, you know," said John.

"Gosh! How was it?"

"Absolutely amazing," said Greg. "It was like his final bid for freedom and almost as if he realized his own mortality."

Greg thought back to the rather final phone call he received from Hugo shortly before Ben and Hugo returned to the UK.

"Or like Icarus, singeing his wings when he flew too close to the sun," said John.

"I think I'm always to going to remember the image of my brother go-go dancing and trying to fly away to freedom," said Helen, with a lump in her throat.

"So will we," said Greg and John together before putting their arms around Helen and having a quiet sob together.

"I can see you're in need of something to lift your spirits," said Alexander, who'd arrived next to them precariously carrying four glasses of pink champagne.

"Who chose the pink champagne?" asked Greg.

"It was Mum's idea first of all," replied Helen.

"And I approved it," added Alexander. "Let's toast Hugo."

"To Hugo!" they all said.

"And to his bid for freedom," added Greg, softly.

"And not forgetting his 10 inches," said Alexander, rather too loudly, and then blushed in embarrassment.

They toasted Hugo again.

Monday, March 7, 2011

From the police's perspective, the case was as cut and dried as it possibly could be. From the taped conversation with the 999 operator to the evidence at autopsy, there simply was no doubt that there was an act of killing and that Ben was the perpetrator. The problem facing the Crown Prosecution Service and Ben's counsel was the issue of mental capacity and whether Ben knew what he was doing and had premeditated Hugo's death.

Ben appeared before the Highbury Magistrates' Court in Islington five days after Hugo's death and he was immediately remanded for psychiatric reports. An initial psychiatric assessment in the Magistrates' Court revealed an intelligent individual with no prior psychiatric history or abnormal personality traits who appeared to have simply gone off the rails and killed his partner. Ben's account of the last six months was intact until the point that he was abducted at the hotel, but beyond that his history was hazy and he became agitated when pressed to explain what had occurred during the week he was missing.

Hugo's parents had had to suffer the appalling experience of formally identifying his body and they were able to help the police fill in some of the blanks, which included informing the police of the abuse and degradation that Ben had endured. And reports from Steven Anderson in the British Consulate and Dr Greg Edwards at the Groote Schuur Hospital confirmed the extent of the underground sex scene that he'd become unwittingly involved with.

Further psychiatric assessment pointed strongly in the

direction of Ben having post-traumatic stress disorder coupled with some degree of Stockholm syndrome, in that Ben viewed some of his captors in a positive light. This particularly seemed to relate to two individuals mentioned in his disjointed narrative whom he called "the t-shirt man" and "the milkman".

The legal and psychiatric conclusion reached was that Ben didn't have mental capacity and a plea of diminished responsibility on the grounds of temporary insanity was put to the court at the crown court. Despite some attempts by the prosecution to persuade the jury that Ben was a thoroughly depraved individual who knew exactly what he was doing, and simply wanted to get his kicks by killing his boyfriend, the jury found unanimously in favor of an acquittal on the basis of insanity and he was detained under a hospital order with restriction to the Roundwell Medium Secure Unit in west London on Monday, March 14, 2011.

Friday, March 11, 2011

Joanna Brown parked her car outside 58 Popham Street, relieved that she still had a set of keys to the apartment. She looked up at the facade of the mid-terrace Victorian house and wondered whether it was doomed to being included on a gruesome murder tour along with Dr Crippen's home in Hilldrop Crescent and Joe Orton's apartment in Noel Road.

Today, she and Helen, Hugo's sister, had the unenviable task of clearing the apartment so that it could be cleaned and rented out to new tenants. Barbara Cavendish planned to come to the apartment later to remove Ben's possessions. They'd spoken on the phone about doing this together but decided that emotions were still too raw at the moment for either to cope with that; blame and recriminations were still unavoidably rather high on the agenda. Joanna heard the sound of a horn parping and noticed Helen pulling up in her Fiat and winding down the side window.

"Is it all right for me to park here? I wasn't sure about parking restrictions."

Joanna looked around for parking signs. "You should be okay but it's probably best to put a note on the windshield anyway."

The two of them entered Hugo and Ben's apartment, unsure what they might find and feeling strangely voyeuristic. The unopened pile of wedding presents was the first thing they noticed in the far right corner of the living room. Joanna bent down and examined the tag on the nearest present: "To dearest Hugo & Ben. Many congratulations! Have a wonderful life together. Love, Rebecca." She started sobbing and reached in her bag for a tissue.

"Are you sure you're up to this, Mum?" asked Helen. "We could always come back over the weekend."

Joanna stood up and put her arms around her daughter. "No, I'll be all right, darling. It's better that the tears come out than stay in." She looked again at the pile of presents. "So what do we do with all of this, then?"

"Let's leave them for Ben's mother to go through," replied Helen. "I'd imagine charity shops would be happy to take all the kettles, toasters and sets of cutlery, and she'd be in her element arranging that."

They examined the rest of the apartment. Apart from obvious things like laptops, a flat screen TV, DVDs, clothes and a shelfful of Hugo's fine art books, there was remarkably little else in the apartment that summed up the two years Hugo and Ben had spent together. Not surprisingly, the bedroom had been systematically examined by the forensic team and even the mattress had been removed. Joanna and Helen shared yet more tears looking at the bed, trying to reconcile clashing images of the joyful physicality of their relationship and the final act that had so abruptly terminated what they had together.

Working out which clothes belonged to whom was straightforward as the closet was divided down the middle, with Hugo's size small clothes on the left and Ben's medium size clothes on the right, and the chest of drawers was similarly divided. Joanna's initial intention was to donate Hugo's clothes to charity but she thought she should spend some time going through them before making a final decision.

Both had secretly dreaded finding pornography in the apartment but thankfully that had all been removed by the police.

Monday, March 14, 2011

Nailing the "whole fucking lot of them" proved to be a monumental and ultimately somewhat unrealistic undertaking for the Cape Town police force, although Sergeant Michelson's keen observational skills helped them to track down two other suspects in addition to Frank Dresden: one of whom had a halo of golden pubic hair cut into the shape of a heart that could easily have been identified in a line-up from ten yards away; and the other had a Prince Albert piercing which could be seen glinting in the light from the overhead bulb. Curiously, the ebony-skinned man in the third video proved to be impossible to track down despite his outstanding distinguishing feature.

Forensic reports eventually came back which definitely established that Frank Dresden had contributed to the contents of the coke bottle and had left his deposits in and around the cold storage room. The other two suspects were found to have left similar evidence, so three successful convictions for male rape and false imprisonment seemed virtually guaranteed. Matching the evidence in the coke bottle with that from the floor of the cold storage room suggested that at least 20 other sources of DNA had engaged Ben in non-consensual sexual intercourse, although some of the evidence was too degraded to be reliable in a court of law.

What was difficult to fathom is exactly why Ben had been sent on his way with the coke bottle inside him, and the nearest they'd come to an explanation was that this was some sort of protection to stop the participants becoming informers. It was also surprising that so much evidence had been left behind given the slickness of the abduction and its sequelae, but perhaps that had been intended as another arrogant taunt to the police.

One anomaly was the forensic evidence obtained when Ben had been seen in the emergency department at the Groote Schuur Hospital: the swabs of dried semen collected by Dr Greg Edwards were attributed to a single individual who hadn't added his DNA to the coke bottle or left any other evidence in the room. The most likely explanation was that Ben had been raped one final time before being sent back to the Nelson Lodge Hotel gardens in the buggy and that the individual responsible had been scrupulously careful right up until he made the fatal error of giving in to temptation. DI van der Merwe was convinced that he was the missing link to the whole business and he wouldn't let a stone remain unturned until he was behind bars as well.

Friday, March 18, 2011

Unlike the Florence Nightingale Hospital, where modernity had been shoehorned into Victoriana, the Roundwell Unit was purpose built to house mental health patients on hospital and restriction orders in conditions of prison-like security. The Old Bailey judge had initially recommended a high-security hospital like Broadmoor Hospital in Berkshire, but Ben's counsel were quick to point out that he wasn't a danger to the general public and had already been to hell and back while in captivity.

Ben settled in surprisingly quickly on the assessment ward in the Roundwell Unit. Although it was hardly four stars accommodation, it was definitely superior to C23 ward in the Groote Schuur Hospital. At first sight, staff found it incomprehensible that this quiet, good looking man could have killed his male partner while making love, but it didn't take long for them to see glimpses of a darker side, particularly after a difficult session with the ward psychologist. And unlike the psychologist in the Florence Nightingale Hospital who'd had Ben teetering rather perilously on the edge of disclosure, the psychologist at Roundwell helped Ben to take the next step to confront what had happened and why he felt so cold and helpless. And bit by bit, the darker side came out into the open and he was actually able to talk about what had happened to him when he was a captive and how it made him feel. Something else that Ben had mentioned recently in a session was receiving a phone call just before he had sex with Hugo on that fateful Saturday morning, although he couldn't recall the contents of the call or who'd been the caller.

Ben was also fortunate to have a sympathetic consultant psychiatrist responsible for his care who was remarkably unfazed by what he'd seen in the videos and was convinced that more lay behind the case than simply psychogenic amnesia or post-traumatic stress disorder. In Dr Simon Shepherd's experience, good looking middle class boys didn't go about killing their lovers at the same time as having sex unless they either had some very aberrant personality development or were high on illicit substances and neither seemed to be the case with Ben. He'd also been gratified to see how quickly his patient had responded to the right sort of psychological therapy. The psychologist had mentioned in the ward round about Ben receiving the phone call and he was wondering whether hypnotherapy might help him recall what had been said. But dealing with the fact that he'd killed his partner would take much longer to heal.

**

Later that evening, when Dr Shepherd was sitting down to dinner with Brian, his partner, the subject of Ben came up in a roundabout sort of way.

"I was reading about the case of that guy who killed his civil partner while they were having sex. It was mentioned in an article in The Times about murders committed within relationships where there was an unequal balance of power. Does that ring any bells with you?" asked Brian.

"It might do. Why?"

"Well, it might sound strange but I remember meeting this guy in Earls Court years ago who seemed to get his kicks out of manipulating people and making them do things they wouldn't normally do. He was a sort of Svengali figure and very sexy with it. His piercing green eyes seemed to look right through you. The trick he seems to have used is a string of words to trigger a post-hypnotic suggestion and he'd usually do this by phoning people. It was usually just minor stuff like making people go shoplifting or do embarrassing things but reading that article got me wondering whether people could be made to do more than that."

"Brian, you may have hit the nail on the head! Can you remember his name?"

"He mainly used the initial 'M' but I'm pretty sure his name was Michael Magister; it's not a name you forget easily. He used to hang out in a rather dubious club called Backdoor in a damp basement."

Saturday, March 19, 2011

Jim and James sat back in bed in James's apartment on High Level Road sharing their post-conjugal cigarette.

"Whew, ours must have been the longest courtship ever," said James.

"Sorry, but I had to be sure it was right. And there was the minor inconvenience of my wife."

"How did she take it when you told her you preferred men?"

"It was a bit of an anticlimax, really. She said she'd always known. She also said my dick was too big for her. And to cap it all, she told me she'd reached the conclusion she ought to be batting for the other side."

"Is that really how she put it? She sounds very butch."

"Unbelievably, yes. And you definitely wouldn't find her in a skirt."

"Well, your dick isn't too big for me. In fact, it's what my dad would've called a 'groot vet wors'." James reached under the covers for a grope. "So what do you think about mine?"

"Well, it's certainly straight and true and I'm relieved that you haven't added the Prince Albert yet."

"Did you notice the tattoos?"

"I don't think I could have missed them. I had Yin or Yang about six inches away from my right eye just a few minutes ago."

The cigarette was passed between them.

"I was going to tell you later but you might as well know now. It's something that's followed on from the Cavendish case. I've been asked to head a task force to tackle LGBT hate crime and I've accepted."

"That's fantastic news!"

"And I'd like you to join me as my assistant."

"Try to keep me away, Detective Inspector."

"I hoped you'd say that, Sergeant."

And James dove under the bedclothes to give him another introductory lesson in gay sex although Jim didn't really need it.

Sunday, March 20, 2011

Although the law is often accused of moving too slowly, that certainly wasn't the case on this occasion.

Following the revelation at dinner, Dr Simon Shepherd contacted an emergency number at the Ministry of Justice on Saturday morning with information which he thought was highly pertinent to Ben's case.

The Ministry of Justice immediately contacted the Chief Superintendent at the police station where Ben had originally been taken to after his arrest.

Phone records for Hugo and Ben's apartment were obtained within hours and they confirmed that a phone call had been received from a cell phone at 8:00 a.m. on Saturday, February 26, 2011 and that this had lasted about 30 seconds.

Later that day, DI van der Merwe's colleague at New Scotland Yard passed on details of the DNA evidence that had been obtained by Dr Greg Edwards from Ben at the Groote Schuur hospital.

Michael Magister was arrested at his south London address in the early hours of Sunday, March 20, 2011 and charged with kidnap, unlawful imprisonment, rape, blackmail and the murder of an unknown male.

DNA evidence confirmed that Michael Magister had raped Ben both orally and anally.

British Airways were able to confirm that Michael Magister had flown out to Cape Town on an earlier flight on Friday, February 4, 2011 and returned to London after Ben had been dropped off at the Nelson Lodge Hotel on Wednesday, February 16, 2011. Border control at London

Heathrow and immigration at Cape Town confirmed these dates.

Reception at the Nelson Lodge Hotel were able to confirm that an unknown white male speaking excellent English had paid for a room upgrade in pounds sterling and had also requested that a message be left on room #202's flat screen TV. A generous tip was gratefully received for that additional service. The hotel was embarrassed to discover that the same white male had been employed as a part-time security guard on account of his language skills and time allegedly spent in the armed forces. His references hadn't been requested.

Michael Magister's bank accounts showed numerous payments of approximately 800 pounds sterling made during the week before Thursday, February 10, 2011 and a large payment of 74,823 pounds sterling made into an offshore account on Thursday, February 15, 2011.

The apparently underage boy sent on his way after being found in Frank Dresden's bed turned out to be his 16-year-old nephew who'd been staying with him while his Constantia parents were enjoying a vacation in Bali. Sexually precocious and appearing young for his age, he'd been easily lured into the daring do activities of mail boy, ransom intermediary and general factotum. His DNA was also found on the floor of the room where Ben had been held captive but this was conveniently forgotten for his parents' sake.

The case of Regina v. Magister was held at the Old Bailey over a two week period commencing on Monday, May 2, 2011. Ben's evidence was heard via a video link to the Roundwell Unit in order to prevent the defendant unduly influencing his testimony. Michael Magister had his hair cut short and he wasn't allowed to shave for several days. He was also obliged to wear a t-shirt and jeans for that part of the trial. Ben had no problem confirming that he was the person who enticed him behind the bushes at the Nelson Lodge Hotel and was then present at the time that all four videos were made. He also confirmed that it was Michael Magister's voice that he heard at 8:00 a.m. on Saturday, February 26, 2011.

Dr Greg Edwards attended the Old Bailey as an expert witness and his eloquent first-hand account of observing what Michael Magister and others had inflicted on Ben in captivity had the jurors and most of the rest of the court in tears. Photos were shown of the cold storage room where he was held captive and of Ben when he was in the emergency department. The jurors weren't required to watch the four videos from beginning to end but they were given a folder of stills from all four videos and from the Nelson Lodge Hotel's security footage.

Michael Magister was found guilty by a unanimous verdict on all charges and received life sentences for each of murder, kidnapping, false imprisonment and rape, 14 years for blackmail, and two years for procuring others to commit homosexual acts, all to run concurrently. In short, the book had been thrown at him and it had stuck. His defense counsel immediately lodged an appeal against all charges on account of procedural irregularities, and in particular the way forensic evidence had been collected.

***

Whilst staying in London for the trial, Greg arranged an appointment through the Ministry of Justice to visit Ben in the Roundwell Unit, which he felt was essential to achieve closure on Hugo's death. Actually, he felt no urgency to rush back to Cape Town as his relationship with John had become increasingly fraught since falling in love with Hugo and then his tragic death.

"Ben, you've got a visitor," said the staff nurse. "He's a doctor, so he must be here to do a report. He's very handsome too. You'd better behave yourself!"

Ben walked into the interview room used for legal and medical visits. The man sitting at the table had short dark hair and warm gray-brown eyes. A few days beard growth complimented his tanned face. He was wearing a suit but no tie and had a folder in front of him.

"Come in, Ben. I'm Greg."

Ben looked puzzled, wondering whether he knew this handsome man.

"You probably don't remember me but we have met before."

Ben still looked unsure.

"Do you remember how you came to be in the hospital in Cape Town?"

"Not really. It's still a bit of a blur."

"Ben, I was the doctor who saw you in the emergency department. My name is Dr Edwards."

Greg noticed a glimmer of recognition on Ben's face.

"Gosh, I do remember something now. You were wearing a white coat and looking down at me."

"That's when you were in the emergency department. I'm afraid you were in a rather sorry state when you arrived in the ambulance."

"That's what the doctor on the ward told me. He also said I did some strange things." Ben looked sheepish.

"You certainly did, Ben."

"Were you there at the time?"

"I was."

Ben looked uneasy. "Are you here to do another report, Dr Edwards?"

"Ben, please call me Greg. No, Ben, I'm not here to do a report."

"So why have you come to see me?"

"It's complicated, Ben. It's about Hugo, really."

"Ah." He looked away. "I'm so sorry," he said, tears welling up in his eyes.

Greg took hold of his hands across the table top. "You weren't responsible, Ben. You were made to do that to Hugo."

Ben looked into Greg's eyes. "I'd like to believe you but it's so difficult to let go. Why did I allow Michael Magister to manipulate me like that?"

"He had a hold over you, Ben. It's really as simple as that. But he's behind bars now and you've got the rest of your life ahead of you. And I'd like to help you with that when you're ready to take the next step and out of hospital."

"Do you think they'll release me?"

"We'll see, Ben, but you've got a strong case. Look, Ben, I'll give you my phone numbers so you can ring me anytime you want. And I'll come back and see you again before I return to Cape Town. I think I owe that to both you and Hugo."

***

Once Michael Magister was behind bars, Ben's own defense counsel lost no time in making a strongly-worded recommendation to the Secretary of State for Justice that

Ben should be discharged from the Roundwell Unit with absolutely no strings attached. Sir James and Lady Cavendish also launched their own courageous crusade against the likes of Michael Magister preying on the vulnerable and bared their souls in the Sunday Times newspaper. They also decided to use the money from selling their story to establish a Hugo Brown bursary at the Courtauld Institute for talented fine art scholars.

An independent forensic psychiatrist examined Ben in the Roundwell Unit and his report basically confirmed what everyone believed about him:

"In conclusion, I believe that the act which lead to the death of Hugo Brown should be viewed in the same way as an epileptic automatism - that is to say, an act that occurred without the volition of the individual, and over which he would have had no control of what he did or who he did it to - which Mr Cavendish cannot be held legally responsible for. I would respectfully recommend that he should be unconditionally discharged from his current hospital order but with the proviso that ongoing psychological therapy should continue to be offered on a voluntary basis."

The sum effect from all the representations, considerable publicity and a hastily convened tribunal hearing was that Ben was released from the Roundwell Unit, off his hospital order and unrestricted, on Friday, May 20, 2011

Friday, May 27, 2011

"Come in, Ben," said the psychologist from the door to her consulting room.

Ben sat down and she leant back to look at him.

"How does it feel to be a free man?"

"Amazing. I still can't believe it, really."

"You've come such a long way since I first met you in the unit. Do you remember how you were ready to bite my head off at the end of our first sessions?"

"I do, but it was probably the only way to get me to fight my way out of the cold, damp place."

"So let's think about what's left for us to do. What are your priorities?"

"Well, first off, I think I need to confront my fear of going back to where it all happened. Greg is coming down to my parents place next weekend and I'm hoping he'll put me up in his apartment if I visit Cape Town. The second thing I need to work on is how to deal with phone calls if I don't recognize the caller. I've still no idea of the trigger that was used to make me kill Hugo, so all I've got is the snip technique you taught me to cut the strings he used to control me. Then there's dealing with the fact that I killed someone I loved and wanted to spend the rest of my life with, but I know that's a long way off and probably for a lot more therapy."

"I can't fault any of that but what's important is how you do it. Exposure is risky and you need to be careful that it doesn't implode and push you back to square one. So you need to choose how and when you do it very carefully, and preferably with someone you trust who can give you support. And if you do go for exposure, you need to pace yourself. So, once you're there, take stock of where you are and then let yourself reconstruct the memories. They could be things you see, hear, smell or feel, and some will be unpleasant. If you can construct a chronological sequence of events while you're there, you'll have done really well, but if you can't don't worry. At some point, you'll know that you've gone as far as you can go and that's the time to pull back and reconnect with the real world and the support you have. The big question is whether Greg as well as you can deal with all of that."

"I hope so. He's strong and copes with anything the emergency department throws at him. He's seen me at my weakest point but he didn't walk away. And what we also have is the link through Hugo. I know he loved Hugo and I hope I'm the bridge to what we've shared together in various ways. I suppose it's a bit like putting a triangular relationship back together where one of the people involved only exists as memories."

"That's interesting but it's still a lot to put on his plate. So are you planning to discuss all that when you next meet?"

"That's the idea although I don't want to put him off."

"The relationship sounds serious. Does he know what he's letting himself in for?"

"I think so but I guess he'll be looking over his shoulder for a bit."

"I'm glad you said that rather than me. But I wonder what you could do to make it easier for him."

"Use call-screening?"

"Certainly; that might come in handy. But most importantly, remember you don't have to prove yourself to anyone. Your family isn't passing judgment any longer so there's no need for you to demonstrate your masculinity. Go with the flow and allow yourself to both give and take."

"That's what Hugo always said, although he had something different in mind." Ben blushed.

"That's good, Ben. Blushing is a sign of allowing yourself to react normally and if it's not caring about who fucks whom, that's absolutely fine. In fact, I'd positively recommend it."

"Can I take it that's doctor's orders?"

"Oh yes, and I'll write a prescription if you like."

Sunday, June 5, 2011

Ben arrived at Thame Parkway rail station ten minutes before the 11:36 from London Marylebone was due. He stood at the platform edge waiting restlessly for the sound resonating down the rails that heralded the train's arrival. As the train pulled in alongside the platform, Ben desperately scanned the interior of the coaches to see whether the person he was expecting was on board. The train pulled to a stop and there was a frenzy of door opening and weekend visitors alighting onto the narrow platform. And just when he thought there couldn't be anyone left on board, he saw Greg step down onto the platform carrying a suitcase and a rucksack. He felt like running up to him and flinging his arms around him in a wild embrace but then remembered he was in Oxfordshire and hadn't even slept with him yet. He walked up to him, trying to remain composed but was sure that his heart was missing every other beat.

"Dr Greg Edwards, I presume."

"Indeed. And you must be The Honourable Benjamin Cavendish. I'm delighted to make your acquaintance."

"The pleasure is all mine, doctor."

The two of them giggled conspiratorially and hugged each other, pausing momentarily for a European peck on both cheeks.

Greg was impressed by the way Ben handled the potholes on the journey back to the family home. He also approved of the tight fitting jeans that showed off Ben's crotch so effectively. He was even more impressed by the sight of the Jacobean manor house with acres of well-maintained grounds that stood at the end of a 100 yard drive.

"Gosh, is that yours?"

"Well, it's not exactly mine, but it's been in the family for a good many generations. It costs a fortune to run, though, which is probably why we're as poor as church mice. Actually, that's not true, but it's what my mother likes to tell people."

"I'm looking forward to meeting your mother. She sounds intriguing."

Ben laughed. "That's a nice way of describing her. Actually, they won't be back until this evening, so we've got the afternoon to ourselves."

"I can't wait." He gave Ben's thigh a gentle squeeze.

The Range Rover came to a halt in front of the grand entrance with a sound of gravel crunching under the tires. The unmistakable figure of a butler came down the stairs to open the passenger door and carry in Greg's luggage.

"Welcome to Hanley Hall, Dr Edwards. I'm Vincent the butler. I trust your stay will be an enjoyable one."

Greg looked amazed.

"You ain't seen nothing yet. We've also got a cook, two gardeners and a handyman," said Ben, smiling broadly.

"I'm not surprised your family is so hard-up."

As they entered the main hall, the butler announced lunch: "Lunch is served, gentlemen."

Ben led Greg into the small dining room which still had a table large enough to seat 10 guests and they sat down opposite each other looking into each other's eyes.

"I'm wondering where to start," said Greg.

"Me too," said Ben, "but as someone said, we have all the time in the world."

"Louis Armstrong, I believe."

The butler came in with a tureen of Vichyssoise soup and ladled it into soup bowls.

"Mr Benjamin, would you like the sauvignon blanc served now?"

"Thanks, Vincent, that would be great."

The butler left them after serving the wine.

"Actually, it's not like this every day. It was mother who insisted on the silver service for lunch. She's a bit of a stickler for etiquette when we have guests."

"I'm relieved to hear that, or otherwise I think I'd have to get a butler back home in Cape Town."

Ben's soup spoon paused in mid-air. "You know, Greg, I think I'll need to go back to Cape Town sometime soon. I've got so many unanswered questions going through my head about what really happened."

"How much do you remember?"

"Quite a lot but there are gaps. I remember the room and I remember the men but I can't recall what they actually did to me. And I remember the smells but funnily enough that hasn't put me off sex."

"I'm glad to hear it." Greg extended his hand across the table to touch Ben's cheek.

The butler came in to remove their soup bowls and then served the main course. He poured some decanted claret into their glasses.

"I'll say one thing, Ben: you're looking remarkably well for someone who's been through as much as you have. They must have fed you well in the Roundwell Unit."

"Well, the food was crap but being there certainly helped. And I'm still seeing the psychologist."

"Where have you got to in the sessions?"

"The bit that we talked about when you first came to see me. The psychologist does her best to remind me that I was just the puppet on the end of some strings but it's hard to shake off feeling responsible for what I did."

"I guess it'll just take time."

"It's a difficult question to ask but are you sure you don't hold me responsible?"

"That's probably even more difficult to answer. To be honest, I guess I did but I know now that you were just the puppet."

"I'm really grateful for that, Greg." He looked deeply into his eyes.

They chewed thoughtfully on the excellent roast beef and sipped the claret.

"Was sex allowed in the unit?" asked Greg.

"Well, it was certainly available but actually I wasn't that interested. Perhaps I was waiting for a tall, dark and handsome man to bring me a box of chocolates."

"Would I do?"

"Ooh, I think so."

"Perhaps now's a good time for our dessert."

"Let's go upstairs."

Ben led Greg out of the dining room up the ornately carved staircase to his room on the second floor. Greg was taken aback by the size, as it seemed to be almost the size of his Bree Street apartment. It also had a magnificent and very enticing four-poster bed.

"I hope the bed doesn't creak."

"Actually, you'll be the first boyfriend to grace my bed, so we'll have to test it and see."

"You mean that Hugo never stayed here?" said Greg incredulously.

"Oh he stayed here but he never felt able to cross the threshold and join me in bed."

"Well, I feel deeply honored."

Ben and Greg slowly undressed each other in the bright light of the midsummer afternoon, feeling the warm sun against their skin. Ben drew Greg over to a full length mirror so that they could compare each other.

"You know, we could almost be twins," said Ben.

"John said the same thing," said Greg.

And they certainly were remarkably alike, with the same dark hair, gray-brown eyes, aquiline nose, strong jaw and tidy body hair distribution over well-defined musculature. The one minor difference was the bulbous head on Greg's dick although Ben made up for this with another half inch in length.

"Have you ever fantasized about having sex with your twin?" asked Greg.

"Oh all the time," replied Ben, bending down to wrap his lips around Greg's splendid dick. "And I'm really enjoying this tasty piece of my twin self," he added as he came up for air.

They crossed over to the bed and lay down facing each other, their dicks touching and jousting for dominance.

"Is it true that you're a bit of an alpha male?" asked Greg.

"Who said that?"

"Oh someone we both loved at one time."

"And you?"

"Oh I'm flexible."

"That's what I hoped you'd say."

And with that affirmation, Ben leapt on top of Greg and exerted his dominance in the way that Hugo had grown used to and his psychologist had done her best to warn him against. Fortunately, Greg proved remarkably receptive to the pounding that his ass was receiving, particularly when Ben took his dick back into his mouth at the same time as fucking him. The bed creaked ominously, but having survived five centuries of civil wars and other unrests, it wasn't going to give up the ghost quite yet. Vincent the butler couldn't help but hear the creaking, but he smiled to himself and was glad that Benjamin had found a new boyfriend. He went to the fridge and took out the bottle of *Moët & Chandon* that he'd chilled for the occasion. He carried the Moët and two champagne flutes on a silver tray upstairs and left it outside the door, walking away quietly so as not to disturb their lovemaking.

Ben lay on top of Greg with their combined ejaculates in danger of gluing them together like evo-stik unless one of them moved soon. Ben thought he'd heard a chink of glass from outside and peeled himself off Greg to inspect beyond the door. He returned with the champagne and poured a couple of glasses.

"The butler sends his regards," said Ben.

"How did he know?" asked Greg, looking surprised and taking hold of the glass.

"Oh Vincent knows everything that goes on in the house. In fact, he could probably tell you my entire sexual history. And the champagne means he approves of you."

"I think a toast is due: To Vincent and us," said Greg.

"To Vincent and us," responded Ben.

"So more sex or more champagne?" asked Greg.

"More of both, I think," replied Ben. "And you can be the alpha male this time."

***

Greg and Ben were finishing having their pre-dinner shower when they heard Sir James and Lady Cavendish's Rolls Royce purring to a halt at the front of Hanley Hall.

"Oh I should have warned you that dinner this evening is formal, which means that we're expected to dress up for the occasion," said Ben.

"Don't worry, I've come prepared," assured Greg.

"I can't wait."

Ben was already downstairs in the drawing room talking with his parents when Greg made his appearance. Their jaws dropped. Greg was dressed in a dark gray, half-length frock coat with a white neck scarf, purple waist coat, black satin trousers and calf length riding boots.

"Wow!" exclaimed Ben. "Mother, Father, I'd like to introduce you to Dr Greg Edwards."

"Count Grigoriy Eduardovitsch Dobrygin at your service, Sir James and Lady Cavendish," said Greg, bowing deeply.

"You're joking!" exclaimed Ben.

"I'm not," replied Greg, smiling broadly. "Unfortunately, I wasn't allowed to carry the Dobrygin dynasty ceremonial sword on the plane."

Needless to say, Lady Cavendish was greatly impressed by this dashing young Count and put her hand against the back of his frock coat as they went into the grand dining room. "So tell me more about your fascinating family, Count."

Ben watched the interaction between his mother and his new boyfriend with amusement. He turned to his father: "Mother certainly seems to have taken a shine to Greg. It's like a costume drama being acted out before our eyes."

"Well, he is rather dashing," said Sir James with a twinkle in his eyes.

"You approve, then?"

"Without the slightest shadow of a doubt, my dear Benjamin. I can see him keeping you in step most effectively."

"You mean, from the likes of Michael Magister?"

"I sincerely hope so, Benjamin."

Ben looked down at the floor, trying to pluck up the courage to say something. "You know, Father, Greg told me about the ransom."

"Ah, I thought he might have. I'm really so sorry, Benjamin, but I had to put my foot down." Ben's father looked uncomfortable.

"I think you did right, Father. Someone had to put a stop to his game."

"That's what I thought, but would Hugo still be alive if I'd paid up?"

"Who knows, but I'm sure he'd have got his pound of flesh eventually and made many more people suffer along the way."

"I'm so very sorry, Benjamin." He put a hand on Ben's shoulder.

"And I'm so sorry for what I've put the two of you through over the years," said Ben, looking directly into his father's eyes.

Ben and his father hugged each other with tears streaming down their faces.

"James, what are you and Benjamin doing?" they heard Lady Barbara calling from the dining room. "You're keeping our guest waiting!"

"Does Mother know what happened about the

ransom?" asked Ben, wiping away his tears.

"Goodness no, that would have been the final straw for her," replied his father.

"It's our little secret, then."

"Agreed."

***

Ben's brief but heart-to-heart talk with his father cleared the way for a thoroughly relaxing week with Greg, and their days at Hanley Hall passed in a blur of picnics and al fresco lovemaking in the grounds and neighboring woods, trips to the Ashmolean and Pitt Rivers Museums in Oxford, pub lunches in Cotswold villages and dinners with Ben's parents. The visit to the Ashmolean Museum had been a real highlight for Greg as he'd been able to see Poussin's 'The Exposition of Moses' close up for the first time.

Waking up on the final day in the four-poster bed, Greg had an important question to put to his host. He snuggled up against Ben and looked into his eyes. "I've been thinking a lot about us over the last few days and I've made a decision. I know I can never replace Hugo, and that it's still early days in our relationship, but I'd like you to come and live with me in Cape Town."

Ben stroked Greg's chest hair and followed the triangle of hair down to his dick. He wrapped his fingers around the head and gave it a firm squeeze. "Actually, I was going to ask you the same thing. I've rather grown to love you and your mushroom head. But this time, I'm going to get my mother's approval, if that's okay with you."

"Do I have to do anything else to earn it?"

"Oh no, I'd say it's all done and dusted. Just smile at

her, say something impressive in your sexy Russian voice and you'll be fine."

Saturday, July 6, 2011

Packing up the few possessions he had and leaving Hanley Hall was emotional for all, but Ben didn't have the slightest doubt that this was the best thing for him, particularly as the tenancy of the Popham Street apartment had ended months ago and his job had been terminated as soon as the advertising company and the rest of the world had learnt of Hugo's death. Despite their concerns about Ben returning to the country where he'd been held captive, his parents understood the rationale for this decision and in the end gave their full approval to Ben moving to Cape Town to live with Greg. Of course, Greg's trump card was that he had all the best characteristics parents could possibly hope for in a future son-in-law, and his title and exotic background were additional icing on the cake for the snobbish Lady Barbara.

Ben's plane departed from London Heathrow late on Friday evening. As it was a one-way ticket, he'd splashed out on business class and found himself back in seat 63J on the upper deck. He thought back to the same flight four months ago when Hugo was in 63K and was relieved that the opposite seat was empty, although he found himself wondering whether ghosts flew business class.

The flight arrived on schedule but early morning in Cape Town this time was cold and wet. As the flight had only been half-full, immigration and baggage reclaim was quick and Ben was heading for the exit with his suitcases just 30 minutes after landing.

Greg was standing at the exit with a sign saying 'The Honourable Benjamin Cavendish' and was wearing a very fetching chauffeur's cap. "May I take your cases, sir? I trust the one with the vibrating dildo didn't cause any problems going through security."

They kissed and hugged and headed for Greg's second-hand Honda in the short-stay parking lot. "Sorry, John took the Mercedes with him and the Silver Shadow is in the auto repair shop."

The short drive from the airport to the City Bowl proved to be hazardous for other drivers on the N2 as Ben seemed intent on ensuring that Greg's dick was still as it was when he'd left it a few weeks before. He reluctantly postponed demonstrating his superior oral skills as Ben pulled into the garage on the ground level of 180 Bree Street. They climbed into the elevator with all Ben's luggage and headed for the fourth story.

"So, Benjamin Cavendish, this is my humble abode," Greg said, dramatically opening the door to the apartment after bending down to pat the sheep grazing on the astroturf.

"Wow!" said Ben, looking around and trying to take it all in. "And all of this is yours?"

"Lock, stock and barrel, though it's a bit emptier since John moved out; he was a bit of a hunter-gatherer of antiques and *bric-à-brac*. But before I give you the guided tour, I want to show you something. It meant a lot to Hugo."

Greg took hold of Ben's hand and led him up to his office on the mezzanine level.

He pointed at the painting. "What do you think of it?"

"Actually, I recognize it. It was on Hugo's laptop as his home screen. I'm guessing it must be by Poussin."

"I'm impressed. It's called 'Self-Portrait: 1649'."

Ben went up and examined the painting. "The detail is amazing for a copy."

"Actually, it's the original," said Greg, grinning.

"Christ! It must be worth millions! How did you afford it?"

"Oh, family money, connections back in Russia and that sort of thing. What does the painting say to you?"

"Well, I'd say it's showing the artist as he is rather than as the public might want him to be. There's sincerity in his face and a hint of humor. Also, there's nothing behind him like other versions of the painting, so he's really just saying take me as I am. And I like the way you've got him hanging over your desk as if he's there to give you his words of wisdom."

"Extraordinary! How did you know all that?"

"Sorry, I cheated. I saw the first few PowerPoint slides Hugo prepared for his Courtauld lecture."

Greg laughed. "You're forgiven. So what words of wisdom do you think Nicolas Poussin would want to give us now?"

"I think he'd say go fuck yourselves senseless."

"I was hoping you'd say that."

Greg lifted Ben up and carried him across the mezzanine level to the bedroom and then gently lowered him onto the bed.

"I had no idea you were so strong," said Ben, seriously impressed by his lifting skills.

"Oh it's in the genes," said Greg, "and I was quite macho when I was in the army."

"Were you fighting off hordes of hunky Cossacks after your body?"

"Unfortunately, no. I was in the medical corps, so it

was mainly female nurses with too much hair on their upper lip."

The two of them sat on the bed undressing each other, finally undoing zippers and letting their dicks stand to attention.

"And now, Benjamin Cavendish, let me show you my new wet room," said Greg, smiling broadly.

Greg and Ben went into the double shower wet room that gleamed with light reflecting from polished granite. The power shower had massage heads to cover the full length of the body and there was a stainless steel bidet with an addition that Hugo would have leaped upon with glee.

"Wow! This is exactly what Hugo always fantasized about having. And is that what I'm thinking it is?" He pointed at the bidet and its attachment.

"It certainly is," replied Greg, with a smutty look on his face. "And guaranteed to reach the parts that douches can only dream of."

Greg and Ben stood under the showers allowing the pulsing water to caress their bodies and used their lips, tongues and fingers to massage the places that the water couldn't quite reach. Greg bent over and Ben licked and tongued his opening, swallowing the water cascading over his buttocks and down the cleft. Ben gently inserted two and then three fingers, moving them around and massaging Greg's prostate. Greg grabbed Ben's dick and guided it into his opening with his fingers still touching the head, enjoying the finger feel of Ben's dick inside him. Ben entered to the hilt and relished the feeling of oneness with his lover's body. Greg stood up with Ben's dick still inside and turned to kiss Ben wetly on the lips. "Time to move to the bench, I think."

The squidgy, orange bench was Greg's latest addition to the wet room. The idea for it came from seeing chairs in the psychiatric cubicles in the Groote Schuur emergency department that were designed to resist anything that might be deposited on them. As well as having just the amount of give to be comfortable, the bench was also heavy enough to stay put on a wet floor.

Ben looked at the bench and smiled. "Good color. How did you know that was my favorite?" He knelt on the bench and wiggled his butt at Greg.

"That's a fine ass you've got there, Benjamin Cavendish." Greg bent down and licked the water off Ben's lower back and let his tongue wander down to the entrance. He tongued deep and licked the velvety smoothness of the inside. His tongue continued its travels around Ben's perineum. He took Ben's balls in his mouth one by one and stroked his dick which looked ready to burst. Greg pressed his mushroom head against Ben's entrance which took his dick in like an old friend. Greg moved slowly back and forth, massaging Ben's prostate. Ben moaned softly and arched his back. Greg flipped Ben over on his back with his dick still inside and held his legs up with both hands. Ben locked eyes with Greg and stroked the full length of his dick slowly and deliberately. Greg matched this with his fucking and they rapidly increased the frequency of their stroking and thrusting.

"God, I love the feel of your dick inside me," said Ben. He groaned, arched his back and ejaculated three long lines of come, one of which ended up in his mouth. Greg withdrew his dick and moved up to stand over Ben's face. Ben took hold of the mushroom head and held it above his open mouth. "More food for me, I think." A handful of strokes later, Greg moaned and came into Ben's mouth. Ben wrapped his lips around the head and sucked and sucked until there wasn't a drop of come left. Greg bent down and licked up the spunk on Ben's abdomen and chest.

"Yum," said Greg.

They lay together side by side on the bench, looking into each other's eyes.

"I've got a little secret to tell you," said Greg. "The wet room was actually your psychologist's idea. The bench was my addition, though. She thought the dark walls would be good exposure therapy. I thought the colored bench would help you to feel comfortable. And I knew that orange was your favorite color."

"Well, it worked. I've decided bottoming is amazing."

"But you didn't like it with Hugo?"

"Not really. His dick was just too big for that. Yours is just perfect, though."

"Thank you most kindly, Benjamin Cavendish." They shared a lingering kiss. "So ready for some lunch?"

"Definitely. All that sex has made me ravenous."

"And after lunch, I'd like to show you something else that Hugo was very proud of."

"I'm intrigued."

They sat down to eat some tapas-style dishes that Greg had bought from a local deli. Ben looked intensely at Greg.

"You know those videos that were made of me?"

That was the one question that Greg felt uncomfortable answering. "Ben, darling, I don't think it's wise to think about them."

"I know, love. But I was just wondering whether..."

"Please don't ask, Ben. You're still way too vulnerable. Perhaps some time in the future."

They continued eating.

"Why did you leave Russia, Greg? Was being gay the reason?"

"It's a long story and gayness didn't really come into it. The Dobrygin family is old school Russia and we didn't fit in politically. Putin detests the aristocracy and enjoyed making life miserable for us. And doctors are paid little more than street cleaners, so getting out of the country was an easy decision for me."

"But don't you miss Russia?"

"A bit. The culture and traditions mean a lot to me. One day I might go back, I guess."

"Why did you change your name?"

"I needed to make a fresh start." He looked a bit uneasy. "But enough about my past, let's go upstairs and I'll show you the little something I was talking about."

They went upstairs to the living room. Ben sat down opposite the flat screen TV while Greg set up the laptop.

The image of Hugo naked and holding his 10 inch dick with both hands like a fire hose suddenly appeared on the screen.

"That isn't..."

"It is."

They watched as Hugo gyrated on the platform under the spotlight, teasing the crowd with his dick which was displayed in its full, humongous glory on giant flat screens around the dance floor. A camera zoomed in on Hugo's buttocks as he spread them wide and teased his entrance with a finger. Hugo's sinuous movements took on an almost manic intensity as the pounding beat got louder and faster, and then he reached the climax, shouted "cock-a-doodle-do", and sprayed his come far and wide over the audience. At the end of his performance, he gave a polite bow and looked at the camera with his winning smile, which is where the video clip froze.

Ben's expression was one of jaw-dropped amazement. "You know, Greg, I never knew he had that in him. I mean, he always produced loads of come but I could never imagine him doing anything like that. In fact, he was usually embarrassed when people mentioned his huge dick. Did he get paid for doing that?"

"3000 rand, I think. And they wanted him back for a weekly spot. John and I teased him about going pro as a porn star. He said he'd call himself Johnny Deep."

Ben laughed. "The night before our wedding, I teased him about someone writing a book about his dick and calling it 'The Adventures of Hugo and his Humongous Dick'."

"Well, he certainly had a few adventures with it while he was in Cape Town. How does that make you feel, Ben?"

"Pleased for him, actually, although I'd have loved to have been part of it. Do you think I was holding him back in some way?"

"I'm not sure, Ben. I think it was more a flowering of his sexuality in a new place and under unusual circumstances."

"And he fell in love with you along the way."

"That too. What do think about that?"

"All right, I think. He always had so much to give and I can see now that sharing with just one person must have been difficult for him. Where you there when he did that performance?"

"Oh God, yes. John and I wouldn't have missed it for the world."

"I'd give anything to hold his dick and taste his spunk again." He started sobbing.

"Come here, darling." Greg hugged Ben and his tears gradually subsided.

"So where was the video shot?" asked Ben.

"At a club called Video, although it had to close down when the publicity about your kidnap came out."

"I'd like to see it if that's possible."

"Are you sure?"

"Yes, Greg."

"Okay, we could try but it'll probably be locked. I've arranged with the police for us to go to Duncan Dock first thing Monday, so we could have a look at Video at the same time, if you're up to it."

"I'd like that."

Greg bent down on his knees and looked up at Ben. "Look, I know I'll never replace Hugo - and I'd certainly never be able to repeat that performance - but would you make me very happy and marry me, Benjamin Cavendish?"

Ben looked deep into Greg's eyes. "I'm not sure that I deserve you, but of course I would, Grigoriy Eduardovitsch Dobrygin."

"That's not bad but I might have to arrange Russian classes before I take you to meet the Grand Duke and Countess back home in St Petersburg."

Monday, July 8, 2011

Greg and Ben arrived at Duncan Dock first thing on Monday morning, and as usual, it seemed deserted. It was also cold and the south-east wind was whistling through the cranes. Jim van der Merwe and James Michelson were waiting for them on the access road which went down to the water's edge. The building that used to house Video was forbiddingly black and monolithic and the Tom of Finland sign hadn't been removed. They didn't really expect to be able to get inside the building and were surprised to find that the padlock on the door hadn't been fully closed. Jim used his DI's prerogative to inspect the premises and they cautiously entered the building. Not surprisingly, virtually everything had been stripped, which gave the interior an even more sinister and unwelcoming feel. The rubber floor was ominously sticky. Jim noticed some light switches and idly flicked them on, not really expecting anything to happen. A single spotlight lit up and shone down onto the only piece of metalwork left in the place, which happened to be the platform that Hugo had excelled himself on that Sunday night.

Greg could see Ben staring up at the platform and wondered what was going through his mind.

"Is that really where Hugo did his turn?" he asked nervously.

"Yes," replied Greg.

Ben went across the floor and stood under the platform with his eyes closed, face turned up and mouth open. The spotlight started flickering weirdly. Ben rotated slowly in the strobing light, imagining Hugo dancing in time with the music, stroking his wonderful dick, and then showering his audience. He looked up at the spotlight and it gave a final flicker, as if bidding farewell.

Ben rejoined Greg, smiling, but with tears in his eyes. "I enjoyed that," he said, kissing Greg. "There's nothing quite like spectral spunk." Greg thought he saw something strangely translucent on Ben's lips but guessed it was a trick of the light.

They left the building and crossed over to the cold storage building where Ben had been held captive.

"Are you really sure about this, Ben?" asked Greg. "We can always come back another day."

"Greg, this is something I have to do now," said Ben determinedly.

James took a bundle of keys from his pocket and unfastened the locks that his colleagues had used to secure the building. The sunlight spilt into the dark room as the door was opened and they could make out the outline of the cage holding the suspension harness which had proven too difficult for the police to remove. Ben let go of Greg's hand and he crossed to the centre of the cage. He slowly looked around the room and started describing his experiences:

"I remember waking up and not being able to move. I had something over my head. I thought Hugo was playing a trick. I was naked and felt so cold." He shivered and wrapped his arms around him for warmth. "I had to pee and heard my urine trickling onto the floor. Someone said "Fucking queer." He came towards me and shoved his dick into me. It was so painful and I thought I was going to pass out. Then he forced his dick into my mouth and I was gagging and couldn't breathe and then he ejaculated over my face. Then someone else said "My turn now" and the whole thing was repeated. I must have fallen asleep and woke up strapped into this thing. I heard the sound of people talking and undressing over there. And then it started all over again and I didn't know how much more I could take. I lost count of how many dicks were forced into me and how much semen I swallowed. I felt so, so sore and bruised. And then I remember feeling the semen trickling onto the floor and I felt so disgusted and humiliated." He started shivering again and looked despairingly at Greg. "But part of me also enjoyed it and I don't know how to escape from the guilt for feeling like that. And then there's what happened next to that man..." He knelt down on the floor and started sobbing uncontrollably.

Greg went across and bent down to comfort him. "It's okay, love, you've done so well to remember. It's time to leave this place and start your new life."

Greg put his arms around Ben and led him outside. He noticed that Jim and James had also been sobbing and were holding each other for comfort.

"I think we could all do with a stiff drink," said Greg.

Friday, October 28, 2011

Ben's relocation to Cape Town had been relatively trouble-free and they decided to have their wedding ceremony in February 2012 when the weather would be at its warmest. Ben managed to get a part-time advertising job with an up-and-coming firm on Long Street. Mental health issues didn't seem to be relevant at the interview, and even the short time he spent in the Roundwell Unit under a hospital order only received passing attention. In truth, Greg's influence, and a previous relationship with one of the directors, paid a large part in Ben being offered the job, although Greg never let on that this was the case. And by bit, Ben's confidence grew to the extent that he found himself enjoying the job and even contemplated going for a full-time position.

One day, at work, after Ben had delivered a succinct and punchy pitch for a new, smaller coke bottle designed to fit in the back pocket of jeans, the receptionist put a call through to him: "Ben, will you accept a collect call? It's from the UK."

Ben immediately said "Yes" and picked up the phone, expecting to hear his mother, who was presumably unable to pay for the call because of her dire financial straits. "Hi, is that you Mother?"

"Hello, Ben, how good to hear your voice. It's been such a long time."

"Who is this?"

"Oh, Ben, please don't pretend you've forgotten me. Let me remind you: I am your master, you are my slave."

"You are my master, I am your slave," intoned Ben,

without the slightest emotional response on his face.

"You know what you have to do, don't you, Ben?"

"Yes."

Ben put down the phone and walked slowly and deliberately through the open plan office, past reception, down the stairs, out past security and down Long Street, heading for 180 Bree Street. He felt extremely horny and hoped that Greg would be home from work. SNIP... He stood briefly outside Long Street Cafe and turned left into Buiten Street. SNIP... He turned right into Bree Street and looked through the windows of Latitude 33. SNIP... He continued walking down Bree Street and had almost reached the garage entry to 180. SNIP...

He suddenly realized what had happened. Better late than never, he thought. He retraced his steps and headed back for the office with the feeling that a heavy weight had been taken off his shoulders.

Sitting down at his desk, he phoned reception. "Hey, Cindy, it's Ben. You know that last call you put through to me? Could you get a trace on it so I can call back on my cell phone? Thanks."

A short time later, the receptionist rang back with the UK number. Ben immediately rang through to Cape Town Central Police Station and asked for DI van der Merwe.

"Van der Merwe here."

"Jim, it's Ben Cavendish. I've got something for you."

"I'm all ears."

"You won't believe it but I've just taken a collect call from Michael Magister and he's up to his old tricks. In fact, I almost went home and killed Greg."

"I hope you're joking, Ben."

"Sorry, I was kidding about the last bit. I used the snip

technique that the psychologist taught me, so I was able to break the control. At least now I know the trigger he used."

"What was it?"

"I am your master, you are my slave."

"Creepy. I'll get onto New Scotland Yard and get them to find out how Mr Magister managed to do that, but now that you know the trigger, he should be out of your hair for good."

"I hope so."

"Will we be seeing the two of you at Hothouse this evening?"

"Oh no, it's our evening in and I've got pizza, a new DVD and a bottle of merlot all lined up."

"Actually, same here. Cozy domesticity seems to be the in thing these days. Do you have any plans for the weekend?"

"I'm taking Greg for a birthday tea at the Nelson Lodge Hotel."

"So no trips into the bushes, then?"

"Definitely not but I might bare my butt on the sun lounger for old times' sake."

"Ben, you're incorrigible!"

"That's what Hugo used to say."

"Do you miss him?"

"Of course, but watching that video from time to time helps, even though I usually end up bawling my eyes out."

"Perhaps he really was too beautiful for his own good."

"You mean, like the boy in the gilded cage?"

"Something like that."

"Jim, there's something I wanted to ask you."

"Fire away."

"Will you be my best man at our wedding?"

There was a brief pause at the other end of the phone. "Ben, I'd be honored to be your best man but are you sure?"

"Of course, silly. I owe you... we owe you so much."

"It goes both ways, Ben. If it wasn't for you and Greg, I'd probably still be with my wife and I definitely wouldn't be heading the task force."

"There was a saying that Hugo had: "Sometimes good things fall apart so better things can fall together." It was something that Marilyn Monroe said and I never really appreciated what it meant before."

"I'll include that in my speech."

"There won't be a dry eye in the house."

"What's going to be the dress code?"

"Oh uniforms, I think. Greg will be in his full regalia complete with ceremonial sword to chase off any undesirables."

"I can't wait, Ben. Where are you planning to have the reception?"

"We were thinking of the Nelson Lodge Hotel, and in fact we've already reserved room #202 for the wedding night."

"Oh no!"

December 25, 2011

The room measured about 10 feet by 6 feet. Opposite the door there was a small window set high in the wall. If he stood on his toes, he could just make out similar windows across the quadrangle but the grime on the window made it all a bit bleary. The length of the narrow bed wasn't quite sufficient to accommodate the extent of his lanky frame, so his feet invariably stuck out and felt the cold of the night. The sheets were changed weekly, although thousands of washings had rendered them an off-white color. The blankets were thin and prickly but he'd got used to that. The pillow was made of some synthetic material which was presumably more hygienic than the luxurious Hungarian duck down in the pillows he enjoyed in his previous life.

Next to the bed there was a desk fitted against the wall and a lightweight plastic chair. The desk was fairly bare, with just a row of his current reading material lined up against the wall and a small moleskine notebook and pens in the center. Pride of place went to Yukio Mishima's 'Madame de Sade' and 'Confessions of a Mask'. His main interest was in writing Haiku poetry. Hours would go by with him making slight changes to one word or another before he felt he could move on to a new line. He didn't really mind if anyone looked at what he wrote as no-one would be able to understand it unless they had a degree in modern languages.

En-suite facilities were at the end of the bed and included a stainless steel sink and toilet. His toothbrush, toothpaste, comb, soap, flannel and safety razor were precisely laid out ready for his next ablution.

Food was provided four times a day: all precisely on time at 7:00 a.m., noon, 4:00 p.m. and 6:00 p.m., and the menu varied according to a weekly roster. Deviations from this were rare and he preferred it when the routine wasn't broken, even if it was a special occasion like today.

So this was his home: meager by any conventional standard but it provided continuity and structure. Everything was exactly as he expected it and he'd come to appreciate the limited aesthetics. And from time to time he offered favors to those who treated him well. He didn't require much back: a collect call to South Africa would do just fine and he knew he'd eventually get through. And he still had plenty of time to complete a book of Haiku poems as a wedding present for a rather special couple.

Afterword

The idea for this novel came from a particularly vivid dream that I had while on vacation with my husband in South Africa a few years ago. The dream went something like this:

We were staying in an eco-lodge reserve somewhere in the back of beyond. It could have been our honeymoon but the dream didn't elaborate on that. The room we had was more of a tent, with fabric and blinds instead of walls and windows. One morning, I woke up to discover that the other side of the bed was empty. The dream sent me frantically searching for my husband but everywhere I went I was confronted by blank faces who claimed no knowledge of his whereabouts. Weirdly, I became preoccupied with the minutiae of how, as a non-driver, I'd get to the next destination of our vacation and what would happen to the car we'd parked back at London Heathrow. The dream then decided I should return to the UK without him to get on with my life as a doctor. And eventually I met someone new. A year after his disappearance, my husband suddenly arrived back in my life but he'd changed and started stalking me at work. Eventually, I gave in and allowed him back in my life and our house. That turned out to be the biggest mistake in my life as he ended up killing me after we'd had the best sex ever. What would Sigmund Freud have made of that, I wonder?

David Ellis
London

Acknowledgements

The Nelson Lodge Hotel doesn't exist, of course, but I have to admit that it is modeled on the Mount Nelson Hotel, which is an excellent hotel in Cape Town owned by Orient-Express. Cape Town hotels in general are renowned for positive, non-discriminatory attitude to LGBT travelers and actively welcome honeymoon couples of all types. Cape Town hotels also employ staff without regard to sexuality, but it's unlikely that even the most ingeniously versatile male staff would offer sexual favors quite as freely as in the novel. Like my fictional hotel, the Mount Nelson Hotel does have beautiful gardens but they don't figure in the Spartacus guide. The reputation of the hotel's afternoon tea remains unsurpassed.

The gay scene in Cape Town is less developed than in American and European cities but it always had a certain freedom of expression that felt quite liberating. With the development of De Waterkant into yet another restaurant and shopping mall, a lot of that has changed. Much more worrying was the murder of Bruno Bronn, the owner of the gay club Bronx, in February 2012, which has been construed as the act of an undercurrent that resents the so-called 'gay mafia'. But none of that really detracts from Cape Town as a terrific destination for a vacation, whether you're gay, straight or anything else.

The author apologizes for any distortions in his depiction of BDSM sex and relationships *in servitude*. The distinction between 'good sex' and 'bad sex' is an interesting one and the predication of consensuality seems to be as good a starting point as ever. As mentioned by DI van der Merwe in the novel, an interesting case in English law is that of R v Brown (1994), also referred to as the 'Spanner case', where a judge ruled that five men engaging in consensual, sadomasochistic sex over a ten-year period, who'd been previously convicted of 'malicious wounding' or 'actual bodily harm', couldn't rely on consent for their defense. English law is frequently an ass (as in the animal sense) and this case proves it. American law generally takes a more rational and less moralistic view of BDSM relationships.

Penis sizes are an endless source of interest and speculation. Reliable, objective surveys are a rarity and the Kinsey Report (1948) wasn't one of them. The average erect penis of an American male is thought to be 5.1 inches, which is behind the UK with 5.5 inches. Two of the characters in the novel way exceed such an average size. Hugo is objectively described, by a physician, as having an erect penis that's 10 inches in length by 2 inches diameter, giving a volume of 31 cubic inches, and placing him quite easily in the 1 in a 1,000,000 category for erect penises worldwide. The 'Milkman' exceeds even that, with quoted dimensions – although admittedly evaluated from a distance and in a condition of distress and with poor illumination – of "well over 10 inches in length and with a girth the size of Ben's wrist", which would put him firmly in the freak show category, although not to the extent of the 13.5 inches attributed to a certain man from New York City whose penis is regarded quite routinely as a WMD by airport security.

Brian Sewell (15.07.31) is a British art critic with a wonderfully acerbic turn of phrase and the author of two volumes of splendidly scabrous autobiography. My references to him are made purely in recognition of his stature as the new and much improved stately homo of England. And the author narrowly missed being added to the notches on his bedpost.

Like the Vulcan nerve pinch, breaking someone's neck by twisting it is more fictional than factual and it's thought that it would take between 850 and 1500 N to fracture the C2 vertebra by twisting the neck, which might happen in novels but hopefully not when you're in bed with your boyfriend. The exception might be those individuals expert in certain martial arts, so please avoid black belts in Taekwondo if you're looking for a new boyfriend.

'Video' doesn't as yet exist but the author would be happy to offer advice on such a project. A rubber floor and comprehensive cleaning contract would come in handy.

Therapy for psychological trauma has a good evidence base but it's easy for therapists to over-identify with patients who've been through extreme traumatic events. The gold standard is cognitive-behavioral therapy. More controversial approaches include eye movement desensitization and reprocessing (EMDR) and somatic experiencing, both of which involve the patient having to re-experience the trauma in order to process it. The key objective is not to retraumatize the patient. This can also occur if debriefing is attempted. Psychoanalytical theories are generally best avoided.

The medical details in the novel reflect the author's many years of medical training and experience, particularly in the specialty of psychiatry. He would be mortified if there were any errors, but if there are, they are his alone.

Finally, and far from least, the author would like to thank Jack Lyle and all at Tenth Street Press for believing in him and 'Captive'.

Biography

David Ellis has worked as a doctor in the UK's National Health Service for 25 years. He was an undergraduate at St Peter's College, Oxford in the 1970s and then a research scholar at Worcester College, Oxford. His first foray into print was when writing on music technology to supplement his medical school grant. He has written books on medical computing and using computers to make music. He co-authored a book and software package to teach anatomy to medical students. He enjoys painting in acrylics on large canvases. He lives in North London with his husband and two cats. They are frequent flyers on BA0059. He doesn't eat meat and goes to the gym daily. This is his second novel.